COLD SHOWER NEEDED

"Now, I'm going to slip into something more comfortable."

The next thing she knew, she was up against the wall with Stone's large, warm body much too close.

"No you're not. I can only take so much." His voice was husky.

Taylor was speechless, mainly because suddenly she was finding it difficult to breathe.

Then Stone's lips descended and the world narrowed to this man and the overwhelming emotions rioting through her. His firm, tender lips demanded a response.

Taylor surrendered, the ember burning at the core of her, blazing into an inferno. His tongue sent shivers of desire through her. He leaned into her, his hardness pressing into her feminine warmth. Her hips rotated against his, seemingly of their own volition, seeking, wanting . . .

"If anything happens here except ripping our clothes off on the way to my bedroom, you're following the wrong script," Taylor murmured.

Stone groaned. "You're not going to make this easy. I have to leave."

"Why?"

"It's not the right time." He grabbed his keys from the coffee table and fled.

Three strikes and you're out, she thought.

BOOK YOUR PLACE ON OUR WEBSITE AND MAKE THE ARABESQUE ROMANCE CONNECTION!

We've created a customized website just for our very special Arabesque readers, where you can get the inside scoop on everything that's going on with Arabesque romance novels.

When you come online, you'll have the exciting opportunity to:

- View covers of upcoming books

- Learn about our future publishing schedule (listed by publication month and author)

- Find out when your favorite authors will be visiting a city near you.

- Search for and order backlist books from our line catalog

- Check out author bios and background information

- Send e-mail to your favorite authors

- Join us in weekly chats with authors, readers and other guests

- Get writing guidelines

- AND MUCH MORE!

Visit our website at
http://www.arabesquebooks.com

A
MAGICAL
MOMENT

MONICA JACKSON

ARABESQUE
☆BET.
BOOKS

BET Publications, LLC
www.msbet.com
www.arabesquebooks.com

ARABESQUE BOOKS are published by

BET Publications, LLC
C/o BET BOOKS
One BET Plaza
1900 W Place NE
Washington, D.C. 20018-1211

First Printing: June, 1999
10 9 8 7 6 5 4 3 2 1

Printed in the United States of America

Special thanks to Marilynn Ault, Marilee Brown, and

all the staff at the Topeka YMCA Battered Women Task Force

ONE

"First, I'd strap my husband on the bed with leather restraints." Denise Whitton's black leather pump beat a nervous rhythm against her briefcase.

"How would you get him on the bed? Would you drug him?" Teensy asked, her meaty fingers digging another handful of potato chips from the large bag cradled on her lap.

Denise's foot stilled. She shifted uncomfortably on the sofa between Teensy, an unkempt woman who must have weighed at least three hundred pounds, and a blond who oozed wealth and self-confidence.

"No, I wouldn't drug him. I'd wait behind a door when he came home from work and knock him out with a frying pan," she said. "Then I'd wait until he came to before I flayed him alive. You know, the death of a thousand cuts."

A collective "ohhh" arose from the diverse group of women sitting in a circle. Taylor Cates sat next to an abandoned flip chart. Someone had tried hard to make the room homey in an overdone country style. Frills and flounces vied with the plethora of homemade crafts. Taylor's group session on restraining orders, court procedures, victim's rights, and other legal matters was seriously off track.

"I liked that old movie, *The Burning Bed,* the blond said. "Remember, the one with Farrah Fawcett, where she burned up her no-good husband in his bed and got away with it?"

"I loved that movie," an Asian woman murmured, surprising Taylor. The woman rarely spoke up.

"I liked the movie where that stalker broke in to attack her and she ended up beating the crap out of him and tied him up, then was going to kill him and bury him out in the garden," a teenager said, adjusting her baby so he could better latch on to her nipple.

"I'd like to do mine like that," a woman murmured.

"I'm going to do mine the easy way. I'm going to get my nine and smoke him clean and simple. I'll just make sure he sees who capped him before he dies," another teenager said.

Dark emotions hung and shimmered in the air.

"There's nothing clean and simple about doing life in prison," Taylor said. "Remember that movies are fantasy. Hard time for first-degree murder is the reality."

The room sobered, and the shadowed impression of fear and darkness that Taylor had felt rising dampened and faded. She expelled a slow breath and ran a hand over her dreadlocks, feeling chilled. Was something going to happen, or had it already come to pass? Did it involve one of these women, or someone close to them? Taylor frowned. Her gift of prescience almost always raised more questions than it answered.

"We ran our mouths again, and Taylor didn't finish telling us about the court procedures," Denise said, looking at Taylor with concern.

"We don't want you to get in trouble," the teenager with the baby said.

"Nobody's going to get in trouble," a grandmotherly-looking woman stopped knitting long enough to grumble. "Taylor here is just doing her job."

"We have times and places and plenty of people available for us to talk to. Ms. Cates has legal things to talk to us about and her time is valuable," said a Hispanic woman wearing a lab coat with the letters M.D. embroidered after her name.

"I suppose you can relate since you think your time is so precious, also," the blond commented.

Taylor stifled a sigh. She had a hard time getting a word in edgewise with this group. "I wasn't frowning because I didn't get my material covered. You needed to talk, and I allowed you to do so. We'll meet here tomorrow, same time, same place. Let's wrap up."

Taylor had sensed how much these women needed to share the poignant sadness of their stories. She'd set her instructional material aside and given way to their need. The sense of wonder at the similarity of their experiences and feelings despite their external differences was still fresh. Pain and guilt had started to be overshadowed by the dawning reality that maybe it wasn't all their fault. Now came the anger frosted with a little pure glee that maybe it was all right to be mad at the son of a bitch. Mad enough to want to kill him.

Taylor looked at her watch in alarm. She was going to be late for her meeting with the director of the center. Again. She hurried to her Honda parked behind the secret location of the Helping Hands shelter for battered women, and rushed to the agency's offices. Marian White was on the phone when Taylor peeked in the door to her office. She gestured for her to come in.

Marian had been with the center since its inception. She had an air of fragile delicacy that complemented her southern magnolia look perfectly. Marian had aged more gracefully than any very fair person Taylor had ever met. Her genteel appearance and soft, southern drawl contrasted with the steely, no-nonsense personality. Marian got things done and took no guff from anybody.

Taylor sat in the chair next to the desk. The strong impressions she'd picked up with the group at the shelter were still with her. Darkness laced the multicolored tapestry of the women's emotions. Something was wrong.

Marian hung up the phone. "You did a fabulous job on the Donnelly case. That was one of the child protection people on the phone."

"Thanks," she said. But Taylor took little satisfaction from a victory rooted in such pain. Her client's husband was a mail carrier from a small Georgia town. He'd been popular and personable, while her client was isolated and shy. His wife's excuses for her frequent hospital visits were always readily accepted, a fall, an accident. When she finally fled to the Helping Hands shelter, he'd said she was having an affair, that she was lying. The town rallied around him and he'd sued for custody of the kids. Taylor had uncovered evidence of abuse that made the custody issue a moot point, and charges were now being pressed against the man.

"Here's your yearly evaluation," Marian shoved a paper at her and grinned.

Taylor smiled when she saw the almost uniform fours for excellence marked across the paper.

"I can't express how blessed we at the center feel in having you on our team. I know you could be making twice the salary elsewhere," Marian said.

Taylor started to demur, but then decided against it. Marian was telling the truth.

"I authorized a ten percent raise and I wish we could give you more."

The money would be more than welcome, Taylor thought. Her budget was getting out of hand. "I appreciate the raise," she said.

"Now, where can we go for lunch?" Marian asked.

They were debating between a new vegetarian restaurant that Taylor wanted to try and Chinese, when a knock sounded on the door.

"Come on in," Marian called.

Two men, obviously plainclothes policemen, entered. Their

expressions were grim. Apprehension ran through Taylor. She feared the worst. She cared deeply about each and every one of the women who came through Helping Hands. The women who returned home to their husbands never believed the worst could happen to them. But all too frequently, it did. More women were seriously injured from domestic abuse than in car accidents.

"What can we do for you, gentlemen?" Marian asked.

"There's been a murder," the older man said.

Marian grayed and Taylor's eyes closed in a silent prayer.

"Was one of our clients killed again?" Taylor whispered.

The detective shook his head. "No. We've come because we need to talk with a woman who we believe is staying at your shelter. Denise Whitton. Her husband was found this morning. He'd been tied to his bed, his throat cut."

TWO

Marian called and told the shelter manager to bring Denise to the office. A few minutes later Denise walked into the conference room where they'd decided to break the news to her. Denise's lips tightened when she saw Marian, Taylor, and the two detectives.

"I'm not in trouble, am I?" she asked with a weak smile.

Nobody answered.

"I have bad news," the older detective said. "Please sit down." Denise sank in a chair, looking scared.

"I'm sorry to inform you that your husband was killed in his home yesterday evening," he said.

Denise sat unmoving. Then she blinked once. "You're lying."

Silence fell. The detectives stared unwaveringly at Denise, perhaps used to this response. Taylor clasped her hands in her lap, feeling Denise's building reaction.

Denise half rose out of her chair, her face suddenly a mask of anguish. "It can't be true. How could he be dead?" She collapsed back into the chair, covering her face as sobs racked her.

One of the detectives pushed a box of tissues toward her.

Denise took one and collected herself with a visible effort. "How?" she asked, not looking at the detectives.

"He was found restrained to his bed by locked, hospital issue restraints. He bled to death from a severed jugular vein."

Denise's head snapped up. "I don't believe it. This is a sick joke you all made up." She turned to Taylor. "You told them what I said this morning, didn't you? You told them how I hoped Jerry would die. How could you do this to me?"

The detectives perked up. "Is this is a confession? You're her counsel?" the younger one asked Taylor.

Taylor's attention was on Denise. "I told them nothing," she said.

"If you're not her counsel in this matter, a confession of murder isn't privileged information," the older detective said.

"Confession? Murder? My husband is dead and you're speaking absurdities to me," Denise whispered while silent tears streaked down her cheeks.

"Despite everything, I loved him. I had this dream that one day he'd realize how wrong he was, and he'd change." Her fingers twisted and untwisted around themselves. "He'd say he was sorry and he'd really mean it this time. He'd never hit me again. I'd go back home, and we'd finally have a baby. We'd be happy and I'd be safe."

Denise turned toward Taylor. "That's all I ever wanted. I know this morning I said I wanted to kill him. But . . . but it wasn't real. I was kidding. I never believed it could really happen." Her voice choked. "I never really wanted him to die."

Marian shifted uncomfortably in her chair. "I'm sorry," she said.

Taylor rarely sensed truth and never sensed falsehood. But she recognized the clear truth of Denise's words. She hadn't wanted her husband to die.

"So you're not giving us a confession," the detective said, disappointed.

"I have nothing to confess."

"So you won't mind telling us exactly where you were between the hours of eight P.M. and twelve A.M. yesterday?"

"I need a lawyer, don't I?" Denise murmured. She turned to Taylor. "Please help me."

Taylor hesitated. "I'm not a criminal lawyer," she said.

"I don't care. You're smart, and I know you care. I'm sorry for my outburst. I know you wouldn't do anything to hurt me. Please help me understand what's going on."

It was strange how Denise said she wished her husband would die this morning, and how he was killed the night before. But Taylor knew better than most that strange didn't mean impossible. Something bothered her about Denise. Something hidden and locked away that she couldn't sense. But Taylor would stake her next paycheck, and the Lord knew she needed it, on the belief that Denise Whitton did not murder her husband.

She identified with her more than any other woman at the shelter, even though their styles were profoundly different. Taylor preferred an ethnic, funky look—dreadlocks and African fabrics in bright colors—and Denise looked like a conservative, executive businesswoman from the top of the chemically fried, bone-straight hair on her head to the expensive, immaculate black leather pumps on her feet. Maybe it was because they were both educated black women from professional families.

Denise clutched the trappings of her life. She clung to her corporate job, ignoring the knowledge that she'd already banged her head against the glass ceiling. She held on to the image of the "picture-perfect" marriage, even though the image shattered behind closed doors, where her perfect husband regularly beat her. Most of all, she wrapped herself around the secret of her own misery. The people closest to her never suspected.

In contrast, Taylor had only worked for nonprofit agencies since law school. She'd never tried to squeeze herself into any mold, never tried to please anybody except herself, especially white folks. Most of all, she never totally committed herself to anything or anybody. There was a piece of her she always held back. So far, her life had worked well, she thought, dismissing the loneliness lurking at the corner of her consciousness.

"I'll help you until you find a good criminal lawyer," she said to Denise, hoping she wouldn't regret her words.

"Were you with a man? Is that why you can't tell us where you went after you left your sister's house?"

"She doesn't have to answer that," Taylor snapped at the detective. She sat beside Denise at an ancient table in a dingy room with cinder-block walls. A lone high-wattage light bulb swung from the ceiling. They were flanked by the two detectives.

It didn't look good. Denise had no alibi during the time her husband had been killed. She said she'd driven through a fast-food place for a bite to eat after work, then she briefly visited her sister. Between seven o'clock and the time she returned to the shelter at 10 P.M., she'd been vague about her whereabouts. Taylor needed to get her out of here before she said something irreparably damaging.

She stood abruptly. "If you're not pressing charges, we're leaving." The older man leaned back in his chair and stared at her with ice blue eyes. They both knew there wasn't enough evidence to hold her. Yet.

"She can't leave the city," the detective said.

Taylor nodded. "Come on," she told Denise.

Denise was in trouble, Taylor thought, worried. She had to have a long talk with her. She was going to have to admit where she went yesterday. Nothing she had to hide could possibly measure up to a murder conviction.

Wendy, the slinky looking blond, met them at the shelter's door. "We're having a brainstorming session about Denise. Come on," she said, grabbing Denise and dragging her toward the living room. Taylor followed.

Quanita, a black teenager outfitted in Tommy Hilfiger gear,

had her leg draped over the arm of the couch. "Girl, you need to get a hold of Johnnie Cochran," she said.

"Shhh, you're going to upset her," Joan, who looked like a suburban soccer mom, said.

"Don't you shhh me. Who you think you are, shhhing me?"

Joan rolled her eyes, familiar and friendly enough with Quanita not to worry about her mouth or her attitude. "I'm somebody who wants to know how Denise got the nerve to do it."

"Yes, tell us how you did it," Wendy breathed, her eyes shining.

"Are you going to get insurance money?" Eva, the doctor, asked.

"Details. We want the deeee-tails," Teensy added.

Denise burst into tears.

"That's enough," Taylor said. She put a protective arm around Denise. "I don't think she did it," she said.

Something that sounded suspiciously like a snort sounded in the room.

"Y'all ever heard of innocent until proven guilty?" Taylor drawled, trying to keep her anger under control.

"But we hope she did it," Amber said, her baby latched on to her breast. Assent shined in the women's faces.

"You hope she does a mandatory twenty years to life? Because be aware, that's what you're hoping for her," Taylor said.

Denise's sniffles echoed in the now hushed room.

"She could go to prison?" Amber breathed. "But look at what he did to her. Farrah Fawcett always got off."

"Oh, so you gotta be white to get off with killing your abusive husband?" Quanita demanded.

"Why are you telling us about your ignorance?" Taylor asked Quanita, irritated. Not waiting for an answer, she turned to the rest of the group. "Dammit, this isn't a movie. This is Denise's life. If she's found guilty, as you all seem to have decided she must be—she'll go to prison."

In the shocked silence, Mai Lin cleared her throat to speak. "That's not fair," she said slowly. There was a long pause as everyone waited for her next sentence.

Taylor sighed when it was apparent that it wasn't forthcoming. "Why don't you go up to your room and get some rest," she said to Denise.

Denise fled. Taylor's beeper went off. She didn't recognize the phone number. Going into the hallway, she pulled out her cellular phone and punched in the numbers. "This is Stone Emerson," a deep male voice answered.

The name registered instantly. Stone was a friend of a friend who owned a successful private detective agency in town. He'd asked her out shortly after she'd arrived in Atlanta.

He was a financially secure, unattached, straight black male in his mid-thirties, and she'd turned him down flat. Now, Taylor adored men, her entire family consisted of men, five brothers and her father. Stone Emerson would fit right in, he was confident, handsome, conservative, and probably bossy and set in his ways.

Her best friend, Kara, thought she was crazy not to go out with him. Maybe she was crazy, but Taylor needed a man like herself. She wanted a free spirit, someone open to new ideas and vibes, interested in the same things she liked and preferably vegetarian. So what if she'd been dating an unbroken string of losers, past and present? Nobody controlled her.

She hoped Stone wasn't paging her to ask her out again.

"Taylor?" He queried again in his deep, sexy voice.

"Yes?" she answered, making sure her voice was crisp and chill.

"I need to meet with you. Tonight if possible."

The man was tripping.

"I said I didn't want to go out with you. And when I said it, I meant ever."

A pause. "You misunderstand. I'm not asking you out. This is business. Wendy McIntyre's husband, George, hired me. He said he got a note saying he's next in line to die."

Taylor clutched the phone tightly. "Do you have the note?" she whispered.

"Why?"

"Bring it if you have it. I'll meet you at the Writer's Cafe, eight sharp." Her fingers still trembled as she clicked off the phone. She felt a headache start to gather at the back of her neck.

She saw Stone first. He was sitting in a corner booth. The booth was private, a little secluded. Taylor's pulse quickened at the sight of him. The man was fine.

She slipped into the booth across from him. Stone nodded at her, relaxed and friendly. Cool brother. There was no hint of the defensiveness she usually picked up when she turned a man down.

The waiter set a steaming cup of coffee in front of Stone.

"I'll have chamomile tea," Taylor said to the waiter.

Then she leaned back and studied him. He gave her a slight, unreadable smile, and took a sip of coffee. So, he takes it black, Taylor thought.

Well, since he was the one who insisted she come, he should speak his piece first. The silence grew heavier, but Stone seemed unconcerned. He took another sip of coffee and studied the people in the cafe. Standoff.

"I talked to Wendy," Taylor said, her voice faintly frosted with anger. "She says she had no idea that her husband received any threat, or was going to hire a private detective. Do you have the note?"

Stone shook his head. "You hung up before I could tell you that the police have it."

"I wish I'd known that before I came down here."

Stone shrugged.

Taylor had a nearly irresistible urge to simply get up and walk away—away from the attraction and temptation of Stone Emerson.

"Why did you want to see the note?" he asked.

Taylor looked at him levelly. "I wanted to touch it. I might be able to pick up an impression of who wrote it."

Stone laughed softly. "Brent said you were way out there. So, you're one of those psychics. Why the law degree? I'd think you'd make more money off the psychic phone line."

Taylor smiled benignly, feeling relieved. This fine brother was proving to be resistible after all. She'd been right not to date him.

"Interesting you think so," she answered.

He had the grace to look slightly abashed.

"The threat is serious," Stone said. "And it could point directly to Denise Whitton."

"Denise didn't do it."

"What makes you so sure? Your psychic senses?"

"Right."

Stone raised an eyebrow and took another sip of his coffee.

"I've had the gift for as long as I can remember. So did my mother and my grandmother before her. I'm a seventh child, so my gift is very strong." She was babbling. She usually never had the urge to explain herself.

"So, are you going to have seven children?"

"Hardly. I would have started before now if I had that sort of massive childbearing in mind."

"It's not too late. Brent told me you were only thirty."

Taylor started to reply and snapped her mouth shut. How did she reach the point of discussing her age and childbearing possibilities with this man? "What do you want from me?" she asked.

"I want to talk to Denise Whitton, and maybe some of the other women. I need to get a feel for the case, see the big picture."

"Investigating Denise Whitton is a matter for the police. And why would you think that one of the women from Helping Hands shelter for women is involved with this? One of our *victims.*"

Taylor emphasized the last word. Some men were always searching for some way to pin the blame on women.

"All the evidence points to Denise Whitton, and she has no alibi," he answered.

"Circumstantial evidence."

Stone shrugged. "So then you don't mind if I interview your client and speak to the other women at the shelter?" he asked.

Taylor leaned back in the booth. She wanted to say no. She wanted to be unforgivably rude and make his job as hard as possible. "The shelter's location is secret. But I don't mind if the women agree to speak to you, but I have to be present, and it has to be at my office," she heard herself saying.

Stone smiled at her, and it was the sexiest, most appealing smile she could imagine on a man.

Taylor rubbed her temple. The simple fact was that she wanted to see him again.

THREE

Stone insisted on walking Taylor to her car. Tense and on edge, she walked silently beside him. She'd had to park several blocks away. Stone hummed a little tune as he walked, seeming so cheerful and comfortable with her moody silence it disconcerted her.

Then, to Taylor's horror, he reached into his jacket pocket and pulled out a pack of cigarettes. Taylor stopped in her tracks, while Stone walked on oblivious, shaking a cigarette out. He stopped a few paces ahead of her and turned, looking back at her quizzically.

"I mind if you smoke," Taylor said, her voice cold enough to chip glass.

Stone sighed and put the cigarette back into the package.

"Smoking is a filthy habit. I don't understand why people would choose to pollute their bodies that way."

Stone gave her an amused glance. "A death wish, I suppose."

Her car was only a block away. Taylor walked faster. How could she be so attracted to this man? Good Lord, he smoked. What else did he do? Probably ate red meat, and spent all his spare time watching sports on TV while he swilled beer.

Stone had no trouble keeping up with her with his long strides. She reached her car door and fumbled for her keys. When she got the door opened, she turned to Stone. "It's a very good thing I didn't go out with you," she announced. "I don't like people who smoke. I suppose you eat red meat, too."

"There's nothing better than a good steak," he said, grinning.

Taylor snorted as she slid into the seat of the car and rolled the window down to release the trapped heat. She turned the key in the ignition. The motor failed to turn over. She tried again. Three times. She closed her eyes at the familiar grinding sound. One more time. Nothing. Taylor beat her hand against the steering wheel and swore.

Stone leaned against the street lamppost, the tip of a second cigarette glowing red in the night. "Need a ride?" he asked, flicking an ash.

"No, thank you. I'll use my cell phone to call a taxi."

Stone chuckled. "You know what, Taylor? You really need to lighten up."

He threw the cigarette on the ground, and ground it out with his foot. Taylor watched with alarm as he approached the car.

"What do you want?" she asked, her voice coming out weaker than she wanted.

He pulled open her door. "Come on. I'm giving you a ride. It's not safe for you to sit here in a disabled car."

Taylor opened her mouth to protest, but he shook his head before she could get the words out. "Let's go," he said. "I want to get some beer before the game starts tonight."

He needed to be driving to the nearest salvage yard rather than riding the streets, Taylor thought when she saw his car. He opened the door to a huge ancient Chevrolet Impala that had once been gold, but was now an indeterminate brown spotted with rust. She had to brush the old fast food bags off the torn plastic vinyl seat and on to the floor with the other garbage, before she could sit down. The ashtray overflowed with cigarette butts, and she wanted to hold her breath all the way home.

Stone slid the key into the ignition and the engine ignited

immediately with a healthy purr. It wasn't fair, Taylor thought, remembering all the money she'd spent for repair bills on her car. By all rights he should be the one waiting for the tow truck.

"There's a car wash a few blocks from here, that will clean out the inside of your car for only ten dollars," Taylor couldn't resist informing him.

Stone nodded, unperturbed. "I'll get around to cleaning out Grandma one of these days. The mess really doesn't bother me."

"Grandma?"

"This was my grandmother's car." He affectionately patted the dashboard. "Lots of good memories in this car. You said you lived in Virginia-Highlands? Do you want me to turn here off Ponce de Leon?"

"Yes. I'm three blocks down in the building on the corner on the right."

He gave her a cheery wave goodbye after he dropped her off, and said he'd call her tomorrow at the office to set up a time for the interview with Denise. She let herself into the apartment she shared. She'd gotten so comfortable with her roommate Tiffany, she dreaded the thought of her ever moving out. Tiffany's own children were close to Taylor's age, but Tiffany had plenty of mothering to spare.

The soft glow of candlelight and the barely perceptible scent of fresh-cut roses assailed her when she walked into the living room. Soft jazz played on the CD, and Tiffany was in a clinch with her new boyfriend on the sofa. They parted hurriedly when she walked into the room.

"Hi, Taylor," Tiffany said, sounding winded.

Dave nodded at her.

"We were just getting ready to go out to dinner, want to join us?" Tiffany asked.

"I'm beat. But thanks for the invite."

She walked into her room and changed out of her office clothes. Taylor felt Tiffany slipping away from her into her newfound love. Knowing the bereft, lonely feeling was normal, even expected, didn't make it hurt less. Tiff deserved a man's love. She was forty-six, still beautiful, and had survived a terrible, abusive marriage.

Tiffany had sworn she was through with marriage, and was going to enjoy herself for once in her life. But this relationship with this new man, Dave, was proving to be serious.

When Taylor went into the kitchen to find something to eat, they had gone, leaving the waft of passion and new love behind. Taylor sniffed and ripped open a bag of salad and tossed it into a bowl with some sunflower seeds and dressing. Sitting in front of the TV, she surfed channels with the remote in one hand, a fork in the other.

She'd hoped Tiffany would stay home tonight. She needed someone to talk to. Setting the salad bowl aside, she picked up the phone to call Kara and then set it back down. Kara would have put her daughter to bed, and she would be spending some private time with her husband.

Kara was busy with her family and there was no time for the hours-long heart-to-heart talks they used to share. These days Kara had those conversations with her husband, Brent. And now Kara was pregnant. Kara was so happy, and Taylor was happy for her. She just missed her, that was all.

She pushed the buttons on the remote aimlessly. She hated it when her sixth sense knew something was waiting to happen—sitting just out of sight behind the black cliffs of the future, waiting to burst out. Vague, diffuse uneasiness moved through Taylor and she shifted on the couch, her eyes focused far away. Her life was going to change profoundly for the better or worse. She was riding the roller coaster up, up, steeled for the inevitable drop that was sure to come.

Taylor had gotten up early to deal with the problem of her car. The car was in the shop and she was driving a rental she could ill afford. She'd gotten to the office late and rushed to the shelter to get there on time for her legal issues group meeting.

For once Taylor got through all the legal information she wanted to share with the seven women at the shelter. The group was quiet today. Too quiet. Denise had left last night. The need for a safe haven evaporated with the death of her husband. She'd left her sister's address, not wanting to go back to the house where her husband died.

An eddy of silent excitement swirled through the house. Denise's main problem had disappeared with her abuser's demise. If only their problems could be solved so easily. Could they work up the nerve to do it? Could they get away with it? Taylor felt the press of unspoken questions. Questions about murder.

Christine, the shelter manager, stuck her head in the door. "All done?" she asked Taylor.

Taylor nodded and rose from her chair. "Any more questions?" she asked the group. Nobody answered and the group rustled as the women got up to leave.

"Marian said to come into the office when you're done."

Marian was doodling on a yellow legal pad when Taylor walked into her office, a sure sign of stress.

"You needed me?" Taylor said.

Marian nodded. "I got a call from the Atlanta Police Department. They want to question the women in the shelter. There've now been two death threats to our clients' abusers."

"Oh, no. I know about one of them. George McIntyre hired a private detective. I met with him yesterday."

Marian rubbed her eyes. "This is getting out of hand," she said. "If the media get hold of this, we're sunk."

She stared at Taylor, determination shining from her eyes. "I refused the APD access to our clients and the shelter."

"Good. They can't force it until they have concrete evidence."

"Until? Do you believe there is a possibility one of our clients . . ."

Taylor hesitated. "I don't know," she said finally. "There's always a possibility."

"The killing and threats could be completely unrelated. It seems much more likely even if they are related that it would be someone outside the shelter. A friend or family member. These women are in crisis, and I won't allow them to be harassed by the police."

Taylor decided that this wasn't the best time to tell Marian she'd agreed to let Stone talk to the women if they chose.

Sure enough, when Taylor got to her office and checked her messages, the first one she heard was Stone's deep, husky voice. He'd left a number. She tapped her fingers on her desk, wondering what to do. It would be much more politic if she called him and said the client interviews were out of the question. But she had given her word. And she'd be lying to herself if she didn't admit she wanted to see him again. She'd lost her mind. What would she do with that red meat eating, smoking slob if she got him?

Giving her head a little shake, she punched the button to continue listening to her messages. Three messages were from Denise, each one sounding more hysterical than the last. The police had already been by to question her again. She'd refused to talk to them until she could get hold of Taylor. She was certain they were going to arrest her.

Taylor ran her hand over her dreads. The fact remained that Denise had no alibi. She was hiding something. Taylor reached for her keys. It was time she found out exactly what.

FOUR

Taylor had lifted her hand to ring Denise's doorbell when she froze, assailed by the sudden certainty something awful had happened. She swallowed. Helplessness swept over her. There was absolutely nothing she could do. She bit her lip, profoundly uneasy. She wondered why psychic awareness was called a gift when all too often it felt like a curse.

In that split second of anxiety, Denise opened the door, and Taylor's head snapped up, startled. "I saw a strange car pull up. I was relieved when I saw you get out. Then you didn't knock."

"May I come in?"

"Of course." Denise led her into a comfortable, simply furnished living room. Children's toys were scattered about. "Sorry for the mess," Denise murmured. "Please sit down."

Taylor sat in an armchair and Denise sank down on a sofa next to her.

"How are you doing?" Taylor asked, with a searching look. A maelstrom of emotion emanated from Denise, with a black cloud of depression building and threatening to overwhelm them all. Taylor sometimes wondered if it was wrong that she hadn't chosen to be a therapist with her ability to sense emotion and atmosphere.

"Not as good as everyone thinks I should be," Denise said. "Now that Jerry's gone, my family thinks I need to get on with my life and go back to work. They don't understand how much his death hurt me, since they found out what he'd been doing to me. They don't understand that I loved him . . . how much it hurts." Denise snuffled and reached for a tissue, wiping her eyes.

"I just don't know what to do," she continued. "I'm going to miss him so much."

Taylor wondered what exactly she would miss, thinking of the horrific stories Denise told of her life with her husband. She shifted, impatient to get to the point. "You were right not to talk to the police without me present," Taylor said.

She leaned toward Denise, her gaze intent. "You are the primary suspect in Jerry's murder. You *have* to tell me where you were the evening he died."

Denise burst into wrenching sobs, and Taylor sat back in her chair with a sigh. This was not going to be easy.

"I'm concerned about your future, Denise," she said after waiting the long minutes until Denise calmed down. "If you continue to withhold information, we don't have a case."

"I don't care," Denise said fiercely. "There are things more important than the future."

Taylor remembered why she didn't go into therapy. She was a little low on patience, and Lord, she hated whining. "What's more important than your life? Do you realize that you could go to prison?"

Denise burst into fresh sobs, and Taylor, getting more frustrated by the minute, resisted rolling her eyes.

There was a knock at the door. Taylor looked over at Denise, who was still quaking with sobs and giving no indication of moving. She'd answer the door herself, maybe it was the police. Maybe a little more questioning would knock some sense into the woman.

She pulled the door open and Stone stood in the threshold.

A slow smile brightened his face when he saw her. "I been trying to get hold of you all morning."

"I was going to return your call later," Taylor said, flustered.

He looked through the doorway. "Is Denise in? I'd like to talk to her."

Taylor stood aside for him to come in.

Ambling to Denise's still sobbing figure, he sat beside her. "My name is Stone Emerson," he said.

"I suppose you're another policeman," Denise said, sniffing.

"No, I'm a private detective." He produced a card and handed it to her. She took it but didn't look at it. "Wendy's husband, George McIntyre, hired me."

Denise stared at the card and wiped a tear off her cheek. "What does that have to do with me?"

"He received a note saying he was next in line to die. Since your husband was the first, I'm trying to gather as much information as I can."

Taylor had leaned against the wall, listening. She straightened and returned to the chair. She felt Denise warming to Stone, maybe he'd get somewhere with her.

"Nobody understands why I'm so upset," she said, shooting a baleful glance at Taylor. "It hurts to lose someone close to you, even if they treated you bad."

Stone nodded, genuine sympathy showing in his face. "I'm sorry," he said simply.

"Thank you," she answered in a low voice. She bit her lip. "What can I do to help you?"

"I need to know where you were between the hours of six and ten P.M. Tuesday evening."

Denise cast her eyes upward. "I can't say. I just can't say."

"It's very important to you to keep something hidden, isn't it? Something that has nothing to do with the murder of your husband?"

Relief shone from Denise's eyes. "You understand, don't

you? No one knew. Not even Jerry. It was so hard keeping it from him . . ."

"You met someone secretly?"

Denise nodded, her eyes filling again. "But it wasn't what you think. I never had a lover."

Stone covered her hand with his. "It's been hard, hasn't it?" he said.

Taylor watched Stone carefully. She could detect nothing but sincerity and sympathy emanating from him.

"So hard," Denise answered. "I can't tell the police. If it got out, I'd lose what matters most to me in the world. My baby. Oh, God, I'd lose my baby." She dissolved into tears on his shoulder, and Stone rocked her in his arms like a child, murmuring soothing words.

Taylor stared at them both in disbelief. Damn, he was good. But there was no point in going too far. He could let Denise go now. She cleared her throat loudly. Denise lifted her head.

"You can't tell," she pleaded. "If it comes out that I'm his mother, his adoptive parents won't let me see him anymore. I couldn't bear that."

"You're not going to see much of him in prison," Taylor said. Stone shot a glance at her, with a tiny shake of his head.

But Denise cocked her head. "I suppose you have a point," she answered.

Palpable relief filled the air by the time Taylor and Stone left. Denise had finally released the secret she carried for long years. Taylor and Stone both reassured her that there was no reason that her child's parentage couldn't remain a confidential matter.

She'd gotten pregnant and given her child up for adoption. Her son's new parents allowed her visitations as his godmother as long as it wasn't revealed that she was his mother. Denise had also been afraid what would happen to her, and possibly the child, if Jerry found out. The strict fundamentalist religion they practiced allowed no grace for sins and secrets of this magnitude.

"You handled Denise well," Taylor said.

Stone nodded and reached into an inner pocket of his jacket, pausing, and withdrawing an empty hand. "Man, I want a cigarette."

Taylor reached for her car door handle. "I'll be leaving soon enough," she said.

"It's not that. I'm trying to quit. I bought those patch things."

Taylor beamed. "Good for you," she said. "You'd do better without those patches though. They'll only prolong the misery."

"Why don't we go grab a bite to eat and discuss the case?" Stone asked.

He looked over Taylor's car while she hesitated. "Nice car," he said. "You just buy it?"

"It's a rental. Why don't you follow me?"

Stone pulled out the keys from his pocket and graced her with one of his crooked, oh-so-sexy smiles that dawned over his face like the rising sun. "I'm on your tail," he said.

Taylor hoped excitement over Denise's alibi accounted for her quickening pulse. Anything, anything but this man.

She drove to one of her favorite vegetarian restaurants in Little Five Points. She waited for Stone while he parked that rolling junkyard he called a car.

"I've never eaten here before. Do they serve foreign food?"

"They serve a few foreign dishes, mainly Indian," Taylor replied.

The restaurant was dim and intimate, and almost empty; it was a little early for the lunch crowd. They were seated quickly in a booth.

"May I get your drinks," a waiter offered.

"I'll have hot peppermint tea," Taylor answered.

"I'll have a Coke," Stone said.

"We don't serve cola drinks," the waiter said. "We have a selection of juices, iced herbed teas, and fruit smoothies."

Stone looked taken aback. "Sweet tea," he said.

"Our teas are sweetened with honey and you add your own. Would you like our green blend, jasmine, chamomile, orange spice, mint blend, or our special of the day, raspberry frost?"

Taylor tried not to giggle at Stone's aghast look.

"I'll have water," he said.

"Perrier? Dannon? Crystal—"

"Tap."

The waiter hurried away to get their drinks. "So do you still think Denise killed her husband?" Taylor asked.

Stone shrugged. "In the heat of passion, it's amazing what we're capable of doing. Do you know about passion, Taylor?"

His voice had sounded almost like a caress. Heat rose on her face and her mouth dried. She opened her mouth and not a sound emerged.

"It's public record that Denise's husband had treated her brutally. Now we discover that she had a child she felt she had to keep secret from him," Stone said.

Taylor watched his hands. He had beautiful hands for a man. Long, elegant fingers, not well kept enough to seem affected. Sensitive hands.

"First, you find out who has the greatest reason to want the victim dead," he continued. "Who has the greatest motive, thus the greatest passion. It takes passion to kill with a knife. A bullet in the head is cold and distant. An impersonal way of killing."

"You seem to know a lot about murder."

"I worked in homicide for three years."

The waiter brought their drinks and produced a pad. "Are you ready to order?"

"I'll have the tofu sandwich with sweet potato fries," Taylor said, not needing to look at the menu.

Stone raised an eyebrow at her. "I'll have a hamburger and fries."

"We don't serve hamburger here, sir. May I suggest the garden burger with sweet potato fries."

"Fine," Stone said after a moment's hesitation.

"You worked three years in homicide? What made you quit?" Taylor asked after the waiter left.

A corner of Stone's mouth tilted upward. "One reason was that I wanted to be my own boss," he answered. "ESP has done well."

"ESP?" Taylor asked.

"Emerson Surveillance and Protection," he answered.

Taylor laughed. "A name after my own heart."

"Are you really serious about that psychic stuff?"

"It's nothing to be serious about. It just is."

"A little psychic power would certainly make my job easier," Stone said, his fantastic smile touching his face again.

"Sorry. You have to be born with it."

"A seventh child, huh?"

"That helps."

The waiter interrupted, bringing their plates.

"I'm starving," Taylor said.

Stone looked over his food a little hesitantly. "It smells good. Looks okay, too." He picked up the burger and took a big bite, quickly followed by a fry. He chewed and swallowed, then made a face. "Sure tastes funky though."

Taylor couldn't stop a laugh from bubbling up. She liked Stone Emerson. She couldn't help herself.

FIVE

"I bet you're heading straight to McDonald's," Taylor said to Stone as they strolled out of the vegetarian restaurant.

"You read my mind, baby."

She shook her head. After the first bite, Stone had left his food untouched. At least he had tried it. She had no respect for people who wouldn't try new things.

Stone headed to his car. "I'll see you tomorrow," he called with a cheery wave.

Against her better judgment, she'd agreed to meet with Stone in her office tomorrow. She'd promised to ask Wendy if she would talk to Stone about the case. Marian would kill her if she found out.

Taylor blamed her poor judgment concerning Stone on gratitude that he'd gotten Denise's story out of her. Better to blame her acquiescence on gratitude than on simple lust for that man. She'd call the boy's parents tonight and see if they'd corroborate the story. It looked like Denise might be off the hook.

Stone rummaged through the pile of papers on his desk. Impatiently, he started sorting the equal disarray of papers on top of one of his bookshelves. Nothing. The cleaners threatened to charge him a surcharge if he kept misplacing the ticket. He'd change cleaners, except the one he used was so convenient to the office. Plus they did a good job on his shirts.

Resigned, he pulled out his wallet. This was the most logical place it would be, so it stood to reason that he didn't put it there. He opened the wallet and gave a whoop of triumph as he spied his dry cleaning ticket in the last place he'd look.

His secretary chose that moment to stick her head in the door. "Are you all right?"

Stone nodded, a grin on his face. "I found my dry cleaning ticket."

She grinned back at him. "A first, I'm sure. A Mr. McIntyre is here to see you. Do you want me to send him in?"

"Tell him to come right in."

George McIntyre strode in, and shook Stone's hand a little too firmly. Stone towered over him, looking down on McIntyre's stocky wide chest and overdeveloped biceps. He wondered why it was always the short guys who pumped iron.

George McIntyre checked him out also, an assessing look in his eye. "You work out, too?"

"No, I never can seem to find the time," Stone answered. He admired McIntyre's dedication. Himself, he only lifted heavy objects if absolutely necessary and only ran when chased. Stone chalked his good shape up to genetics and a fast metabolism.

McIntyre looked around for a seat, and finally moved a stack of papers off a chair next to Stone's desk and set them on the floor. "Do you mind?"

"Of course not, take a seat," said Stone, too late.

"I tried to call Arthur Robbins this morning," McIntyre said.

Stone raised an eyebrow. Arthur Robbins was the other man who'd also received a death threat. His wife was apparently staying in the shelter also.

"I couldn't get in touch with him. One of his sons answered the phone and said he was also worried. He said his father never does anything unexpected and if he was going to be out, he'd have let him know."

Stone picked up a pencil and twirled it between his fingers. "It's still early afternoon. He could have had a doctor's appointment, could have stepped out to the store."

McIntyre rubbed a weary finger across the tip of his nose. "I know. This thing has me really on edge. It's my wife, you know. If she could have me killed, she'd do it in a heartbeat. She wants control of my money, and I made the mistake of telling her over my dead body." His lips twisted.

"I built this business from nothing and I'm not going to leave it to a woman to ruin. Everything Wendy touches, she screws up. Her main value is she's ornamental. She lets those looks go, and she's nothing."

Stone kept a bland, noncommittal look on his face, but his contempt for this man was growing by the second.

"She screws around, detective," McIntyre continued. "I bet she's got some man to do me in. They'll split my money. She probably had that other woman's husband killed to throw the law off her scent."

"You have evidence your wife is having an affair?"

McIntyre's face grew red, and his fists clenched. "I don't need evidence. You should see how she flaunts her body around. If I didn't watch her every second . . ." He stared at Stone, his eyes narrowed. "You know where she is, don't you?"

Stone suddenly stood, and proffered his hand. "We discussed this before, Mr. McIntyre. My only interest in this case is the personal threats to you. But, I appreciate your concern," he said. "I'll look into the matter with Arthur Robbins."

McIntyre stumbled to his feet. "Thanks, Detective Emerson. I need to get back to work. This thing has got me all wound up. Man, when Wendy comes back home, I'm going to teach her a lesson . . ."

"I have an appointment," Stone said, his voice purposely soft.

"Oh, sorry. I'd better go. Uh, thanks again." The man finally scrambled from Stone's office a mere second before Stone gave in to the impulse to throttle him.

What made these men into the monsters they'd become? What allowed them to feel it was their right to control, to dominate, to hurt? Stone couldn't understand it. He always tried to have an open mind, not to judge people—but it was hard not to despise these men, these abusers who hurt the ones weaker than them, the ones who loved them the most.

Taylor stood in front of the shelter's opened refrigerator door. She lifted the lid and stared inside one container of leftovers, then another. Meat, meat, and more meat. Ugh. She never understood the fascination with eating dead animals. She grabbed two apples and a banana on the way out of the kitchen. She was starving and the fruit wouldn't hold her for more than an hour or so.

Wendy entered the kitchen and stared at the menu posted on the large bulletin board.

"Your turn to cook?" asked Taylor.

"Yeah. And I hate meatloaf."

"So do I. Can you make substitutions?" Taylor asked, having visions of bean and brown rice patties, salad on the side.

"In the house meeting yesterday, they said no more substitutions and to stick to the recipe. The other night, Quanita's casserole surprise didn't turn out quite right, and we had to eat it or go hungry."

"How did it taste?"

"I don't know. I took one look, and was so surprised I decided to go hungry," Wendy said with a grin, taking out a roll of hamburger from the refrigerator.

Taylor munched on an apple. "I've been wanting to talk to you alone. Your husband hired a private detective."

Alarm immediately fired in Wendy's blue eyes. "To find

me?" she whispered, her hands starting to tremble as she crumbled the crackers into the bowl with the hamburger.

"I don't believe so. He and another man whose wife is at the shelter got written messages that they would be next to die."

"What do you think that has to do with me?" Wendy asked, not looking up from the bowl.

"The detective wants to talk to you."

"About what? If I had the stomach and the means to kill my husband, God knows he'd be dead already."

Taylor looked at the purplish bruises on Wendy's face, her arms, all her exposed skin, and wondered what could make a man beat a woman so. And what could make a woman tolerate it? She knew the theories and the psychology, but she couldn't imagine the reality of living such a life of fear and terror.

"He wants to talk to all the women in the shelter." Taylor handed her Stone's card. "There's no need to reveal your whereabouts to him. And I have a strong feeling he won't say anything to your husband."

"If he came to you, he already knows where I am." Wendy's eyes darted around frantically. "Oh, God," she muttered.

Taylor gently embraced her, willing her to calm. "Wendy, you're safe. Right now, you're safe, and that's what matters. You shouldn't contact Stone if you're frightened."

Wendy nodded and pulled away. She slipped Stone's card into the pocket of her jeans, and reached for the onion and the knife. "Thanks for letting me know what's going on," she said.

Wendy had closed down, iron barriers erected to shut off emotion, to shut away fear. Taylor felt at a loss, as if she'd made some sort of faux pas. She lingered a moment while Wendy concentrated on cutting the onions, then slipped from the room. There was nothing more to say.

* * *

Taylor walked through the shelter's large dining room to the living room on her way out. Two of Teensy's children and one of Joan's kids were lying on the floor watching a show with a blaring laugh track on TV. Bea Robbins, an older black lady, was sitting in an easy chair knitting.

"I've got something to ask you," Bea said in response to the nod Taylor gave her as she passed through the room heading for the door.

Taylor paused and moved to the sofa. "How can I help you?"

"It's about my husband. Now that Arthur's out of jail, I want to get him out of the house. I want to go home. This living pillar to post is killing me. I have a home and I have my things that I worked all my life to get. I asked my daughter to talk to him . . . but my kids don't want to get involved."

Taylor felt Bea's pain. Not knowing what to say, she laid a hand on her arm in silent comfort. Bea laid down her knitting, dug in the pocket of her housedress for a tissue, and dabbed at her eyes. "It's not right what my kids are doing. It's as if they blame me for not putting up with Arthur anymore and having him arrested. They think it's my fault for tearing apart the family."

"Change is tough, Bea. It's a big change for them to see you so strong, but it's a good change. Give them time to adjust. I think I'm going to get you on the docket for divorce proceedings week afer next. We have to see where it goes from there as far as you getting possession of the house. Right now, it's purely a legal matter, and you know legal matters take time."

Bea nodded and blew her nose. "I've given my all to my family my entire life. It's time that I have a little peace before I die. Arthur never could bring himself to treat me like a human being, so I'm treating myself like one and getting the hell away from him. But it ain't fair that I got to be the one to give up everything."

Bea picked up her knitting needles and looked Taylor in the

eye. "I used to wish that old man would have a heart attack or stroke or something and now I wish it more than ever. But that devil is healthy as a horse. It's true that the good die young. Arthur Robbins is so evil he'll probably live to a hundred and twenty."

Taylor smiled. Bea was something else. It took great inner strength to break the patterns of a lifetime, and Taylor admired her greatly. She was going to do all she could do to get Bea settled back into her life. This time in the shelter had been hard on her.

"I'll talk to your husband's lawyer tomorrow, and see what I can do to speed things up."

"Thank you, baby," Bea said, her knitting needles clacking in rhythm.

Taylor left the shelter into the summer night air. She took a deep breath, cleansing her lungs of the debris of shattered dreams and broken lives. Weariness tinged with slight depression assailed her. Then, as she unlocked her car, she reminded herself not to take for granted the new hope that always permeated the shelter. The hope for happiness, real love, and a better life the women gained after painfully casting off their misery. That hope was what made her work worthwhile.

"Our agency's policy is to neither confirm nor deny the presence of anyone in the shelter," Taylor said to Stone as he lounged in her neat office the next morning. He must be at least six foot three inches she thought. Six foot three inches of brown perfectly toned man-flesh. He must work out.

"Then how am I to interview any of the suspects?" he asked.

Taylor leaned forward. "Number one, the women in our shelter are not suspects. They are victims and don't you forget it for a moment. And number two, if any of the women want to talk to you, they'll get in touch with you, on their own time and with their own dime. I'll just tell them who and where you are."

"Is that the best you can do?"

Taylor moistened her lips. "In this matter, yes."

Stone looked deep in her eyes. Taylor realized her office was too small, much too close and stifling despite the air-conditioning.

"What do I have to do to satisfy—" Stone started to say.

Marian stuck her head through the door and Taylor bit her lip. Things were just getting interesting.

"The police want to talk to us."

"Again? I thought they'd dropped Denise as a suspect."

"This is about something new." Marian darted a glance at Stone.

"This is Stone Emerson. He's a private detective handling threats related to the Whitton case."

There was a pause. A long pause.

"So, have you heard what happencd?" Marian asked Stone.

"No. What's going on?"

"Arthur Robbins has just been found. He's been murdered."

SIX

"George McIntyre was in my office yesterday worrying about Robbins," Stone murmured after Marian dropped her bombshell about Bea's husband's death.

Though Taylor was shocked at the news herself, she couldn't help feeling a tinge of relief for poor Bea. The woman could finally go back to her own home, sleep in her own bed. Bea had never left the shelter since she arrived. Thank God there was no way she could fall under suspicion.

"We'd better go, they're waiting for us in the conference room," Marian said to Taylor.

"I'd like to come with you," Stone said, rising also.

Marian shrugged. "Whether they let you stay is up to them."

When·they entered the conference room, Stone nodded at the older detective, the same one who'd met Taylor after Denise's husband was killed. The man nodded back.

"How's it going, Charles?" Stone asked.

"Could be better." The detective's hand hovered near his jacket pocket and withdrew.

"I'm trying to quit, too," Stone said.

"Makes you long for the good old days, when nobody gave a damn about smoke and lung cancer."

Then the detective leaned back in the chair and stared at Marian and Taylor with ice blue eyes. "It seems you have a problem at your shelter."

* * *

Marian had segued into steel magnolia southern belle mode. The detective seemed fascinated with Marian's ladylike, firm outrage at his demand that the shelter be searched and all the residents questioned.

Once it was decided that the search was out of the question, Taylor decided not to fight the sudden urge she had to escape. She picked up her purse and walked out of the conference room and away from the building.

She'd thought she'd accustomed herself to strong emotions and heavy forebodings, though feeling accustomed was not the same as feeling comfortable. She suspected her hard shell in the face of other's strong emotions was just that, a shell, a device thrown up to protect herself. Was it a form of cowardice to be too afraid to share the pain?

She heard someone gaining on her and looked back at Stone. He'd followed her, his long legs easily catching up with her and keeping perfect pace. He lit a cigarette. Taylor glanced at him, and the expression on his face was preoccupied, absorbed.

"Sorry," he said, intercepting her glance, and started to throw away the cigarette. She shrugged. He took another drag before he tossed the cigarette into the street.

Stone walked silently beside her. She was grateful to Stone for not trying to carry on a conversation.

They reached the Atlanta Underground, and Taylor walked briskly inside. She headed straight into a gaudy bar. Stone sat across the tiny table from her, and a waitress approached.

"Margarita. Make it a double," Taylor said.

"I'll have a Coke." Stone thrummed his fingers on the table. "I'd never have taken you for a drink-before-sundown type of person."

"Everyone has vices," Taylor said.

A hint of a smile appeared at the corner of Stone's mouth.

"What brand do you smoke?" Taylor asked.

"Marlboro."

"Figures."

"Why do you say that?" Stone asked.

"You know, the rugged, independent Marlboro man."

"That white guy is a product of Madison Avenue. And he's defeated me once again."

Taylor nodded. "It's very hard to quit any bad habit. Any sort of stress is likely to do you in."

The waitress brought their drinks and Taylor took a long swallow.

"You seem rattled. Before, you've always been so cool."

Taylor took another swallow of her drink, and set it carefully on the table. "This situation is going to seriously compromise the agency . . . and maybe even my job."

"I'm not even psychic, and I can tell more is on your mind than that."

Taylor narrowed her eyes and took another sip of her drink. The tequila hit her gut and warmed her from the toes up.

"You're right." She moistened her lips. "Every time I look around lately, you're right behind me." The atmosphere subtly changed. The air between them became charged, tense.

"Hmmm. You're not saying this is about me, are you?"

"Do you want it to be?"

Stone was watching her lips. Heat shimmered between them and it wasn't from the Georgia sun. "Direct, aren't you?"

"Very."

"Why did you turn me down when I asked you out?" Stone asked.

The man also knew how to get to the point, Taylor thought. "You scared me. You remind me of my five brothers and my father. I sense that easygoing facade of yours is just that, a facade. You like to have control in your relationships."

"A date isn't a relationship."

"With me it would soon be."

"You're pretty confident."

"Only when I have good reason to be."

He chuckled. "I suppose I don't mind giving you the reason."

Taylor leaned forward and looked deep into Stone's eyes. "You cloud my thinking. It upsets me."

"Are you serious?"

"Dead serious. I'd like to get this out of my system. My place is ten minutes away."

Stone looked away, toward the waitress. She hurried toward them and laid down the check. Stone set a ten down on the table and gestured for her to keep the change. Then he turned to Taylor, his eyes somber.

"I'm going to have to take a rain check on the invite. To be honest . . . Lady, you scare me."

Taylor stood up in a smooth motion. "Thanks for the drink," she said, taking care to keep her features unperturbed. She strolled out of the bar without a backward glance. She'd walk alone back to her car. She wanted to put a few city blocks between her and Stone Emerson before she gave in to the mortification she was feeling.

For once Taylor was happy Tiffany was out when she let herself into her apartment. She needed the space and time to herself to mull things over. She went into her adjoining bathroom and turned on the hot water and threw two handfuls of chamomile scented bath salts into the tub and watched as the water turned a soothing green.

She put on an Aretha Franklin CD. When she lived with Kara, she'd gotten hooked on the sound . . . Aretha . . . Etta James . . . blues and old soul. Dropping her clothes into a puddle on the bedroom floor, she went into the bathroom and stirred the bath water with her toe while Aretha moaned that she would never, ever love a man the way she loved him.

The water was almost too hot. Perfect. She sank in, slowly

parboiling, her brown flesh turning ruddy mahogany. Taylor loved her color of rich brown earth, red-tinted like the Georgia clay. It often seemed silly to her, the significance people attached to skin color. The colors of the earth. How could pale glass-toned sand be more or less beautiful than rich black earth? Different, yes, but each as valuable and necessary as the other. White sand, yellow clay, brown loam, black earth, and every gradient in between, all the children of the earth reflected their kinship in their very skins.

A tiny high window let in the rosy setting sun. The hot steam released the green odor of the profuse hanging ferns in the bathroom mixed with the apple-sweet scent of the chamomile. She inhaled deeply, feeling the tensions and stresses of the day dissolve. The emotions and energies of others washed away in the bath water.

She tried to take her full measure of the simple pleasure of the bath. But the ever-present image of Stone kept intruding past all her barriers. The moment she first met Stone a couple of years ago, she'd felt a flash of significance. It had scared her to death and she'd fled, and had been fleeing ever since.

Destiny brought him into her sphere once again. She'd decided not to flee or fight. She'd wanted to give in and be done with it. She'd thought they'd kick it a few times and that would be that. He'd be out of her system, and she'd have the upper hand again over her emotions. Deodorize him of the stink of cigarette smoke and Stone would make one fine man.

But he wasn't about to make it easy for her. She still could hardly believe he'd turned her down without blinking. He'd wanted her. She was an attractive, young, healthy, reasonably in-shape female, and his hormones were functioning fine. But he wanted her on his terms. And that was the problem. Taylor wasn't about to bend to any man's terms.

There he was, hovering at the edge of her consciousness, invading her reality, and she couldn't make him fade into nonsignificance. Taylor sighed deeply. Lying back against the inflated bath pillow, she let the cooling green water lap against her body. She needed to take the man to bed. Easily done, and only a matter of time. She had to play the game. Most men couldn't take the direct, let's-get-down-to-it approach from a woman.

Once she had him, he'd be out of her system, and she could have her life back, free of unsettling feelings. Not to mention the strong premonitions of a lifetime tied to and ordered around by Stone Emerson. He was completely wrong for her.

Taylor got out of the bath, and massaged sesame oil into her skin until it gleamed. She was slipping a sky-blue cotton caftan over her head when she heard a woman's voice say clearly, "Two gone, the rest to go."

A quick intake of breath, and a rush of adrenaline. Tangible sensings such as otherworldly visions, mysterious sounds, odors, and touches unsettled her profoundly. And she'd happily wait until she was a spirit herself before she sighted another ghost.

Two gone, the rest to go. A prophecy, a warning. She shivered. A killer was out there, someone close to her. Someone she knew. The abusers of the women at the shelter . . . their husbands, their lovers—they would die. She knew. And there wasn't a thing she could do about it. The men were going to die. That was as certain as if it had already happened. But a host of other possibilities lay hidden below the horizon. Other men died, or were harmed irreparably, too. When Death walked, Death wasn't finicky.

Taylor reached for her pack of Tarot cards and sat crosslegged in the center of her bed. Taking a deep breath, she shuffled the cards slowly, and though loath to lay them out, she formed them into a simple Celtic cross. She stared at the confused message. From the jumble she read, the road would not be easy. Dangers and obstacles, heartbreak and betrayal abounded.

She reshuffled the cards. The cards fell in almost the exact same pattern. A statistical improbability. Taylor gathered the cards up, knowing that sometimes they misled. She prayed that this was one of those times.

Rising, she placed the cards carefully on a shelf, then picked tiny white buds from a plant and dropped them into a small amethyst bowl of water. She lit a blue candle and released words into the air.

Sometimes the small things made a difference. Sometimes small things balanced the universe to its good.

SEVEN

Stone moved into the smoking section and lit up. "Another Coke?" the waitress asked.

"With Jack Daniels." He was a fool to turn down an offer of free, no-strings-attached . . . Right about now, he could have Taylor Cates heels over head—which was exactly the position he favored her in.

So why not? He could take it. Boy, he could take it, give it, whatever she wanted, and for however long. She'd made it clear enough that it wasn't true love she was seeking.

The problem was that she had his nose wide open. He wasn't lying when he told her she scared him. For some strange reason, prickly, dreadlocked, way-out-there Taylor Cates was who he wanted. He hoped he hadn't totally pissed her off by refusing her offer. Ah, well, she'd get over it.

Taylor was so different from the women he usually dated: socially conscious, correct, processed-haired, black American princesses. Women who would rather be snatched bald than boldly invite a man to bed.

Stone stubbed out his cigarette, and took a sip of his drink. In due time, he'd give her what she'd asked for. In full measure. Meantime, he'd have to be patient. Premature sex could ruin the relationship he hoped to have.

He left money for the drink and a generous tip.

When he entered his apartment, his dog Ernie almost

knocked him down, a hundred and thirty pounds of love and doggy-spit. "Whoa, boy, ready to go out for your walk?"

Ernie took off and returned with his leash dangling from his mouth. Stone collared the dog, and headed for Piedmont Park. Ernie strained at the leash as he made for his favorite fire hydrant.

"Nice dog," a woman said. Stone smile pleasantly and drew Ernie aside so she could jog past. She slowed down and matched their pace.

He checked her out. She was petite, light skinned, straightened hair pulled back for her run, great shape. "What kind of dog is that?" she asked.

"He's a mutt, rottweiler, Saint Bernard and German sheperd."

"He's interesting looking. By the way, my name is Amy."

He had no urge to bite. "Stone Emerson. Nice to meet you, but Ernie and I need to get home."

She didn't miss a beat. She nodded, smiled, and jogged on down the path. Stone watched her go without regret. The image of the ever-so-irritating Taylor Cates just wouldn't leave his mind.

When he and Ernie got back, he noticed the red blinking light on his answering machine. Nine messages. He threw a frozen dinner into the microwave, and turned on ESPN before he hit the button.

Five messages from his answering service, four regarding George McIntyre's calls, two from old girlfriends, one from his mother, and another from one of his sisters.

He lifted the phone and punched in George McIntyre's number. The man picked up on the first ring.

"This is Stone, I'm returning your calls."

"Thank God you've finally called back. I need to meet with you now."

Stone let the silence play out, waiting for him to give a reason.

"I heard about Arthur. I'm next in line. I have a bad feeling about this. Maybe I need to pay for some protection."

Stone couldn't disagree with him. "I'll be over in an hour."

It was at least a forty-five-minute drive to the northern suburbs where George lived. He ate his dinner in three bites and grabbed a bag of Doritos on the way out the door.

Taylor had tossed and turned most of the night, and woke up a full hour before her alarm rang. She was at her desk early this morning, but had barely gotten down her first cup of coffee when Marian stepped into her office, looking worried.

Taylor spoke before Marian opened her mouth. "We do need to get some strategy together for public relations, in case the media puts this together, and they will. We also need to present a united front to the police."

Marian beamed. "You read my mind. I shouldn't have gotten so upset with that detective. We need to work well with the APD, and we usually do. But this is a touchy matter with all the issues of confidentiality and client safety involved."

"I'm going to get in touch with some of the other shelters to see if they've dealt with a similar matter."

Carol, the social worker, stuck her head in the door. "I got a message in my voice mail from the newspaper. They want to know if they can interview a shelter resident. Anonymous, of course."

"I'll get back to them," Marian said. Carol nodded and withdrew.

Marian turned to Taylor, a question in her eyes.

Taylor shook her head. "Even if one of our clients agrees to be interviewed. I don't think it's a good idea right now. They're all on edge because of the murders, and probably would talk about it."

Taylor stood. "Let me brainstorm a while, and I'll get back with you around eleven. I need to get over to the shelter now.

I want to meet with the residents, and I have a court appearance."

Taylor squinted against the bright morning sun as she headed for her car. A contrast to the darkness waiting for her at the shelter. Someone there was the killer. She felt it.

A large group of women and children were finishing breakfast. Taylor smiled and waved at the greetings they gave and went into the kitchen and helped herself to a biscuit, and another cup of coffee.

Christine sat down next to her when she settled down at the table. "We got in two new women yesterday with three kids. We're bursting at the seams. Funny how we fill up when the temperature gets above ninety."

"Bea gone yet?"

"I've just got her packed. Her daughter's picking her up at ten. I'm taking her stuff over to the agency in a few minutes. Want to help?"

"I would, but I need to speak with the clients before they all scatter."

"Eva's gone to the hospital already. One of her patients had a turn for the worse. She'll probably be leaving soon. We're still trying to get her into somewhere untraceable. We're having a hard time with the utility companies."

"We decided to get them turned on in the agency's name," Taylor said. "So, she'll probably be leaving in a few days."

"Great, two beds open. I got six kids doubled up, and it's not working out too well."

"Christine, I got a problem," Teensy said, leaning on the table. "That new woman, Kay, you put in my room isn't working out. She took over my kid's closet space without asking. And she said I needed to keep the kids out of the room except at night. We can't take her smell either. You have to do something."

Taylor jumped from the sudden clang of cookery. She looked

around and saw the woman in question standing in the kitchen door, a tall, attractive white woman with an unruly mane of red hair and heavy makeup. Obviously she'd heard. "I need to get a new room. Don't even let me get started. That woman doesn't even try to control those wild kids of hers."

Teensy rolled her eyes and moved away.

"I need a ride down to the social service office, I got an appointment at nine thirty," Quanita interrupted.

"What about the bus?" Christine asked.

"I don't have money for the bus."

"I'll get you a pass. And I can't do a thing about room re-assignments until some beds open up. You all are going to have to cope."

Teensy's roommate burst into tears, flinging her flame-red hair from her face. "If you don't get me out of that . . . woman's room right now, I'm going to go back home to my boyfriend and let him kill mc. I don't care. I just don't care anymore."

Christine handed her a tissue.

Joan, the ex-soccer mom, approached. "Taylor, the dry cleaners doesn't open until ten. I don't know if have time to get my suit out before court."

"Don't worry about it, as long as you're clean and neat."

Joan bent down and whispered in Christine's ear in a stage whisper. "When Bea goes, if I got to put up with a family, I will. That new woman does have a smell. Gas, I think."

Christine nodded, her pleasant expression unchanging through all of this. Taylor didn't know how she stood it. She'd worked in the shelter once when Christine took vacation, and by the end of the week, she was nearly crazy, and had to take a vacation herself to recover.

"I'll meet with you in my office in half an hour," Christine told the still sobbing redheaded woman. "I've got to go talk to the new family. We're having a problem with the rules already," she said to Taylor.

"I need to get with everybody for a few minutes before they all scatter. Is there any way you can watch the kids? It's important."

"Better do it now, then. I'll get everyone together in the living room. You need to make it quick, I'm swamped already," Christine said. "Listen up, everybody. Taylor's got a mandatory meeting in ten minutes. Living room. Adults only."

There were no groans forthcoming. Taylor supposed the women had a good idea of her topic and didn't mind any meeting where they might hear more about the murders.

"I'll only take a few minutes," Taylor said when everybody finally was settled in the living room. "I know you need to get started with your day." She nodded at Bea, who just entered. "I know the recent murders are foremost in everyone's minds."

"I wonder who I can give the word to that I want mine to go next," Quanita said. Nervous laughter rippled through the room.

"I need to remind everyone about confidentiality. Any breaches whatsoever can result in your being barred from any shelter in the area indefinitely. But it's more important than that. This threatens the very existence of the shelter."

She looked around slowly at all the women in the room. She finally had their attention. Nobody would be here if it wasn't absolutely necessary for them and their children's safety. Communal living was a pain, but it was a price each woman here was willing to pay.

"Confidentiality includes speculating about any events concerning any shelter resident without tacit agency approval. That means interviews and casual conversation. Understand?"

"We need to talk about this among ourselves. It is strange, two men being murdered, with us the only connection between them," Teensy said.

"You're right. Discussing this among ourselves is different. I'm going to make it a point to be at group at seven." Taylor stood. "We'll talk more about it then. Remember confidentiality."

Christine stuck her head in. "Joan, your caseworker wants you to give her a call right away."

Taylor's fists clenched as she watched the women as they scattered. She had an ulterior motive for getting them together. She'd opened herself up, reaching for a clue as to what was going on, reaching for anything. She'd slammed against a black wall. That was something she'd never experienced before, a barrier. She always could at least detect the emotions of the moment in a person. Who could cast up a barrier to mental probes?

The obvious answer made her shiver. Someone who had considerable mental powers herself. Someone who could detect Taylor's probing. It was outside Taylor's experience. She'd never met anyone else with true second sight. She couldn't ignore the knot that curled in her stomach. Fear. She was afraid of what would happen next.

EIGHT

George McIntyre was standing in his doorway before Stone even got out of his car. He waited, fidgeting as Stone approached. "It's about time you got here."

His comment didn't seem to call for a reply, so Stone stepped past him through the door. "Nice house," Stone said as he looked around, admiring the strong, masculine decor, unusual in a home on this scale. Homes this grand usually reflected the woman's dominant touch in interior design.

"Why don't we go into my office?"

Stone followed George to a room that looked more like a library than an office, with a comfortable leather couch and chair, bookcases reaching to the ceiling, a massive desk.

"Have a seat," George said, heading for a bar against the far wall. "Want a drink?"

"No, thanks."

He sank into the buttery leather and watched George pour himself a generous amount of bourbon.

"You should have listened to me. I warned you about Robbins." George stood across from Stone, assuming the pugnacious waiting posture of a sparring partner. Or maybe a bantam cock?

"You're absolutely right. I should have listened to you. Now a man is dead." Stone leaned forward, looking earnest. "We have to carefully consider what we're going to do next."

George relaxed. "I'm gonna need some protection. You handle that don't you?" He walked over to the couch and sat down.

"I have some excellent bodyguards."

"A bodyguard? Maybe that's a bit much."

"That's what I meant by protection. You have a state-of-the-art security system installed here?"

George nodded. "But a bodyguard? It would look strange at the office. You know, like I couldn't protect myself or something."

"You want someone who blends in, who doesn't look like obvious protection." Stone nodded sagely. "You want a woman."

"A woman! What's a woman supposed to do if something happens?"

"You'd be surprised."

"No. No woman. I'd be wasting my money."

"So you want a big burly guy following you around day and night?"

George looked glumly into his drink.

"I got just the woman for you. Turns out she's available, a rare occurrence. Why don't you give her a try for a week or two. I tell you, you'll be surprised. Anne's very competent."

"I find that hard to believe. But I can't go on like this. That first guy who was killed was big. Someone tied him down, and took him out with hardly a struggle. Maybe another pair of eyes at my back will be enough." George flexed his muscles. "I can handle anything that comes along. Even protect the girl, if I have to. I work out, you know."

"Yeah, you told me." Stone stood. "I'll give her a call. She should be here first thing in the morning. Let me give the house a quick once over before I go, then activate the alarm system." He got his wallet out, and pulled out a card. "Here's a picture of her. You shouldn't let anybody else in until she arrives."

George studied the card. "She's attractive. I like blonds, but she looks like she couldn't protect a fly."

"Believe me, looks are deceiving."

"Might be kind of fun, after all," George said, taking a sip of his drink. "How much is this going to set me back?"

Stone told him. Then he left the room to do his walk-through while George was still choking and sputtering. He felt pretty good. There was no one better than Anne to set George straight on his odd ideas about women.

Taylor touched Joan's hand as they waited on the court docket, trying to soothe her and send her strength. So much depended on this court hearing. After twelve years of marriage and beatings, Joan had finally gotten the strength to call the police. They came with flashing lights and arrested her husband. She'd told Taylor her neighbors were still talking about the spectacle of seeing her husband, a respected banker, led away in handcuffs.

He got out of jail the next day, and Joan took her kids and fled, genuinely frightened for her life. Although the police observed him pushing her, they saw no evidence of grievous battery. Joan had hid her scars and bruises well, and took to bed with a case of the "flu" after particularly serious beatings.

They had a large house, and he always made sure the kids were in the basement rec room, and they were in their private suite before he started the beatings. He denied everything, and said she was crazy and jealous, an unstable woman and a dangerous mother.

He was trying to get sole custody of the children with limited visitation for Joan. Joan's parents were dead and her in-laws supported their son totally. Her only brother lived out of state and wasn't all that interested in her personal problems. Over the years, she'd become estranged from the few friends she had. Joan was alone and facing the biggest battle of her life. She needed Helping Hands, not only for shelter, but for the community and emotional support the agency offered.

Taylor's heart had sunk when she'd seen the judge assigned to today's docket, an older white man who had a history of lecturing parents and making quick, surface judgments. From Taylor's personal experience, she knew the judge could care less about the custody of a lower-class black woman's children. But the judge was certain to take a special interest in this case.

"All rise," the bailiff said.

The judge entered.

He sat, and the court followed suit. Taylor darted a quick glance at Joan. Her upper lip was beaded with tiny drops of sweat, and she was pale and drawn. Taylor hated that she had to go through this. She already had a very good idea of the judge's decision.

Judge Gold studied the folder while the bailiff announced their case.

"I sat up most of the night worrying about this sad situation," the judge intoned.

Taylor wanted to roll her eyes. She'd love to see the day when Judge Gold said he stayed up all night worrying about a black welfare mother's family dispute.

"I understand this is the only police report pertinent to this matter?"

"Hmmm," the judge said at the opposing counsel's affirmative answer. "No prior evidence of spousal abuse? I see here statements of the children's social workers attesting to absolutely no evidence of the father abusing them in any way."

He looked over at Joan.

"Why are you suing for sole custody?"

"I believe I'd be the better parent. We were barely married for six months before Harry started hitting me . . ."

"Objection."

"Sustained."

"We have evidence here of Ms. Spencer's insane jealousy—"

"Objection—irrelevant," Taylor said, not surprised by the judge's response.

"Overruled."

Opposing counsel continued, "She thought he was having an affair at the office. I have affidavits from several office employees attesting to her many disruptive calls during working hours."

"Hearsay," Taylor's voice rang out. "Move to strike."

"Overruled."

Joan's face crumpled. "It's not true," she whispered.

The judge put on his half-framed reading glasses. "I see from the financial statements that Harry Spencer was the household's sole financial support for twelve years. I've banked at the bank you work at for years, by the way, fine institution," he said, nodding at Joan's husband.

Taylor's heart sank. It was all over, not even a decent skirmish.

The judge turned to the table where she and Joan were sitting. "Your husband's job was paramount to family survival, and the disruption you caused possibly harmed his career. I understand that you're not supporting yourself at this time, is that correct?"

Joan said, "I'm going to get an apartment. I used to work as a secretary, and I plan to take a refresher course . . ."

"Do you realize that you have no chance of providing your children with what your husband can easily give them. Did you think of them? Did you think of anything besides yourself?"

Joan's eyes filled with tears, and she choked, but no words emerged. Her husband looked smug. Taylor wished the judge would keel over with a heart attack that very moment. She hoped there was a special hell for fools, criminals, and stupid judges. Together.

"My judgment is that the children be given over to their father for temporary custody with reasonable visitation rights for the mother until Joan Spencer can provide evidence of appropriate housing and sufficient income. I'll reconsider this case for joint custody in ninety days."

He handed the file to the clerk. It was over.

Joan was frozen in shock, her eyes glassy. "No, no, no . . ." she started to moan. Taylor prodded her to the door. She needed to get her out of the courtroom before—

"I can't believe it. Judge!" Joan screamed in anguish. "You don't know what this man is capable of, please don't do this to me and my kids."

The gavel pounded and the deputies came to drag Joan from the court, still screaming and sobbing.

Taylor gave the judge a long look, raised her chin, and turned to follow Joan. Sometimes you had to experience the system before you truly believed it. She hurried to comfort Joan and tell her the battle was only just beginning.

An hour after the appointed time, Taylor knocked on Marian's door. "Sorry, I'm late."

"Bad time at court?"

"The worst. Gold was the judge."

"Crap. Our client lost custody, didn't she?"

"Temporarily. I don't know why we even bother to show up at court when Gold's presiding. He's so predictable. I've got some irons in the fire though. If Joan can get herself on her feet, she'll be okay."

"Easier said than done. She's been isolated and broken down for twelve years . . ." Marian shook her head.

"I think Joan is stronger than she realizes."

"God, I hope so," Marian murmured.

"I talked to all the shelter residents about confidentiality this morning. But I think a leak's the least of our worries."

Marian fished for her purse and stood up. "Let's talk about this over lunch. The least of our worries, eh?"

"I believe someone at the shelter is the killer."

Marian sat back down. "Don't say that out loud. What makes you think that?"

"Say I have a hunch."

Marian stared at her. "After working with you for two years, I never discount your hunches anymore. What can we do?"

Taylor bit her lip. "I don't know. I can't see any way to stop them. I get the feeling that this person is relentless."

"There'll be another murder attempt?"

"I hope not, Marian. But we have no choice but to wait for the next move."

NINE

The shelter group was more subdued than usual, Taylor thought. Christine was there, along with Linda, one of the night shelter staff. Carol, the social worker who usually led the groups and did individual counseling, sipped a cup of coffee. Taylor exchanged greetings and went into the kitchen to get a cup of tea before they got into full swing. All the children were downstairs in the basement playroom/nursery with child-care workers.

Joan tearfully told the group what had happened at her court appearance.

"How can judges get away with not taking into account the fact that the husband was abusive?" Teensy asked.

Quanita snorted. Taylor knew she was wise to the ways of the legal system.

"The judge is the absolute power in his or her courtroom, especially when there's no jury," Taylor said. "Without evidence corroborating the allegation of abuse, such as the police witnessing actual abuse, statements to doctors, or documentation of injuries on the hospital records, it's simply your word against theirs."

"Nobody would lie about their husband hitting them," Wendy said, arms across her chest.

"No one usually does," Carol said. "Joan, what do you need from the group to help you through this hard time?"

"Everybody's been so nice to me. But I really need everybody's support now." She blew her nose and wiped her eyes with a tissue. Quanita crossed the room, and leaned over and hugged Joan, whispering something in her ear.

Taylor considered Quanita and Joan an unlikely pair. They'd forged a solid friendship at the shelter. There was no one better than Quanita to tarnish Joan's suburban middle-class naïveté and ready her for the world's reality and hard knocks, Taylor thought.

"Whatever we can do," Wendy murmured.

Kay, the redhead, raised her hand to speak. "I need a room reassignment. Now that Bea's gone, Joan has an empty bed in her room."

Joan blanched.

"I'll see about room reassignments tomorrow. I need to remind you that things are always changing, and you all must be flexible," Christine said. "We may get an admission tonight, and have to juggle everyone around. That's a reality of the shelter. We do the best we can, but remember nobody is guaranteed any specific room or bed, merely a bed, and sometimes the kids don't even get a bed to themselves," Christine said.

"Since I been here, once we got real full and people had to sleep on the couch or on one of the roll-away beds," Teensy added.

"We try to avoid those kinds of situations, but I'd rather change everyone's bed assignment than have no shelter for a woman in danger. We're not about personalities here." Christine set her can of Coke firmly on the table to emphasize her point.

"No, you're not going to like everybody, but we expect politeness. Everyone has to be tolerant and flexible. Failure to adjust to your coresident's personality and idiosyncrasies is not an option," Carol said.

Taylor admired Christine and Carol. They kept the shelter running smoothly, considering they were dealing with a group of women and kids thrown together, most in the worst crisis of their lives. There hadn't been any riots or mutinies yet, and only the occasional fist or food fight.

"Bea called me and said she was ecstatic to be home, and everything is going well for her. She wants to give everyone her love," Carol said.

"She's lucky, all her problems just died," Joan said in a bitter tone.

There was an almost audible intake of breath. Taylor set down her teacup carefully. "It's scary, and it looks bad for us. Two men died who were abusers of residents at this shelter. But it could be coincidence," Taylor said.

Eva stared at her. "You don't believe that it's a coincidence. It only makes sense that one of us, or someone that knows us, did it."

"Tell me who, so I can pin a medal on their chest," Wendy quipped. "We might love our husbands and all, but there isn't a single one of us who wouldn't be a whole lot better off with them dead."

"Amen," Joan said fervently.

"It doesn't really do any good to speculate. We need to prepare ourselves for possible police interviews and a barrage of publicity if it comes to that. Our anonymity may be compromised," Taylor said.

Eva shook her head. "I can't risk it coming out where I'm staying. My husband would hunt me down, and maybe torch the place. Especially if he knows there are only women here. He's afraid to mess with me at the hospital because of the restraining order, and I always have security close by."

"If my boyfriend found me, he'd come by with his boys," Quanita said. "I don't know what they'd do, but it wouldn't be good."

"We would close down and relocate you before we released

the location of the shelter to the public," Taylor said, and Carol nodded.

"I know it's a lot to ask, but try not to worry. Continue working on your plans to rebuild your lives, and don't allow anything to get you off track from what really matters," Carol said. "Yourself and your kids." Her gaze fell on Mai Lin. "I'm not trying to put you on the spot, but I wanted to make sure you didn't have anything to add. How do you feel about all this going on, Mai?"

Mai lifted up her hands, which she'd held neatly folded in her lap, and stared at them. "I'm happy for the women who lost their husbands. Maybe now they'll be able to live." Mai Lin's voice was low but fierce.

Taylor watched her with concern. They'd all been worried about Mai. She never really spoke or opened up. They'd only been able to cadge bits and pieces of her story out, never the whole picture. Taylor's impression was of a woman profoundly beaten down.

Mai Lin lowered her hands. "My daughter died. She was the love of my life, my only child. Her husband killed her. He beat her to death, along with my unborn grandson. If only someone had killed him first."

Everyone was silent. It was almost as if they were afraid to say anything that would break the spell of Mai Lin's sharing.

"My fault. She learned how to endure from me. Her father frequently disciplined me in front of her. I thought it shameful to complain, even to cry. I thought I made it better if I endured the pain without a cry."

She studied her hands. "My daughter married a man new from Hong Kong. A very traditional man, like her father. From me, she learned how to be a wife. She learned her lessons well. The neighbors never heard her cry out, not even the night she died." Her chin sunk deeper on her chest. "I kill my only daughter as sure as he did."

A collective, slow exhale.

Carol cleared her throat. "Your story almost moves me to tears, Mai. But you must remember violence is always the choice of the abuser, never the victim. I applaud and admire your courage in breaking free of your husband. I can't imagine . . ."

Mai Lin nodded her head slowly and neatly refolded her hands in her lap. "Thank you," she said,

Taylor shuddered from the depths of the pain she was feeling from this woman.

"That's deep," Quanita said. "I don't see how you can think you killed your daughter. Ain't it cultural for y'all to be kind of cool and restrained? You can't fault yourself for your culture. I sure don't."

An infinitesimal flash of humor touched Mai's face. "No, you don't. I guess that is a good thing."

The desire to talk about the murders paled under the impact of Mai's confession. Also, Carol never made a big deal of introducing the new residents. She gave them time to settle in, to recover somewhat from the acute crisis that brought them here before she put a spotlight on them in any way. They had enough pressure simply adjusting to the shelter life.

Taylor surveyed all the faces in the room. Mai Lin, quiet and restrained, recovered from her confession, which was as startling as a complete emotional breakdown from anyone else. Eva looked tired. She was, by far, one of the brightest people in the room. She had the medical knowledge to know plenty of ways for people to die.

Quanita, raised with violence, and murder was simply another unpleasant fact of life. Wendy stood to inherit a small fortune if her husband died. Teensy was a take-no-guff practical type, big and strong enough to subdue a man. Joan was the last of the original group of women in the shelter when Denise's husband died. Joan who might lose her kids, and from whom Taylor had glimpsed hidden depths of strength and will.

Taylor ticked off the new women—Kay, the high-strung red-head, and Laura, a young black woman with three kids, who was very quiet and soft-spoken so far.

The staff. She'd never suspected the staff! Christine and Lily were the primary day shelter staff, the shelter manager and her assistant. And there were around eight other paid staff members who covered nights and weekends. That didn't count the office staff, who were in and out. Any one of almost twenty women could be the murderer.

Taylor was sure it was a woman. The memory of a female voice whispered, "Two down, the rest to go."

"Do you have anything else to add?" Carol was asking her.

"No, that's it, unless somebody has questions."

"No questions? Then let's call it a night."

Taylor was rinsing out her teacup when Wendy approached. "You know that detective you told me about? That one my husband hired?"

Taylor laid the cup in the dish drain. "Yes, I remember."

"Well, I want to talk to him. I figure it won't hurt, and the more I find out what George has up his sleeve, the better."

"Okay. I'll give him the message."

"Thanks, Taylor. And by the way, if George turns up dead, forget I ever said anything about wanting him killed. I don't want to go through what Denise did."

"I sincerely hope you won't have to."

TEN

Taylor checked her watch yet again. Stone was due to arrive at her office in ten minutes to meet with Wendy. She'd been on edge all morning. The last time she saw him didn't end at all well from her standpoint, her cheeks burning a little as she remembered her invitation, and his easy refusal. "Lady, you scare me," he'd said.

So she'd been forward, brazen even. All right. She'd put their budding relationship back on ground she was comfortable with. He wouldn't consider a relationship beyond a physical fling with a woman like her. Men thought women who were forthright about their needs were only good for one thing. And that one thing was good enough for her.

Coward, a tiny voice whispered in her head. You're copping out. You're wildly attracted to Stone Emerson, the man scares the drawers off you, and you can't handle it. You want to blow it, to turn him off so bad you don't have to deal with your feelings, and worse, the possibility he'd reject you. You're going to make certain it never comes to that, you fool.

"I guess I'm a little early."

Taylor flinched in surprise as the object of her reflections stood directly in front of her desk.

"Uhhh . . ." Not a single coherent word dared to emerge from her mouth.

Stone dropped into a chair. "You seemed deep in thought."

"Uh. I was thinking about . . . the murders. It doesn't look good for the shelter."

"Looks a whole lot worse for the men in your clients' lives."

"If they weren't abusers, their women wouldn't be here, and they wouldn't have a problem."

Stone arched that sexy right eyebrow of his. "Abusers or not, they don't deserve to be killed so brutally. Nobody does."

"The killer is a woman," Taylor said, mainly to fill the awkward silence that descended after his last point.

"How do you know?"

Taylor shrugged and looked away.

"Do you know of some evidence that I'm not aware? My contacts in the APD said they'd turned up nothing concrete."

"No evidence. Say I have a feeling."

"Taylor, you're going pretty far with this psychic stuff. Murder is nothing to make light of. Abusers or not, those men had mothers, children . . . people who cared about them."

Taylor stood, and walked to her window. "People rarely believe me, and the ones who do tend to believe everything anyone tells them. I've been called a flake, an imposter, you name it. So I don't talk about it. The gift has been no blessing to me, I'd be better off without it. My knowledge usually isn't specific enough or full enough to make a difference. It just nags and worries at me. Makes me feel as if I should be doing something, standing in the way of the flow of fate, so that the eddy will turn another way."

She turned back to the desk and sat down. "I never should have said anything."

Stone regarded her. "How do you know the killer is a woman?" he repeated. His face showed no hint of mockery, just a touch of concern.

"A woman's voice said, 'Two down, the rest to go.' I knew it was the killer. I felt the touch of her mind . . ."

Stone blinked. "Anything more specific?"

Taylor lowered her eyes. "No." She bit her lip. "There's this one thing. I strongly feel it's someone connected with the shelter."

"The APD feels that, too."

Taylor shot a sharp glance at Stone.

"So what do you think would help you get more specific information on the killer?"

Taylor folded her arms across her chest. "That's a pretty sudden transformation from skeptic to true believer."

"I never said I was a true believer. I know there are many things in this world I don't understand. Something tells me you're not the type to lie or play games. I'm giving what you say, a chance."

Taylor felt a secret place in her heart start to crack. He trusted her and didn't believe she was simply a flake. And with the crack, came an instant of knowing that the time would come when this man's opinion of her mattered more than anything else in the world. A future of dependence, body, heart, mind, and soul on Stone Emerson.

She slammed shut that open place in her heart, that place where Stone Emerson seemed to belong. Alarm filled her as she flashed back to her adolescent rebellion and young adult surge to break free and establish her independence despite the controlling men in her life. Her feelings for this man threatened to take away the identity she'd fought to establish, to replace Taylor Cates with somebody who only wanted to please Stone Emerson.

She panicked. Taylor moistened her lips and leaned closer to him. Direct eye contact. Thrust out breasts. Thighs slightly parted. She felt Stone's gaze intensify and the thermometer notched up a few degrees in the air-conditioned office. Good. Men were so predictable, so easy to understand and direct.

"My invitation still stands," Taylor said in a husky voice.

Stone looked totally confused for a moment, then visibly pulled himself together.

"Taylor, quit it," he said, sounding exactly like her oldest brother. "I know what you're doing, and it's not going to work with me."

Feeling disoriented, she repeated, "What's not going to work with you? Are you saying I'm not going to get you into bed?"

A slow smile curved his lips. "I'm not saying all that. Kara and Brent told me all about you, and what you're showing me ain't it. Give up, girl. I'm not going anywhere. Do you ever get a feeling that some things are simply meant to be? I do. We're meant to have a real relationship, Taylor, in spite of all you're trying to do to scare me away or turn me off. It's not going to work."

She closed her eyes. Lord help her, the man had read her like a book. Was he psychic, too? What the heck did he mean that they were going to have a real relationship if he wouldn't even take her to bed?

"We'll talk more about this over lunch, my choice this time. What do you think's keeping Wendy?" he said.

George peeked out of the peephole at the petite blond standing at his door. He glanced at the photograph in his hand. It was her all right. Although how this little woman was supposed to be a bodyguard was beyond him. She squinted in the bright sun and the movement betrayed the fine network of lines around her eyes. Cute, but a little worn around the edges. Great shape, though. That's really all that counts, George thought. It wasn't the face you . . .

"Aren't you going to let me in?"

George opened the door. "Stone told me to make sure it was you before I let anyone in." He brandished the photo at her. She cocked her head to the side, assessing him. "Anne Riley," she said, proffering her hand. He took her hand, expecting the little lady to try and bone crush him considering her occupation and all. Her handshake was firm, but surprisingly ladylike.

"I'll be your new assistant at the job. I'll be close by observing you at all times. I need you to make sure this is possible."

Trying to take charge already, huh? "Just how close are you going to get to me?"

She lifted an eyebrow. "Close enough to do my job." She stared at him, and he shifted uncomfortably under her gaze. "You can make all the innuendos you like, I don't care. Just make sure you don't act on any of them."

So, she thought she was a tough cookie. He'd set her straight. She cost him a pretty penny and he planned to get his full value. He'd watched enough TV to know what bonuses were added on to the bodyguard deal. George smiled. "Forgive me. I'm under a lot of stress right now."

Anne shrugged. "Am I dressed appropriately for your office?"

She had on khakis, loafers, and a white, crisp cotton shirt.

"You'll do," he said. He let her lead the way out of the door. That was something else that was going to change soon. He was the man, so he led, or he refused to play. That was simply the way it was. He didn't make the rules of this world, he just followed them.

Wendy knocked on the door just in time to avert Taylor's impending nervous breakdown. Stone had gone in search of a cup of coffee and left Taylor with her dour thoughts. Did he actually tell her to quit it? Why, when she'd heard him say that a relationship between them was meant to be?

"Sorry, I'm late. Where's that detective I'm supposed to talk to?"

"He went to get some coffee."

"I called George's office to leave a message for him about when my brother was coming to pick up my things. He picked up. He was in the best mood. He said he got a replacement for me, and he was going to give in to the terms of the divorce settlement. He said he wanted me out of his life so he could move on."

Taylor waited, sensing listening was the best thing she could do for Wendy right now.

"Stupid me, all he put me through, and here I am upset he's got another woman. I should be relieved." She wiped a tear from her eye. "So, what does that detective want to talk to me about?"

"I think he wants to find out if you know anything about the threat to your husband's life."

Stone strolled in, steaming cup of coffee in his hand. "Ms. McIntyre?"

"Yes, sorry I'm late."

He sat down. "That's all right. I'm Stone Emerson. Your husband hired me last week."

Wendy tensed. "Did he ask you to find me?"

"That's not the job I agreed to do. He hired me because of the threats to his life. Did Taylor tell you that I will keep our meeting confidential?"

"Yeah. She said you could be trusted."

"I appreciate that. I don't have any long interrogation in mind for you. I just wanted to ask if you knew anything about these threats to your husband."

"He told you I did it, did he?"

"He thinks that's a possibility."

"That paranoid son of a bitch." Wendy stood up and paced the tiny office. "Although he's got a good point."

Taylor held her breath.

"He knows if I could, I'd string him up and relieve him of those masculine jewels he's so fond of in a hot second." She stopped a mere foot away from where Stone leaned against the office wall. "George knows if I had the means to kill him, he'd be a dead man already." She turned away and resumed pacing. "I need a cigarette," she muttered.

Stone reached into his shirt pocket and pulled out a pack of Marlboros and handed her one.

"Thanks." Wendy stuck the cigarette between her lips. "Is that it?"

Stone nodded.

"Bye, Taylor," she said on her way out the door.

Taylor looked after her. "Well, that was mighty productive," she said, a sarcastic tinge to her voice.

"It was," Stone answered. "That woman has nothing to do with the murders."

ELEVEN

For once, Taylor didn't mind the traffic on the drive out to Kara and Brent's Stone Mountain home. There was a strange Ford Taurus parked next to Kara's minivan. She must still be doing hair, Taylor thought. She went around to the side door to the basement level where Kara had a beauty salon outfitted.

There was no immediate answer to her knock, understandable because of the pounding blare of music. Taylor pushed the door open, and Kara looked up, curling iron in hand.

Obviously pregnant, glowing and beautiful, she grinned at Taylor. "Good to see you, girl. I'll be done in a moment, make yourself at home."

Taylor smiled back at her and nodded at the woman in the chair. Walking out to the family room, she picked up and hugged Kincaid, Kara's two year old. A teenager danced to the music of Blackstreet. Taylor returned Kincaid to the floor and the toddler scampered around, dancing and giggling. Taylor joined them, her slim hips easily swaying to the beat of the music.

"Dance, Auntie Taylor, dance." Kincaid said.

Taylor laughed and kissed her. "I missed you, baby."

Kara and the woman with the new 'do entered. Even though Taylor wouldn't be caught dead with the woman's style, she did look nice. Her hair was bone straight, frozen into place, and wouldn't last more than a few days without intensive intervention. Taylor didn't see the point.

She managed to keep a straight face as the woman handed Kara a check for seventy-five dollars. Lord have mercy, obviously she'd entered the wrong field.

"You look sharp," Kara assured the woman as she walked out the door.

"That hair is so sharp and hard, it could cut somebody," Taylor murmured, after the woman exited.

"Quit, girl. Please, don't get started on hair." Kara touched her long relaxed hair, styled simply in a soft pageboy.

"I just don't see why we can't be natural. Now, you know that hair of yours ain't nothing like you were born with. The Bible says Jesus had woolly hair. What's wrong with wool?"

"Not a thing, except it's hard to comb through. Variety is the spice of life, we can change our hair texture and color, and we do. We're not the only race that does it. And haven't we had this conversation before?"

"Guess so, but it's one of my favorites."

Kincaid fussed at the babysitter and Kara scooped her up in her arms. "It's nap time."

Taylor kissed the child. "Night, night, baby," she said. Kincaid waved goodbye as her mother carried her out of the room.

Taylor wandered into the kitchen and poured herself a glass of wine. When she returned to the living area, Kara was paying the babysitter.

"Kincaid was happy to see that bed," Kara said after the teenager left.

Taylor followed her to the kitchen and watched as she poured a glass of apple juice. "What's been going on with you and Brent? How's that baby doing in there?"

"The baby is doing great. Oh, I have news! I can't believe I haven't told you yet. Yesterday, at my ultrasound, I found out I'm having a little boy."

Taylor grinned. "Fabulous. How's Brent taking it?"

"He's thrilled. Although he said he wouldn't have minded being the only man here in a house full of females."

"I grew up in a house full of men. Even though I have my own bathroom now, I still don't sit on the toilet without checking if the seat is down."

Kara giggled. "I still can't get Brent completely trained." She gave Taylor a considering look. "By the way, I overheard Stone tell Brent that he's seeing you."

"He is seeing me, but it's not what you think. One of the reasons I've been so busy lately is because of the agency. Two of the shelter residents' abusers have been murdered."

"My goodness. Do you think someone at the shelter is responsible?"

"I don't know. After the first murder, two men received threats on their lives. One is dead, the other one hired Stone."

"I don't know what to think. Scary that someone you work with every day could be a murderer."

"It's very scary."

Kara's finger circled around the rim of her glass. "I got the feeling that Stone wasn't just talking about a work relationship. He's been attracted to you for quite some time. I never could understand why you wouldn't go out with him. He's one of the nicest guys I know."

Taylor shifted. "Something about him makes me want to run and hide. He's so much like my brothers . . ."

"What's wrong with that? Brent's lucky that I met and fell in love with him before I met any of your brothers. They are sooo fine."

"You've never had to live with them. They're bossy and controlling. I love them, but they drive me crazy. I couldn't even date until after I left home. If my father didn't chase away every boy I had the slightest interest in, my brothers did. I complied with the pressure to conform to their mold up to a point. I went to law school. But no farther."

"When I went with you to visit your family, it looked like they adored you. It must have been wonderful to grow up with such love and concern." Kara sounded wistful.

"The grass ain't always greener. I think after mother died everybody was overly concerned with protecting me. I felt like I was being suffocated. The problem is that Stone seems so much like them. You know I wanted a different sort of man. I can't imagine spending a lifetime cramped, struggling to be free."

"Just because Stone isn't some new-age flake doesn't mean that he's some bossy control freak. Although I know exactly what you mean about being confined by outside forces; I grew up in a similar situation. But I don't see how dating Stone has anything to do with what you're talking about. He hasn't asked you to marry him, has he?"

"But it might go there. I'm psychic, remember."

"Oh." Kara leaned toward Taylor. "I think you're just scared. I've met some of the guys you chose to date. They might look good, but Stone is head and shoulders above any of them. You want Stone, and you're afraid to face it."

Taylor frowned. "I'm not scared of anything. I know I want Stone. I planned to go ahead and kick it with him and get it out of my system, but he turned me down. Twice."

Kara paused midsip of her apple juice. "You asked him to bed twice? And he said no?"

"Yep. Pissed me off, too."

"Taylor, you don't go around asking men to bed, especially men you want to pursue a relationship with. Since the beginning of time, men have preferred to be the hunter."

Taylor gave her an arched eyebrow look. "Exactly. I would have killed two birds with one Stone, got Stone out of my system and out of my hair, too."

"I don't understand why he turned you down. I've seen how

he looks at you," Kara muttered. Suddenly a smile curved her lips. "Taylor, I think Stone's got your number."

"I know he does," Taylor said, her voice miserable.

The sound of a key turning in the front door came from upstairs. "Brent must have come home early. He's cut back on his caseload to spend more time with me and Kincaid." Kara struggled to get up out of the overstuffed couch and Taylor gave her a hand. "Here I am barely six months pregnant and lumbering already."

Taylor followed her up the stairs. Brent was standing in the foyer looking at the mail. He immediately put down the letter when he saw Kara and kissed her tenderly. Taylor felt tears coming to her eyes as she watched them. They had so much love in this home, and Kara deserved all of it. Love, happiness, and warmth seeped from the very walls.

"It's good to see you. Stone mentioned you the other day." Brent said, a glint in his eye. "He's outside checking your car out. He said you just got it out of the shop."

Taylor's mouth dried. "He's outside? Looking at my car?"

A small smile touched Brent's lips. "That's what I said."

Bemused, Taylor walked outside, and indeed the hood of her car was up and Stone was bent over the engine.

"What are you doing to my car?"

Stone stood up and wiped his hands with a rag. "Just making sure they took care of the problem. Cars are my hobby. You say they replaced this part. Did you pay for a rebuilt model?"

"No. They said they put a new one in."

"Did you ask to see your old one?"

"No."

Stone shook his head. "This is definitely not a new part. They jerry-rigged this wire. It could give at any time, and leave you stranded. You got triple A?"

Taylor shook her head.

"Take it back to shop first thing in the morning. This time

I'll go with you." He put down the hood, and walked to the house.

Taylor stared after him. Then she gathered herself and hurried after him back into the house. Stone and Brent's voices came from downstairs. The scent of food wafted from the kitchen. Kara was standing in front of the stove, stirring food in a pot. "Are you going to stay for dinner? I'm making pasta primavera so you can eat, also."

"No, I don't think so. I need to get home."

"You're running away from Stone."

Kara made the statement flatly, a fact. Taylor felt momentarily irritated, then shamed. She'd been as blunt, and as free with her opinion with Kara over the years. She never liked people who couldn't take what they dished out. Or refused to face themselves.

"Damn straight. I'm getting out of Dodge while I still have time."

Kara looked startled, then laughed. "I still think you're making a mistake. You could do much worse than Stone."

"You're right, he's probably the one. But I'm not ready for the one, and I don't want him to be it." She grabbed her purse. "I gotta go."

Kara opened her mouth, then shut it. She wiped her hands on a dish towel. "Wait. I'll see you out."

Taylor had barely started to pull the door open when she heard Brent's voice. "Are you leaving already? I thought you'd stay for dinner."

Her heart sank. She'd thought she'd made a clean getaway.

Stone approached and leaned casually against the wall. "I'll see you tomorrow," he said.

"I don't want you to bother."

He smiled, revealing rows of perfect, white teeth. "No bother."

Kara hugged her. "I know our lives are getting so busy, but I haven't seen near as much of you as I'd like."

"I know. I'll try to come by for lunch sometime like I used to."

"Good. You take care of yourself." Kara's eyes were worried.

Taylor nodded and walked to her car, consciously trying to stroll nonchalantly rather than the near run she felt like making. She felt Stone's eyes on her back. He was watching her walk away. Uncharacteristically, she felt acutely self-conscious. Her brothers had always teased her about her flat "white girl" butt. What would Stone think . . . ?

She squelched the thought, climbed in the car and inserted the key into the ignition. She waved goodbye at the group at the door and turned the key. A brief whine, then nothing. Panic rising, she turned the key again. Silence.

"What did you do to my car?" Taylor yelled, erupting out of the front seat.

"Not a thing except test the wires. I told you they wouldn't hold."

"They held just fine until you started messing with them."

Kara said, "Taylor, I think you should calm down, and—"

"It wasn't your car he sabotaged."

Brent sniffed the air and dashed in the house.

Stone hadn't said a word. He was still leaning against the door jamb, hands in his pockets, an amused expression on his face like this was all going on about somebody else. Taylor wanted to go over and kick him to wipe that smug expression off his face.

Instead, she put her hands on her hips and glared at him. "Well, what are you going to do?"

A baby's wail sounded and Kara turned inside, with a worried look back at Taylor and Stone.

Stone drew his keys out of his pocket. "The first thing I'm going to do is to take you home. Tomorrow morning, I'll take care of your car. Don't worry about it."

Taylor folded her arms against her chest. "How am I supposed to get to work tomorrow?" She turned to the car and shook her head. "How am I supposed to pay for all of this repair work and the rental cars?" she asked herself.

"Like I said, don't worry about it."

He leaned into the door. "Brent, Kara, we're gone."

"The pasta boiled over," Brent yelled from the kitchen.

Stone walked toward Taylor. "Tell Kara we said goodbye," he yelled back.

Stone took Taylor's arm gently and guided her to his car. She obeyed him mechanically, sliding into the seat. He slid in beside her and Taylor had a sense of déjà vu. She belonged beside this man. A sense of continuity rippled through her. She'd been next to him before, many times, and she'd continue beside him again, many times. This was more than déjà vu, it was déjà doom.

TWELVE

The atmosphere in the car thickened. Acute consciousness of Stone's breathing, his heartbeat hung in the air. His feelings. Warm, open, overhung with passion. Taylor bit her lip. A whirlpool of inevitability opened up to spin her down within. However, she fought against the tide of fate—

"Wanna stop at McDonald's?"

"What?"

"Do you want to stop at McDonald's? I'm hungry. If you want to go in somewhere and sit down and eat, that's all right, too."

Taylor shook her head, physically trying to shed vestiges of her mood and foreboding.

"I like Wendy's better," she said.

A few minutes later, Stone pulled up to the drive through. "I should have asked if you wanted to go in," he said.

"That's okay. I'd like a baked potato, broccoli only and a Caesar salad.

Stone said her order into the microphone. "Double classic combo with Coke," he added.

They got their food and Stone reached into his bag and grabbed a handful of fries.

"Do you know that the trans-fatty acids in the shortening they use to cook those fries raises your cancer risk?" Taylor asked.

"Breathing raises your cancer risk. I need to lighten you up. Sometimes you take things entirely too seriously. Or are you only that way with me?"

"Only with you."

"Nice to know I'm special to you."

Taylor gave a slight snort and stared out the window. They drove the rest of the way to her apartment in silence. By then, she'd made a decision. Three times was a charm.

Stone expertly parallel parked the large car near her building.

"You're welcome to come in," she offered. "I might have some pie to go along with the burger and fries."

Stone gave her an easy grin. "I never could resist pie. Apple?"

"Cherry."

"That's even better."

Taylor opened the door, for once hoping that Tiffany was out. The apartment was empty and dark. She flipped on the light. "Make yourself at home."

She went to pour herself a glass of wine, which she sorely needed, and got a real fork to eat her salad with. Then she heard the TV come on. When she returned to the living room Stone sat on her couch munching his burger and fries in front of a sports channel. "I hope you don't mind that I turned on the TV," he said.

She did mind but now was not the time to say so. She sat beside him and sipped her wine, her appetite gone.

"Very nice place you have here," he said. "Lots of plants."

"I love greenery, and I've always had a lot of plants wherever I've lived. I share this apartment with a roommate. She's out right now."

"Ummm," Stone replied. Taylor could almost believe he was uncomfortable, shy even, if it wasn't so unlike him. The thought made her feel a little better.

With a quick movement, she turned off the TV. "I have a CD I want to put on."

She hesitated, then slipped one by Teddy Pendergrass in the player. "You like old school, I hope?"

She turned to Stone, who had stopped chewing his hamburger and was watching her closely.

"Now, I'm going to slip into something more comfortable." She cringed as she heard the old cliché drop from her lips, and turned toward the bedroom.

The next thing she knew, she was up against the wall with Stone's large, warm body much too close.

"No, you're not. I can only take so much." His voice was husky.

Taylor was speechless, mainly because suddenly she was finding it difficult to breathe. Stone's eyes stared down into hers. Her only thought was how interesting it was how many gradients of brown there were in his eyes. Her only feelings were those that were the direct result of Stone's body touching hers. His hard male body. Oh, Lord.

Then Stone's lips descended and the world narrowed to this man and the overwhelming emotions rioting through her. His firm, tender lips demanded a response from her. Taylor surrendered, the ember burning at the core of her, blazing into an inferno. His tongue sent shivers of desire through her. He leaned into her, his hardness pressing her feminine warmth. Her hips rotated against his, seemingly of their own volition, seeking, wanting . . .

He buried his face in the sensitive area of her neck, trailing kisses from her earlobe to her collarbone. They strained to one another, a long, slow grind.

An incoherent murmur came from her lips and Stone raised his head, and pulled away from her. He closed his eyes in a visible battle for control.

"If anything happens here except ripping off our clothes on

the way to my bedroom, you're following the wrong script," Taylor murmured.

Stone groaned. "You're not going to make this easy. I have to leave."

"For God's sake, why?"

"It's not the right time yet." He swayed toward her, then backed away. "I have to leave now." He grabbed his keys from the coffee table and Taylor heard the sound of the door closing behind him as he fled.

You'd think the hounds of hell were chasing him, she thought, and cherished that image for a moment. She dropped on the couch and stared glumly at the leavings of his hamburger and fries. Three strikes and you're out, she thought.

Teddy crooned, "Turn out the lights, light a candle . . ." All Stone had to do was follow Teddy's instructions, she thought bitterly.

"I'm going to make it so good for you . . ."

"Oh, shut up," Taylor muttered and flung a throw pillow at the speaker.

Stone sat behind the wheel of his car, still breathing hard. It had taken every ounce of will he had not to do her right there against the wall. God, she was sweet. He couldn't remember when he'd wanted a woman so much. He must have been out of his mind to go into her apartment.

He needed a cigarette, and groaned when he felt his empty shirt pocket. He'd quit again. He dug in the ashtray for a long butt as he started the car and pulled away from the curb. He found one and lit it, pulling in a long drag of a much needed smoke. He'd quit again tomorrow.

Taylor was playing hell on his resolve. He bet he'd have a whole lot less problems quitting cigarettes if he went ahead and took her to bed. It was usually when Taylor reduced him to an inner quivering mass of desire, that he found the need for a cigarette overwhelming. Sex was what she wanted, but he was determined not to give in to her wiles right now. He was determined they were going to have a relationship. But she had to learn that there were some things that she couldn't control—namely, him.

"Why don't you show a little leg more often, honey?"

Anne looked steadily at George, and decided to ignore his crass comment. Usually her opinion of her clients went up when she knew them better. At least she usually understood them better. But this man was impossible. She wondered what his wife had seen in him. It wasn't that he was an ugly man. He actually wasn't bad looking. He was just so . . . obnoxious. His wife had married him for the money, likely.

Anne crossed her legs, feeling uncomfortable under his stare. She'd worn a tailored pair of linen shorts with a matching jacket to the job today. She'd stick to her customary khakis from now on.

"Did I tell you I really like that getup you have on?"

"Many times," Anne replied drily.

"Makes you look more feminine with that sweet little shape of yours."

Anne leaned back in her chair, weary of his banter. "When are you going home?"

He winked at her. "Soon. And I got a treat waiting for you when we get there."

Anne stifled a sigh. "I've told you several times I'm not going to accept gifts from you."

"You'll like this one."

There was no point in arguing with this man. For someone who ran a successful business, he was decidedly thick in the head.

He made a big production of opening the car door for her. She glanced around her, alert for any threatening signs. From her study of the police records of the previous murders, the threat to George was real, and dangerous.

He scurried ahead to open the door of the house for her. She rearmed the security system, wondering what she'd make for herself to eat. She'd quickly disposed George of the notion that she was going to cook for him. She'd told him to handle his meals the way he usually did and she'd handle hers.

She heard his heavy breathing about four feet behind her and dreaded turning around. What did he want now?

"I'd like to cook dinner for you tonight," he said.

"No thanks," she said, walking toward the kitchen.

George blocked her way.

"Excuse me?" she asked, her voice icy.

"I don't know why you're so unfriendly. I've tried to be as hospitable as I can." Then he leered at her. "You're trying too hard to pretend you don't feel the sparks between us."

"Excuse me?" Anne repeated, raising a blond brow. This bozo had to be kidding.

Then he reached out and pulled her to him.

Anne made a quick move, allowing the momentum of his body to work against him, and he landed heavily on the floor. She went and stood over him. He blinked up at her, dazed. "You tripped me on purpose," he accused.

"I didn't trip you, and it was my full intention that you hit the floor. Consider it a warning. Don't touch me again."

She left George lying on the floor and made her way to the kitchen. Peanut butter and jelly sounded good. It would be even better if George stocked some bananas in his pantry.

THIRTEEN

The doorbell rang and Taylor pulled the pillow over her head. It couldn't possibly be morning yet. Must be a bad dream. The shrill sound rang again. She groaned, rolled over and sat up in bed. She immediately regretted the move. Her head throbbed and the inside of her mouth felt like sandpaper.

She shouldn't have polished off that bottle of wine after Stone left. And to top it off, someone was leaning on the doorbell. She looked at the clock, 8:07. She was going to be late to work, and obviously Tiffany hadn't made it home last night, a frequent occurrence.

She tore the covers back and swung her legs off the bed. Whoever this was had better have a very good reason to be ringing her doorbell at 8:07 in the morning or they were going to be throughly cussed out.

She peered out the peephole and blinked. Stone stood there, with a pleasant expression on his face, but he wasn't letting up on the doorbell for an instant.

"Okay! I'm here. What do you want?" Taylor called through the door.

She was wearing an oversized, raggedy, paint splotched T-shirt and panties and she looked like morning hell. No way she was letting him in.

"I'm here to take you to work. You have no car, remember?"

Taylor sagged against the door frame. She'd forgotten. Unless she wanted to bus it to work, and she was late already, she needed that ride.

"Okay, I'm going to unlock the door. I'm not dressed, so wait a second before you come in."

She unlocked the door and took off toward her bathroom in a sprint. She heard Stone entering immediately, the dog. She closed her bedroom door and had a flash of a vision of them together, joined and fevered, making love under a hot, steamy shower. She groaned and locked the door behind her. A true vision of a future time, when she was wholly in love with Stone, body and soul.

Stone stared at the spot on the wall he had Taylor up against last night. Then he heard the shower start and visualized her naked brown body with rivulets of water streaming down. He wrenched his mind away from its treacherous meanderings, and gave her apartment a closer look.

Decorated in white and neutral shades, with plants everywhere, it was light and airy, like the outdoors. He liked it. African sculptures were scattered here and there, and African patterned cloth graced the walls. He wandered over to the book shelves and his eyes widened as he perused the titles. She wasn't kidding about being into this New Age stuff.

Polished rocks, crystals, and other objects he didn't recognize covered the shelves. He touched a beautiful pink-gold crystal, and withdrew his hand quickly as he thought he felt warmth and a slight vibration. He must be imagining things.

He reached out again and picked the crystal up. It did feel warm, but the room was warm. He studied it closely. He really liked this rock. He briefly considered asking Taylor if he could have it. Then he frowned. What was he thinking? It was just a rock. He placed it carefully back on the shelf.

He heard the shower turn off, and he visualized her toweling her body off, and wished with all his heart that he was that towel. He wasn't enjoying playing hard to get, so why was he holding out? She'd made it clear that she wanted him and he wanted her, so why weren't they going at it? He could have wakened up in her arms this morning.

If he was going to be in close contact with her, he wasn't going to last much longer. And weren't the constant turn-downs killing their budding relationship quicker than a quickie would? He would have moved on without a backward glance if a woman had said no as often as he had. Unless he really wanted her. Unless she was worth the wait. Did Taylor think he was worth the wait?

She came out of the bedroom wearing blue jeans and a brightly colored top tucked in. Her dreads were pulled on top of her head and wrapped with a scarf. An Egyptian princess, she took his breath away.

"Do you like my crystals?" she asked moving close to him. Her signature scent was warm and musky with green undertones. He loved it.

"I especially like this one," he laid his hand on the pink and gold one.

He watched Taylor draw in her breath and glance at him from under her long lashes. She put out her hand slowly and touched it also.

An electric current ran through them. Stone gasped and knew she'd felt it, too, from the surprise in her eyes.

He removed his hand from the stone. "What the hell?" he muttered.

Taylor removed her hand more slowly, and studied her leather loafers.

"Taylor, what was that?"

Taylor gave a tiny shake of her head. She wasn't going to answer him. He took a deep breath. It was probably nothing. An overactive imagination, hormones or both.

He took a step back and looked at her. She was attractive,

true, but it was more than that. She was everything he wanted in a woman, and he wanted her badly. "I don't have to be in the office right away, do you?" he heard himself ask.

She turned to him. Her eyes were wide, and if he wasn't mistaken, frightened.

He took two steps to her and touched her cheek. Her soft lips mesmerized him. He started to lower his head.

And she stepped away. "I need to get into work," she said.

Touché, Stone thought, and withdrew his keys from his pocket. "Let's go," he said.

He saw the frightened look fade and a small smile curved Taylor's lips before she turned to leave.

The warm glow from the morning stayed with Taylor the entire workday. Stone had finally made a move toward her. She suspected he wanted her as much as she lusted after him, but his refusals had shaken her confidence. The episode with the crystal threw her. True love, it had said as clearly as if it had spoken. If it was to be true love, wouldn't her bondage to Stone be a sweet one? Maybe she should give herself up to fate. She had lived with her brothers and father eighteen years plus and survived their loving control and dominance.

Anyway, when he'd asked her to go to Stone Mountain with him tomorrow, she'd accepted. She'd never found the time to go to the amusement park, so instead of doing her laundry Saturday afternoon like she usually did, she was going to spend it with Stone. And it was shameless the way she looked forward to it, and that following night, especially the night she'd surely spend with him.

Tiffany was in the kitchen when she let herself into the apartment. Taylor shrieked, and ran to her. "I feel like I'm welcoming back a stranger," she said.

"I'll be spending a lot more time here," Tiffany said.

Taylor poured a ginger ale. "What's up with you and Dave?"

"We had a major blowup. It's not going to work out. For a while I thought he was the one. We moved so fast it kind of accelerated things, I think."

"I thought you basically moved in with him."

"For all intents and purposes, I did. Once the gloss wore off our relationship, his true self started showing, and I didn't like what I saw."

"I'm sorry, Tiff."

She shrugged. "That's okay. Much better to find out now than later. I wasted too many years in a miserable marriage to settle for any less of a relationship than what I want." She turned back to the stove. "I'm making a potato and cauliflower curry. You don't have plans? Are you going to eat here?"

"Sounds great. I'm starving. Nope, no plans. But my arid love life is finally showing signs of rain."

"You met a new man?"

"Well, I've known him for a while. He's Brent's best friend."

"Is that the private detective you said had the hots for you when you first came to Atlanta?"

"Yes. He's back in my life again, he's working on a case that peripherally involves the shelter residents. I'm going to go out with him tomorrow."

"That's great, Taylor. I remember meeting him over at Kara's once when she invited me to dinner. I wondered then what you were thinking of when you turned him down. That man was fine, really nice, too."

"He's not my type."

Tiffany turned away from the stove and faced Taylor, frowning. "You really need to get over that hang-up you have about strong, black men. I know you told me that it's related to your five brothers and your father, but it doesn't make sense. Believe me, there's nothing better. Those too-cute, weird, usually married, little boy, wimp types you dated in the past can't hold a candle to a strong, black man."

"Whew. You got their number. But I don't agree. Just because I want a man to have interests in common with me, and to be flexible and easygoing doesn't make him less than a man."

"Just makes him a wimpy, weird man."

"You calling me weird, girlfriend?"

Tiffany grinned. "If the shoe fits. But, I admit, you wear that shoe well, unlike that last guy, what was his name? Maxwell. Lord have mercy, that man needed medication. I walked in here once and he was talking to the plants. And if that wasn't bad enough, he told me they answered him."

"Now we agreed you were going to leave poor Maxwell alone. I don't see what he has to do with Stone anyway."

"Exactly. Being with a strong black man like Stone will do you good, Taylor. You need to give him a try."

"I've been with strong black men my entire life, and it hasn't done me that much good except drive me crazy. You haven't met my father or my brothers yet. They treat me like a dainty, irrational, not-too-bright child," Taylor muttered.

"No, but it looks like I may get to meet some of them. Your dad left a message. He and some of your brothers are coming to Atlanta for the weekend. I saved it for you."

FOURTEEN

A light tap on her door woke her. "Taylor, your Dad and your brothers Jared and Donovan are here. I'm cooking them breakfast."

Taylor rolled over and looked at the clock with one eye. Seven thirty-five in the morning. "I'll be out in a moment," she croaked.

"Take your time. Your family is delightful, I'm having a great time."

Tiffany always got up with the birds, also. Taylor never did understand people like her father and Tiffany who got up early when they didn't have to. She rolled out of bed, and headed for the shower. Ever since she'd begun seeing Stone again, sleepless nights were becoming a habit.

After her shower, she pulled on a pair of cutoffs and a cropped T-shirt. Noticing the T-shirt and panties she'd dropped on the floor on the way to the shower, she shrugged. She ignored them while she applied a little mascara and lipstick. As she turned to walk out of her room with the bed rumpled and unmade, she paused.

Her dad visited and instantly she segued into seventeen-year-old rebellion mode. Taylor sighed and picked up her dirty clothes from the floor and threw them into her hamper in her closet. She spread her comforter and arranged the pillows.

There. Just because her dad and most of her brothers were neat freaks, she didn't have to be a slob.

Then she instantly thought of Stone, slob extraordinaire. Even though at first, she was appalled at the state of his car, maybe it was an endearing trait after all.

Dad and her brothers were chowing down in the dining room when she walked in. Jason Cates stood up, his face beaming at the sight of his daughter. Taylor hugged her dad hard as he folded her in his embrace. She'd missed him and "the boys," as she referred to her brothers, much to their dismay.

"Let me get at little sis, Dad." Jared, her favorite brother wrapped her in a bear hug. "Since it looked like you weren't going to make it home to St. Louis anytime soon, we had to come and check you out."

"I'm doing great. Just busy at work. How about you guys?" She dropped a kiss on Donovan's forehead, who hadn't missed a beat cleaning his plate.

"We've added a brilliant surgeon from Pennsylvania to the practice. I'm slowing down a bit and gearing up for retirement."

Taylor looked at her Dad, eyes full of love. A handsome man at fifty-five, he'd aged gracefully, with a close-cropped beard and an only slightly receding hairline with salt and pepper hair that accentuated his brown skin.

"If anyone deserves a rest, it's you," Taylor said. Her father had managed to have a thriving practice as a cardiovascular surgeon and carry on as a loving, single father. Her mother had died in childbirth along with her twin sister. She'd heard her father had been devastated but determined to raise six children—the newly born Taylor, three toddlers, and the other two barely in school. He'd always been able to afford plenty of household help, but still it was no mean feat.

"Come and get a plate," Tiffany called from the kitchen.

Taylor went into the kitchen and admired the feast Tiffany prepared. Wholewheat pancakes and fruit salad. Ham and cheese omelettes. "This looks so good. I'm sorry I wasn't awake, I didn't mean for you to go to such trouble, Tiff."

"It was a pleasure. I planned to cook breakfast for us anyway, and visiting with your father and brothers was an unexpected treat. They are charming, Taylor. I don't know what you're talking about looking for a man opposite to them. Doesn't make sense. I'd be breaking my neck trying to find someone that could match up to them."

"They are great guys. It's just that they want to control my life. And you wouldn't believe how bossy my dad is."

"I'd call it strong. He's a surgeon for God's sake. Plus with all those kids, five boys? He'd be a fool not to take the reins." Tiffany opened the refrigerator. "I thought I had another quart of orange juice back in here."

"I drank it. Sorry," Taylor said, feeling guilty.

"Why did your dad never remarry?"

"I don't know. It certainly wasn't for lack of offers. I had so many women playing 'Mommy,' it was pathetic."

"I bet. He's extremely handsome."

Taylor raised an eyebrow at Tiffany. "Now, don't you start. I'm telling you the line is long, and nobody's ever caught him yet."

"I wouldn't dream of standing in line," Tiffany said with a smile.

"Good." Taylor heaped a stack of pancakes on a plate. "I think it was so hard growing up because I craved his approval so much. My brothers, too, especially Jared."

"Is Jared the oldest?"

"No the second oldest. Donovan is the youngest. You haven't met the twins or David, the oldest, yet."

"Twins?"

"I didn't tell you my mother had two sets of identical twins? Besides my sister and I, she had Trent and Trey. They're three years older than me. Donovan and I are just a little more than a year apart. My father said that one reason she died is that carrying five children in just over a three-year time span severely weakened her."

Tiffany shook her head. "So sad that she couldn't see her children grow up."

"Oh, she saw. That's what held her to the earth so long. She only moved on when we all got out on our own."

Tiffany opened her mouth, then snapped it shut. "Sometimes I wonder about you, Taylor."

"Everybody does, Tiff."

They sat in the living room relaxing over coffee after breakfast. "You still haven't told me exactly why you're in Atlanta?" Taylor asked.

Her father's eyes twinkled. "I was going to let Jared give you the news," Jason said.

Taylor turned to her brother, "Well?"

"I'm getting married."

"What!" Taylor shrieked. "I can't believe it. I'm tickled. So who's the lucky girl?"

"Her name is Benita, everyone calls her Bennie. We're in town to meet her family and get fitted for her gown."

"I can't wait to meet her."

"Her parents have invited all of us to dinner tonight. She wants to ask you to be a bridesmaid."

"I was worried about you, bro. I thought you were enjoying that open field too much. I'm happy to see someone bagged you. How did you meet her?"

"She's doing her residency at Barnes. She's fantastic, Taylor. You're going to love her."

"Where—" Taylor stopped midsentence. "Oh, Lord, I forgot. I have a date. What time is it?"

"A few minutes after ten," her father said.

"He's supposed to be here at ten. Maybe I can catch him on his cell phone."

The doorbell rang just as Taylor picked up the phone. Taylor slowly replaced the phone on the hook. Too late.

Tiffany glided to the door and let Stone in while Taylor was mentally kicking herself. She wasn't ready for Stone to meet her family. It made everything seem so . . . serious.

Stone was introducing himself and shaking Jared's hand when Taylor reentered the living room. She could tell her dad was checking him out carefully. Good, she thought. Dad would set him straight. Dad had gotten rid of more boyfriends than Taylor could count.

"Stone Emerson, is that it? So what do you do?" Jason asked casually.

Ahhh, the interrogation begins, Taylor thought, mentally rubbing her hands together.

"I own a private detective agency here in Atlanta. ESP Services." Her father's eyebrows shot up.

"I've heard of it. I had a friend that needed some work done here in Atlanta before he could get his insurance claim settled and he used you."

"Yes, that's pretty much what we do. A lot of insurance-related work. We also handle many cases for lawyers."

"So you don't spend all your time out on the streets investigating colorful murder cases?"

"Hardly. I'm usually hunkered over a computer. Though lately, the case I'm working on with Taylor is mighty interesting."

Everyone looked expectant. "We'd better keep the details confidential. It involves shelter residents," Taylor said.

Stone nodded and draped an arm over her shoulder in a proprietary way. "We were going to Stone Mountain. It would be wonderful if you could all join us."

"I don't think—" Taylor started to say.

"I'd love to go," Jason said.

"It's been a long time since I've been on a roller coaster, and Bennie is going to be tied up until later this afternoon."

"Drop me off at my friend's house," Donovan said. "I promised to be there by noon."

"She's the reason Donovan came with us," Jared said.

"Not so, I'm looking forward to meeting Bennie's family. I just need a little diversion on the side."

"Right."

"I rented a van at the airport, so we'll all fit in comfortably." Jason turned to Tiffany. "I hope you're going, also."

"I wouldn't miss it."

"You can tell me more about your detective agency while Taylor changes," Jason said to Stone.

Her heart sank, then the familiar rebellion flared up. "Change? Dad, I'm not going to change."

"Surely you're not going out like that."

"I'm thirty years old, and I can go out like I please."

"Not with me. Even if you were sixty, you'd still be my daughter."

Taylor raised her chin and crossed her arms over her chest.

Jason raised a cup of coffee to his lips and turned his attention back to Stone. "Oh, be sure and put on a bra, while you're at it," he said as an afterthought.

Taylor turned on her heel, so furious she was shaking. She closed the bedroom door behind her a touch too hard.

He'd been here only a few hours and already she was pissed off. Taylor ripped a pair of tailored Bermuda shorts off a hanger. She slipped into a bra, and tucked a soft silk T-shirt into the waistband of the shorts. Surveying herself in the full-length mirror as she drew her belt through the notches, she wondered if now she looked good enough to please him. Tears suddenly stung her eyes. It seemed that nothing she ever did fully pleased her dad.

* * *

By the time they'd reached the amusement park, Taylor had calmed down. She'd known her father, a staunch Baptist and a deacon in the church, would be offended by his daughter wearing Daisy Dukes out of the house. So why had she pressed the issue like a rebellious seventeen-year-old? She sighed to herself. Oppositional was the word for her behavior, a pattern she'd continuously played out with her father and her brothers.

She'd volunteered to drive since her dad and Jared were unfamiliar with Atlanta. She'd just dropped off Donovan at his girlfriend's place in Decatur, and Jared, Stone, and her dad sat talking and laughing in the back, while Tiffany sat up front with her. Just as she thought, Stone fit in perfectly with them.

The trill of a beeper interrupted her thoughts. "It's me," Jared said. "Bennie wants to get in touch with me. Can I use your cell phone, sis?"

Taylor handed it over. A few minutes later Jared said, "Good news, Bennie is finished with her fitting and she wants to go with us. Do you mind swinging by to pick her up? I think it's a little out of the way though."

"Of course I don't mind. Where is she?"

"Her parents live in Alpharetta."

Almost an hour later they pulled into an affluent subdivision of a half million dollar plus homes. "Girlfriend got bank," Taylor said under her breath to Tiffany.

"Right here," Jared said.

Taylor pulled into the circular drive of an imposing home and Jared got out of the van. A few minutes later he emerged from the house, a woman clinging to his arm. Taylor tried to keep her jaw from dropping, but it hit the floor anyway.

Her brother's fiancée was white.

FIFTEEN

George sat in the den in front of a blaring TV. Anne did her final walk through the house, making sure everything was secure before she turned in. Happy the day was over, she was looking forward to a warm bath and bed. As far as she was concerned, she was earning every penny on this job. George stretched her nerves to their limits with his smarmy overtures. She'd tried to warm up to him, knowing her coolness and distance only made a man like him try harder. But to no avail, treating a woman with respect seemed to be beyond his capacity. She despised the man.

She entered her suite, locked the door, and ran the bath water, generously sprinkling in handfuls of blue mineral salts. Pinning up her chin-length blond hair, she shed her clothes and sank into the bath.

Later, after the water cooled, she toweled herself off, pulled a clean nightgown over her head and slipped between the sheets, loving the feel of clean sheets, silk, and lace against her freshly bathed body. Expensive, scandalously feminine nightclothes and underwear were her one indulgence.

She'd barely drifted off to sleep when she heard the click of a lock in the door. Awake instantly, she'd hardly had time to raise her head before George fell on her, knocking the wind out of her with his stocky body.

"I'm sick of your games, bitch. It's time I got what I paid for."

He grunted as he pressed her body into the mattress. Anne forced her muscles to relax, as George groped her body, pleased at her seeming acquiescence. "I knew you wanted it," he panted.

Within the next two heartbeats, the time was right, and she moved, quickly as a snake, and with a twist of her body pushed him off of her.

George hit the floor with a growl of rage. He started to stand up and lunge at her, but she jabbed his eyes, and with a flick of her bare foot against his stomach, he was doubled up in pain gasping.

"I'm going to put you in the hospital, bitch," he screamed.

Anne faced him, about seven feet away, seemingly relaxed in the dark room. When he came for her again, she was ready.

The third time George hit the floor, blood streamed from his nose and mouth, and he didn't get up.

Suddenly light flooded the room, and an attractive woman with long blond hair stood there gawking at her. "So you're the whore my husband moved in? Get your clothes on and get out of my house," the woman shrieked.

It took Anne about two minutes to comply.

"George, you told me that you wanted me back, you begged me to come home tonight. How could you do this me?" Wendy approached George who was still lying on the floor in shame at having his adulterous sex game interrupted.

"George?"

She gave a little scream as he rolled over and she saw the blood covering his face. "My God, George, what happened to you?"

"Call the police, I've been assaulted," he moaned.

"Who assaulted you? Was it the murderer?"

George's gaze darted wildly around the room. "Is she gone?"

"Did that woman you were screwing have an accomplice?"

"No it's just her. And I wasn't screwing her."

Wendy slowly replaced the phone that she'd picked up. "Then why was she standing over you in a dark bedroom?"

"She's crazy. She attacked me!"

"Are you telling me that a woman who looked smaller than me, kicked your ass and left you on the floor bleeding?"

George looked at a loss for a moment.

"It wasn't a woman," he said finally. "I think it was one of those men with their thingie's cut off. One of those freaks."

Wendy slung her purse over her shoulder. "I'm leaving."

"No! Wendy . . . it's true, it was my bodyguard. A real woman couldn't be a bodyguard. I can prove it." George fumbled for his wallet. "Here." He handed her a card. "This is the owner of the detective agency I hired, call him and ask. Just don't go and leave me again, Wendy."

He looked so pathetic sitting on the floor with blood smeared on his face. Wendy wished with all her heart that it could have been different—that she could have the marriage she once dreamed of. The family.

"I'll make everything up to you. I promise. I was a fool losing my temper with you. It won't happen again, I promise."

"Promise?" Wendy asked hopefully. Maybe he wouldn't hurt her again, and they'd be happy. The thought of starting all over, alone and with nothing and nobody was terrifying.

"I promise with all my heart. I love you more than life. You know that. That's why I get so jealous."

It was true. Nobody had stuck with her the way George had. Even in the end, she'd left him. "You won't ever hit me again?"

"Never. It'll be like we dreamed. All your things are still here. And I'll buy that boat we talked about."

George always provided for her. Anything she wanted, really. Now, she didn't have her own bed to lay her head down on. She loved him. She married him, didn't she?

She sat on the floor next to him and touched his cheek. "I'm not going anywhere. My home is here, with you."

He gathered her in his arms and kissed her tenderly, and she believed anew in her dream of love, marriage, and family. She'd never given up her hope. It would be the last thing that would ever die.

Taylor paced the floor of her apartment. Tiffany watched her with concern and munched potato chips. "I can't believe my father said that Stone was one of the family. My God. I used to count on my dad being predictable at least. His record of scaring off any male interested in me was unbroken."

"Your dad and Stone did hit it off. Jared liked him, too. You must admit you two make a nice couple."

"I told you he was just like them."

Tiffany munched on a potato chip and stared thoughtfully at Taylor. "You were pretty quiet when you met Benita. She's awfully nice, and they seem so much in love."

Taylor held up her hand. "How could somebody with a name like Benita not be a sister? I don't understand."

"And here I was, thinking you're psychic."

"Don't get me started, Tiff."

"Who, me?" Tiffany asked innocently.

"Do you realize how many sisters would have sold their souls to get with my brother? Do you realize the shortage of available, successful, black men? So my brother, a doctor, the cream of black manhood, goes and gets himself a white chick."

"From the way they tell it, it seems like they simply fell in love."

"Believe me, there are plenty of fine sisters, doctors also, if that was what he wanted, to fall in love with. That's why it's so hard to get a good black man. If they aren't in prison, they're gay; if they aren't in prison or gay, they're homeless or living with their mamas. And the three left are marrying white chicks . . . What are you doing?"

Tiffany was choking and waving a magazine wildly around in the air.

"I'm clearing out the smoke issuing from your ears. If I didn't know you better, I'd swear you sound a bit, should I put it nicely, biased?"

"I'm not a bigot. I'm talking about numbers here. It's just not fair."

"Well then, why don't you go out and take a handsome, successful white man from the white chicks, and I do believe that would even up the tally."

Taylor gave her a disgusted look and stalked from the room.

"I really had a good time with your dad," Tiffany called after her.

"I bet you did," Taylor answered, and heard Tiff's answering chuckle.

She threw herself on the bed and stared up at the ceiling. The afternoon and evening had been one fine family affair. Jared and Beenie, excuse me, Bennie, Dad and Tiffany, who Taylor spied Dad checking out in a decidedly unfatherly manner, and her and Stone. Everybody looooved Stone. Her dad practically came out and asked when the wedding was going to be.

Stone and Jared looked like brothers strolling together. The same height and build. Both with ready smiles. Shoot, maybe it was her obligation to get with Stone to save him from the clutches of some white chick.

Okay, so she was wrong. But Jared was her favorite. Taylor didn't know if she'd be crazy about anyone he married at first. Hard to believe anyone was good enough for her bro. This Bennie girl seemed nice, and more important, she seemed to make her brother happy. She'd give her a chance. That was only fair.

SIXTEEN

Mondays were generally the pits, Taylor thought, nursing a cup of coffee at her desk, but this Monday was proving to be a veritable sinkhole. Gazing dismally at the stack of papers heaped on her desk, she knew she'd be in court most of the day with her favorite bigot, Judge Lawrence Gold, presiding. She'd opened her briefcase and started to transfer the stack of papers from her desk when the premonition crept into the edge of her consciousness like an incoming tide. An impression of emotion in color.

As she dropped back in her chair and buried her face in her hand, the feeling spread over her like viscous black oil. Violence and death, revenge and retribution. "Three gone . . ."

Taylor's head snapped up at the woman's husky whisper, but of course no one was there. She gripped the edge of her desk as sensations continued to flood through her. A whimper of pain, the color of blood, the feeling of pure satisfaction. Pleasure at a job well done, a difficult task carried out. The certainty of justice, deep blue, almost black. Harsh justice. Then it was gone, as quickly as it had come.

Taylor took a deep shuddery breath. She didn't want to think about the too certain fact that someone was going to die, murdered in a wash of blood and pain.

Her phone rang and she started. Taylor bit her lip and picked up her extension, her pulse increasing. It must be Stone. She hadn't hard from him since their outing Saturday.

"Hello, Taylor, this is Maxwell. I hadn't heard from you for a while so I thought I'd give you a call."

Her heart settled down to her shoes. "Hi, Maxwell, uh, good to hear from you."

"There's a collective chant for us to raise the vibration of world consciousness at the Metaphysical Bookstore tomorrow evening. Want to go?"

The no almost immediately dropped from Taylor's lips, but she pulled up. She wasn't dating Stone. She'd resolved not to have a relationship with him. He wasn't her type. Maxwell was her type—handsome (not as fine as Stone, a treacherous voice whispered) and they were both vegetarians with similar interests. Maxwell would never try to control her. With him, she was firmly in charge.

"Okay, I'll meet you there, though, I'm planning to work late tomorrow."

"Fabulous, baby," Maxwell's voice dropped an octave. "I missed you."

Uh? "Well, I'll see you tomorrow."

Taylor hung up the receiver slowly. Suddenly, chanting to raise the vibration of world consciousness seemed kind of silly.

George tasted the steak. Acceptable. But not quite as good as it could be.

"How do you like the steak?" Wendy asked anxiously.

George shrugged and Wendy's face fell. "I tried hard to make dinner real nice for you, honey."

"Where did you get the avocados you put in the salad?" George asked casually.

"I-I went to the store."

"You left the house without me? I thought we talked about that."

Wendy folded and refolded her napkin. "I've been wanting to

discuss that some more with you. George, I don't think it's right . . ."

George laid down his knife and fork on the plate. "Who asked you to think?"

Wendy bit her lip. "I get bored in the house all day," she said, the words coming out in a rush.

"So, you don't appreciate this nice house I gave you. What else don't you appreciate? Go ahead, tell me."

Wendy paled. "I appreciate all you do for me. It's just that—"

"Just that what? You're an ungrateful bitch?"

She bit her lip again, and looked down. George saw she had her hands clenched, her knuckles white. She had the nerve to be mad.

George laid his knife and fork on the plate. "Am I making you angry?" he asked softly.

Wendy gave a tiny shake of her head "I'm not mad."

"That's good. Because I am. Everything you own, wear, and put in your mouth is mine. And you question my right to make the rules? What is the rule, Wendy?"

She sat there, saying nothing. He struck the table hard, making the dishes jump and clatter. "What is the damned rule?" he roared.

"I don't leave the house without permission."

"Why do we have the rule, Wendy?"

Her lower lip trembled. "I can't hear you," he said softly.

"Because you love me," she whispered.

"Finally, you got it right, you dumb bitch." He got up and Wendy flinched.

He picked up his hardly touched plate of food and threw it in the trash. Tears ran down his wife's face. The woman was always sniveling and whining. Getting on his nerves. But he was a patient man. He wasn't going to whip her like she deserved.

"I'm going to order a pizza," he said as he left the room.

* * *

"That Beano stuff might work to clear up Kay's gas problem. Eva, what do you think?" Teensy asked innocently.

"Quit stuffing your face and that might clear up your fat problem," Kay shot back.

Taylor tried to keep a straight face. One thing about Kay, she gave as good as she got.

"You two are making inappropriate attacks on each other. The purpose of our group is to address problems in a constructive way," Carol, the social worker, said.

"My husband is leaving messages with everybody, begging me to come home. He says we can go to counseling together. I'm tempted to give him another chance," Eva said.

"Why do you want to give him a another chance?" Carol asked.

"Well, it only happened once. It's not like he drinks or kicked my butt every Saturday night."

"Last week you told me the first time I got hit I should have booked. You said that the first time your man hit you was the last time," Quanita said.

"I know. But I've been thinking about things. Anybody could make a mistake once. I don't think he's going to beat me again."

"But you got everything set up so well to go ahead on your own. You got lots of money to get your own apartment and everything," Amber said, a touch of envy in her voice.

"I don't have lots of money. I'm a resident. I make twenty thousand dollars a year. I've been running away from Ben, not because I'm scared of him physically so much as I'm afraid to face what I've done to him."

"What you done to him?" Quanita said. "He's the one who put your ass in the hospital."

"Everyone has to make their own decisions in life, and it's not our place to judge. But I do want to add that couples therapy is not recommended for couples with a history of domestic violence. I strongly suggest if counseling is the road you wish to take, that your husband seek individual therapy, preferably with a male counselor experienced in domestic violence issues," Carol said.

"I'm thinking about going home to Mama," Amber said. "I don't think Billy is going to do anything to me. I heard he got another girlfriend already." She cradled her sleeping baby closer to her chest, looking troubled.

Carol sighed and looked at her watch. "We're going to have to wrap up. For those who don't know already, I want to announce that Helping Hands has suspended taking new residents into the shelter."

"Where are women that have to get away going to go?" Joan asked.

"We're referring them to other shelters in the area."

"Too bad they didn't suspend it last week," Teensy mumbled, darting a look at Kay.

"I heard that." Kay stared at Teensy belligerently.

"This meeting is over," Carol said.

Taylor walked into the kitchen to rinse out her teacup. She'd tried to sense something she could pinpoint from the women. Any sense of violence or premonition. She couldn't even perceive the black wall she had sensed earlier. She couldn't perceive anything at all that wasn't from her five senses. It almost seemed as if someone or something had thrown up a shield that blocked her off completely.

Someone approached her from behind, and Taylor jumped, startled. She swung around and stared into Kay's heavily made up face. "I wanted to ask if there was any way I could get a transfer to another shelter. I'm tired of everyone dogging me here."

Taylor turned and rinsed her cup, buying herself a few seconds to collect herself. "The problem is that the other shelters are getting full, especially with their taking our referrals. Since you have a bed here already, and there's no emergency, it would be difficult to get a transfer for you," she answered.

"Everybody here makes me sick. I'm going to have to go back to my boyfriend and let him kill me, just wait and see." Kay flung herself out of the room.

Taylor shook her head, grateful as ever that she'd never had to put up with living in a shelter.

Wendy shifted in her husband's arms. He was relaxed and sated from their lovemaking. Now, was the time to ask him. She reached up and kissed his chin. "Honey, you were wonderful, perfect. I can't imagine anyone pleasing me the way you do."

George smirked. "Anytime," he said.

"Remember when you said I could have what I wanted for my birthday if I was good? Have I been good?"

"You've been very good. Very obedient for a change."

"I've tried hard to make everything right. I really want things to be right between us."

"Uh-huh."

"I saw an advertisement for a group tonight of men only. Husbands getting together to discuss how they can better manage their wives."

"That sounds like a good idea. You women need all the managing you can get."

"For my birthday, I wonder if you'd go. It's all men, and I think it might make our good marriage even better."

George lifted up on one elbow. "Do they talk about sex stuff?" he asked frowning.

"Oh, no. There's no way you need to improve in that department. It's mainly dealing with how to cope when your wife gets on your nerves. I know I get on your nerves all the time, and I hate doing that. A minister leads the group."

"You got your heart all set that I do this, don't you?"

"I wish you would."

"Okay, sweetie, I'll think about it. Now, roll over and stick your legs in the air. Let's see if I can make you holler again."

SEVENTEEN

Dr. Brown surveyed the group of men in the room. The Men's Alternatives to Violence group had more participants than it ever had since the agency's opening. Nothing like a few murders to give abusers the impetus to change.

"It said it was a woman, but it was a man, one of those freaks with their dicks cut off. It tried to rape me," one of the new guys was regaling the group.

"What did you do, man?"

"Why, I kicked its ass, of course."

"Which is never an appropriate intervention," he interrupted. "I want to welcome all the newcomers to the Men's Alternatives to Violence group. I'm Dr. Alonzo Brown, a minister of the New Faith Church, and I am your group leader for the next sixteen weeks. Please, let's go around the circle and introduce ourselves . . ."

George was the name of the man who complained of his assault. Dr. Brown looked at his notes. George's wife had recently returned to him.

"Bill, can you tell us what might have been an appropriate intervention to the assault George suffered?" he asked a long-term group member.

"You should have called the police after you got the freak offa you. If you beat his ass, you could have been the one hauled off to jail."

"Exactly." This instance of victimization was too good to pass up, he thought. These men had a history of difficulty empathizing with the victim. "George, how did it feel when the man overpowered you?"

George looked uncomfortable and squirmed a little in his chair. "I didn't say he overpowered me, he jumped me, that's all."

"Okay, how did you feel when he jumped you?"

"It made me mad. I wanted to kill him."

"So, being attacked made you angry. Did you feel that you did anything to provoke the attack?"

"Hell, no!"

"What if that man thought you were sexy, that the shirt you wore revealed your awesome biceps, what if the way you walked turned him on?" Laughter rippled through the group. "Do you think that man would be justified in attacking you then?"

George looked pissed. "Just what is it that you're getting at?"

"Only that violence is never justified by anything the victim does." The minister looked at each man in turn. "How many of you have felt your wives deserved their beating at your hands? That they didn't do something that you expected, or they screwed something up? They were flirting with another man, or your dinner wasn't prepared how and when you liked it?"

The men shifted uneasily. "Every single one of you believed your wife or girlfriend deserved the whipping you gave them."

A man spoke up. "It's a husband's God-given right to be the head of his household. For the wife to be in proper subjection, we have the responsibility to discipline."

Dr. Brown's hand hit the podium next to him and the sound resounded like a bullet. "That's a load of hypocritical manure," he roared. "You stand here piously and spout scripture to me to defend your violence and evil. 'They will cry out to me on that day, Lord, Lord, and I will tell them I never knew them.' Have you heard that verse before?"

He straightened his tie and composed himself. "Excuse me, blame my passion on the fact that I'm a Christian minister. But I preach the gospel of love not tyranny and violence.

"I want a show of hands. How many were ordered by the court to attend these sessions?" Half the men in the room raised their hands. "And why are you other men here? Speak up."

"My wife said she'd leave me if I didn't come."

"I want to go back home, but my wife said I had to get counseling first."

"I want to make my marriage work."

"My girlfriend wanted me to."

The man who'd been assaulted, George, hadn't said anything. "How about you?"

"I want to make my wife happy. She wanted me to come," George said after some hesitation.

"Anybody nervous about the murderer?" the minister asked.

Almost everybody in the room raised their hands. He chuckled. At least they were honest.

The whine of a baby greeted Taylor when she arrived at the shelter the next morning to meet with Joan. "Amber's baby has colic," Joan said in answer to Taylor's questioning look. "He cried all night. It's driving us crazy."

"Poor baby."

She and Joan had just settled into their discussion with paper spread out over the dining room table when Kay burst into the room, Quanita on her heels brandishing a candlestick. "She's going to hit me!" Kay cried hysterically.

"Quanita, put that down, you know better," Taylor snapped. Quanita set the candlestick on the table and directed a stream of unprintable words at Kay.

"Calm down, Quan," Joan said. "Tell us what's going on."

Quanita sent Kay a look of pure disgust. "Just keep that bitch away from me," she said and stalked from the room.

Taylor stood and gathered her papers. "Are you okay, Kay?" she asked.

"I'm all right," Kay said sullenly.

Taylor waited for her to tell her what was going on between her and Quanita, but it looked like Kay didn't want to say anything.

"Do you want to continue this over at my office?" Taylor asked Joan.

"Good idea," Joan answered.

"I just gave my opinion of her boyfriend. I was very complimentary. I don't know why she went off. Those people are so touchy," Kay blurted out.

Taylor raised an eyebrow.

"I didn't mean you," Kay said hurriedly. "I meant people like Quanita."

"And what sort of people are those?" Joan asked, frowning.

"Uh, people who lose their temper real quick."

Joan looked disgusted.

"I saw him skulking around this morning," Kay added.

Taylor set down her briefcase. This could be serious.

"You saw Quanita's boyfriend around the safe house? How did you know it was him?"

"She described him real good."

"Hold that thought, because you're going to have to give that description to the police." Taylor pulled out her cell phone and at that moment the tinkle of broken glass followed from the back of the house followed by a woman's screams.

She punched in 911. "There's a possible intruder and assault at 555 Jensen." She raced off after Joan and Kay to find out what was happening.

Quanita brandished a chair at a broken window in Amber's room. Amber huddled in a corner with her baby, both whimpering, while Mai Lin crouched beside them, an arm around Amber's shoulders.

The sound of sirens rose in the distance. "What happened?" Taylor demanded.

"A black man tried to break in here. When Amber screamed, he ran away," Mai Lin said.

"Did anyone else see him?"

"I don't think so, only Amber," Mai Lin answered.

Taylor shook her head and went to let in the policemen who were starting to arrive.

The police finished taking their statements and left the house. Taylor stood on the porch and watched them go. Then she heard the sound of shouting within the shelter. What now? She followed the hollering and screaming to the living room. Amber, Mai Lin, and Joan watched Quanita and Kay face off in full-fledged battle. Taylor watched a few seconds before she pulled out her cell phone to call the police back to break it up. She valued her own hide too much to ever get between two people and their fight.

Kay was coming out the worse for the battle. She fought like a girl, throwing her arms out and slapping to counter Quanita's punches. Taylor flinched as she heard the sound of flesh striking flesh as Quanita landed a solid right to Kay's jaw.

"Could you return to 555 Jensen, two of our residents are fighting. Yes, one car is fine. No sirens please."

Quanita had changed her tack. She methodically ripped the clothes off Kay's back.

"I got five dollars on Quanita," Joan said. Taylor darted a look at her.

"Ten dollars on Kay," Mai Lin said, surprising her. "I have a feeling . . ."

A sound of ripping cloth. Quanita had pulled Kay's skirt off.

Then Taylor's jaw hit the floor for the second time that week. The equipment showing through the thin nylon of Kay's bikini panties wasn't of the feminine variety.

EIGHTEEN

Christine, the shelter manager, entered with a sack of groceries. Taylor struggled down the stairs with a suitcase. Sacks, boxes, and luggage were lined up at the front door. "What's going on?" Christine asked.

"You don't really want to know, but I guess I'm going to have to tell you. We're packing up Quanita's and Kay's things. They had to leave." She dumped the suitcase down by the other luggage.

"Why? What happened?" Christine set the sack on the dining room table.

"Quanita and Kay got into a fight."

"Oh. Well, I expected Kay to tangle with someone before she left."

"Oh, but that's not all. Kay is a man."

"Get out of here."

"I'm not kidding. Quanita ripped off her clothes and Kay's family jewels were displayed for all the world to see."

"Daaang," Christine said. "Where are they now?"

"The shelters are all full and the police took them over to the homeless mission."

"They aren't going to last long there."

"I know, but what else could we do? Most of the staff is upstairs now, packing up their stuff. I can't believe how much stuff Quanita had. Lord."

"I can't believe that Kay was a man. Hell, she looked better than me. Sheesh."

"Don't worry, she didn't. Makeup can work wonders."

Taylor had barely made it back to her office when her phone rang. "Hello," she said, still distracted from what happened over at the shelter.

"Hello, Taylor." Relief went through her at the sound of Stone's husky voice. "I had to go out of town unexpectedly for a few days on a case."

No, she hadn't been worried about not hearing from him. Not her. "I was worried when I didn't hear from you." Was that her voice? What was wrong with her? Taylor pounded the side of her head soundlessly with her open hand.

"I missed you, and I want to see you," he said simply.

Her heart melted. What was it about this guy that got to her so? Give it up girl, a little voice whispered.

If only he would take it. "I'd like to see you."

"Tonight? How about dinner?"

"Fine."

"I'll pick you up after work."

"How about six thirty?"

As soon as Taylor hung up she remembered she'd promised to meet Maxwell for the chant. Shoot. There was no way to get in touch with Maxwell because he worked temporary jobs. She wasn't inclined to cancel with Stone. Taylor thought for a moment, then she smiled slowly. This would be a great opportunity for Stone to meet some of her friends.

Stone agreed quickly to her change of plans and said he was looking forward to meeting her friends. She'd ordered a vegetarian pizza, cola for him, bottled water for her. Taylor was starving, so she nibbled a piece of pizza as she waited for him to show. The plan was they'd eat here in her office, then they'd go to the bookstore.

Her heart leapt and Stone peeked around her office door. "Smells good in here," he said.

He approached as as naturally as a husband or a long-time boyfriend, he leaned down and lightly kissed her lips. "Tastes good, too."

Taylor's appetite drained away like someone had pulled a plug. She regretted that she couldn't have more of him, right here and now. He looked wonderful, smelled wonderful, a mixture of sandalwood, earth, and forest. Fate, that's what it was, fate that she be led by men all her life. Her gaze fastened on Stone's lips, as he devoured two pieces of pizza at once. Maybe a sweet destiny.

What had she been thinking to invite him to something like that? He'd think she was stupid, flaky at best. The whole scene would be embarrassing.

"You said we needed to be there by seven. We'd better go," he said, grabbing a Coke and another two slices of pizza from the box.

Taylor followed him slowly out the door.

They turned into the parking lot of the Metaphysical Bookstore. Stone parked his car and had his hand on the door handle. "Hold up. I want to tell you something," Taylor said.

Stone turned to her immediately.

"When I said this was a group of my friends getting together to talk about world conditions, I misled you."

Stone blinked.

"I'm going to meet an old boyfriend here for a chant to raise the vibration of world consciousness," she said in a rush.

"For a what?"

"A chant to raise the vibration of world consciousness."

Stone appeared to absorb this. "You're going to chant?"

Taylor nodded.

"What are you going to chant?"

"Healing mantras. When voices are combined together, the power is increased . . ."

"To vibrate the world consciousness?"

"Are you making fun of me?"

"I wouldn't dream of it. Give me an example."

Taylor took a deep breath. "Ohhhmmmm. Pure in heart, mighty with desire, grant us the transmuting power of your violet fire."

"Is that it?"

"Well, there are others, but yes, basically that's it."

"Oh. Dare I ask how this is going to raise the vibration of world consciousness?"

"Look, if you don't want to go, I understand."

"I wouldn't miss it for the world. Let's go, I want to meet this old boyfriend of yours before he starts chanting."

He was a little on the small side, but he was built like a brick outhouse, Kay thought. And the bulge in his pants was promising.

"So, Milton, where do you stay?"

"I'm still at the house. Quanita's afraid to call the Housing Authority to try and get me out because she's afraid they'll kick her ass out, too, if I tell them I been staying there the whole time."

Good, she needed a place to stay so she could get out of this hellhole mission. The projects weren't her first choice but they'd have to do.

She ran a carefully manicured hand over Milton's chest. "What if I make you forget about ever wanting Quanita back?"

"I don't think you can."

Kay leaned back from him and crossed her arms across her chest, her eyes narrowing. "I got second thoughts about getting some from you anyway. Quanita said you were sorry in the sack."

"What!"

"Faster than a bullet, and smaller than a pistol." Kay held up her thumb and forefinger about three inches apart.

"She's a damn liar!"

"I don't know if it's worth the trouble to find out if she was lying," Kay said. "She told everybody you couldn't find your way around a woman if it was high noon and you had a map, a guide, and a compass."

"I'm gonna kick that heifer's ass."

Kay smiled. That was more like it.

NINETEEN

"Taylor!" Maxwell called, as he hurried out of the bookstore. "It's great to see you." Then he caught sight of Stone.

"Maxwell, this is Stone." A tiny frown showed between Maxwell's brows, but Stone was as affable as usual as he shook Maxwell's hand.

"There's been a change of plan. We're not going to chant," Taylor said.

"We're not? Honey, I was so looking forward to it," Stone said. Taylor shot him a murderous look.

"Well, okay," Maxwell said, shifting from foot to foot. "Taylor didn't say she was bringing her new boyfriend."

Stone smiled at him, showing his teeth. "That's probably because she didn't know I was coming."

Taylor wanted badly to get out of there. "I'll wait in the car."

She wheeled and walked to the car and got in. A few moments later Stone got in. "If you wanted to stay, I wish you hadn't let me embarrass you. I'd really be interested in seeing you chant."

"I bet you'd have gotten a good laugh out of it."

"No, I have too much respect for other people's beliefs to laugh. Anyway you never told me what the chanting was supposed to accomplish."

"I did tell you to raise—"

"World consciousness, right. But how is chanting supposed to accomplish this? Seriously."

Taylor sighed. "You know when you go to church and the choir's singing praising God, and the song is so good the entire congregations jumps to their feet and joins in?"

"Uh-huh."

"Everybody in that church is raising the vibration of world consciousness through the glory of their words and upraised voices. We were just going at it a different way."

"Chanting is the way people who can't sing raise world consciousness?"

A laugh bubbled out of Taylor's throat. "I suppose you could say that, because I sure can't sing."

"Frankly, neither can I. So, what do you want to do tonight?"

What she wanted to do was to jump his bones. "I'm not sure. Do you have any ideas?"

"I'd like to take my dog out for a walk. The dog-walker I usually use called in sick. I was only out with him a few minutes before I went to your office."

"Okay. What sort of dog do you have?"

"He's a mutt. I've had him for seven years. You like dogs?"

"I don't dislike them, but actually, I'm more of a cat person."

Taylor watched him drive. She'd heard you could tell the way a man handled a woman from the way he handled his car. Stone didn't drive fast or impatiently. He was competent, safe, and handled the huge car deftly. The way he weaved in and out of the traffic showed he wasn't afraid to go for an opening, to take a risk. She couldn't wait to see how he lived.

Stone turned the key to his apartment door, and Taylor jumped back against the far wall of the hallway in terror as a large dark shape exploded out of the door.

It jumped on Stone in an ecstasy of joy, and Taylor took a closer look. It was far too large and ugly to be a dog.

"That's not a mutt, that's a mutation," Taylor said as Stone held his dog back from greeting her also. As big as that dog was, it certainly would have knocked her over with its enthusiasm.

"Don't talk about Ernie, you'll hurt his feelings."

Taylor gave the dog a skeptical look.

"Let me dash in and get Ernie's leash. I'll be right out."

Then Stone was gone and Ernie promptly jumped on her. Taylor gave a strangled scream as they both tumbled over and Ernie proceeded to wash her face with dog slobber. She gagged from the hot dog breath Ernie exhaled in her face and tried to struggle up. Ernie had no intention of allowing her to gain her feet. The damn dog probably weighed more than she did.

"Help, I've fallen."

Stone appeared. "And you can't get up. Down, Ernie," he commanded in a stern voice. The dog whimpered and laid down beside her. Stone held out a hand and helped Taylor to her feet.

She tried to brush the dog hair off her clothes and failed. Then she touched her wet and sticky face. "Keep that dog off me from now on," Taylor said in measured tones. "I have to wash my face."

"You look okay."

"I have to get the dog slobber off my face, now."

"Well, okay." Stone reluctantly let her into his apartment. Taylor could see why he was reluctant. The place looked like a tornado had hit it. Geez. "The bathroom's the second door to your right."

Taylor steeled herself to confront his bathroom, but the room was surprisingly clean if you disregarded the towels thrown on the floor. Even so she could never, ever live with him. Not in a thousand years. Stone and that dog would drive her bonkers within a day. They were both complete slobs.

Ernie behaved himself well on a leash. Twilight fell as Taylor and Stone strolled through Piedmont Park. The air was sweet and sultry, a breeze softly caressing them. The night promised to be magical, and Taylor understood magic.

"I'd love to know what you're thinking," Stone said.

"About magic."

"You believe in magic?"

"As much as I believe in breezes, and radio waves and other things you can't see."

"Do you consider yourself a witch?"

"No. I don't practice that religion." The she smiled up at him. "But I am magical. I was born that way."

"So, what do you consider magic?"

"Simply the perception of higher levels, the ability to use some senses and powers that are dormant in the majority of people."

"What about witchcraft then, and the different types of magic? What type of magic do you practice?"

"There is only one type of magic. The difference is how you use it. Myself, I operate under the simple tenet of do no harm. And I also apply the Master Jesus' directives."

"What's that?"

"First, love God with all your heart, then love your neighbor as yourself. Pretty straightforward when you get down to it."

"So you practice good magic, white magic?"

"Relatively so."

"What does that mean?"

"We all define good and evil within ourselves. In our hearts, so to speak. The intention counts as much as the result."

"That's deep. I have a cartoon idea of magic, the fairy godmother versus the evil witch."

"It's either simpler or more complicated. There are people who make magic their life's study, and people who use the gifts that come naturally without a second thought, much like you taste and see and touch."

"So those psychic hotlines really do work?"

"Not really. There's no way that foresight is that predictable or the answers that pat."

Stone smiled down at her. "You're an interesting woman, Taylor. Do you want to walk toward this homemade ice cream place? They have outside tables."

By the time they purchased their ice cream, the evening had deepened to blue. The vanilla ice cream tasted homemade, and the evening had cooled to perfection. Taylor gave a sigh of contentment.

She saw Stone gazing at her intently, and knew as clearly as if he'd spoken, that the time was right. She'd surrendered to destiny and tonight he wanted to make her his. She shivered a little, reluctant to let go of her baggage so easily.

"You haven't smoked all evening. How's quitting going?" she asked casually. No way could she date a smoker. She could take the red meat, she could clean up his apartment, maybe she could even get used to the mutt, but smoking . . . no.

"It's going. I quit almost every day."

"At least you haven't given up. I'd have a really hard time being in close proximity with a smoker for a long period of time. It really turns me off."

Stone looked glum. "You were right about those patches. I think they make it worse."

"I've got some ideas we can try."

"Like what?" Stone looked a little worried.

Taylor gave a mysterious smile. "You'll see."

Her beeper went off. Her home phone. It must be Tiffany, and it was unusual for her to beep her. "Excuse me," Taylor said as she pulled out her cellular phone.

"Tiff, what's up."

"I'm sorry to bother you, but I was wondering when you'd get home. I have fantastic news." Excitement bubbled in Tiffany's voice.

"What is it?"

"I can't tell you over the phone. You're not going to believe it!"

She'd never heard Tiffany so excited. She'd better get home. "I'll be home in a bit," she said, casting a regretful look in Stone's direction. Tonight wouldn't be the night.

TWENTY

"That was Tiffany. I need to get back home."

Stone nodded. "We'd better start back to my place."

Stone interlaced his fingers with hers on the walk back. It all fell into place, perfectly right, Stone next to her, their hands touching. Even with that monster mutt tagging along.

They didn't talk much on the drive to her office to get her car. Something had changed subtly in the balance between them—unvoiced, but there nevertheless. A bond was forming between the two of them that transcended all the baggage Taylor usually brought to male/female relationships.

Stone pulled up to her car. When he bent his head and touched her lips with his, the message that they exchanged in their kiss was unmistakable. No more games, this was the real deal.

Tiffany paced the floor. A whole bag of Oreos lay on the coffee table. Half of them were missing. It must be heavy, Taylor thought. Tiffany usually avoided Oreos like the plague.

"What's wrong, Tiff?" Taylor asked.

Tiffany grabbed a handful of Oreos out of the bag and munched one before she answered. "Nothing's wrong. I just made the biggest, most incredible decision today. I've accepted a job in St. Louis."

"What! I thought you loved your job here. I had no idea you were job-hunting."

"I wasn't. Jason called me and told me a friend of his, the president of WomenHelp Foundation, was desperately seeking a fundraiser, and I'd be perfect. It's an opportunity I can't turn down."

"My dad called you and got you a job?" Taylor asked, reeling.

"He didn't get it for me. I had an extensive phone interview and I know the VP from my Washington days."

"But you have a good job."

"I have a rooty-poot job and you know it. Now, I'll be doing what I love for an organization I've admired a long time. I start next week."

"What!"

"I told you they were desperate."

Taylor sank onto the couch. Dad had deprived her of a roommate. And a dear friend. She wanted to kill him.

"Daddy didn't waste any time making his move."

Tiffany frowned. "That wasn't it, though I wouldn't mind if it was. His motive was to help out a friend in need. Also, he said he saw right away I'd be perfect for the job."

"But next week? Tiff, what am I going to do without you?"

"You'll be okay. I'm going to leave all my furniture to you. I'm only going to take my clothes and personal items."

"Where are you going to stay?"

"The foundation offered me a hotel room until I find a place. But your father kindly offered to let me stay with him until I find a place."

"You're going to live with my father?"

"It's not like we'll be living together alone. Three of your brothers still stay at home."

Taylor said nothing, and picked an Oreo from the bag.

"I can take the stipend the foundation pays me for living expenses and buy new furniture instead of blowing it on a hotel room."

Taylor chewed the Oreo and picked up another cookie.

"I thought you'd be happy for me."

"I don't mean to be negative. It's just that I'm surprised. This is incredibly sudden. And I can't believe my dad is going to let you live with him."

"Don't keep saying that. I'm not living with him, just staying with him, a guest in his home, until I get my own place."

"I'm going to miss you, Tiff, but I suppose the opportunity is fantastic."

"The job is fantastic."

"I was talking about my father."

"Oh."

"Even though he gets on my last nerve, I'm crazy about him. Take good care of him."

"Taylor, I'm just a temporary guest."

"Yeah."

Tiffany dropped down beside Taylor and gave her a hug. "I'm going to miss you, too. But you know things always change."

In a flash, Taylor saw life as a river, sometimes turbulent, sometimes calm, always moving, tributaries breaking away and joining together. "You're right. The only thing certain about life is that as long as you're alive, nothing will ever stay the same."

Kay looked around to make sure no one was close enough to overhear before she put the coins into the pay phone. "She's leaving now. Yes. She'll be going that way to catch the bus because her interview is on North Ave. Okay, I'll meet you there."

She carefully hung up. Milton didn't know it yet, but Quanita was about to be history, and he'd be next. Rushing out, she hailed a taxi. "Take me to Southgate Place," she told the driver.

On the way to Quanita's house, Kay imagined how much fun she was going to have teaching Quanita a lesson. That Milton was one dumb nigger—she had him pinned under her mani-cured thumb. No, there wasn't a thing to worry about. That would be the end of Quanita, and Milton would be in jail. She'd be set to move in.

The taxi driver burned rubber as he pulled off after he'd dropped her off. Why was he pissed? He didn't do anything to deserve extra. He should be happy she paid him. She used the key Milton gave her and walked into Quanita's place. It would do. She went to look in the refrigerator, she might as well have a snack before Milton got back. She was hungry.

Kay licked the last of the peanut butter from her fingers when Milton walked in the door. She stared at him, disbelieving. "Where the hell is Quanita?" she demanded.

"I couldn't make her come."

"I didn't tell you to make it a choice, you dumb . . ."

"Who do you think you're talking to?"

"I'm talking to you. We made plans. You said you wanted to get Quanita back for what she did to you."

Milton looked at her through narrowed eyes. "If I did what you wanted me to, Quanita would never come back. She'd split for good. I know the girl. And what do you get out of this anyway? You don't know me. You ain't got no reason to help me out."

"I was trying to help you out. If you're too stupid—"

Milton grabbed her and was dragging her toward the bed-room.

"Let me go this instant!"

"You're sure quick to call somebody stupid, bitch. I'll let your ass go when I'm through with it. Then I want you to clear the hell out of here."

He threw her on the bed. She screeched and tried to struggle up, but for someone that little, he was strong. She panicked when he exposed himself, and pushed her miniskirt up her thighs. What would he do when . . . ?

He paused, not even breathing. "You muthaf__ freak," he snarled, and the first blow was to the side of her head.

"Not the face. Just don't hit me in the face."

"You like it, freak, when I hit you anywhere else?" And her head snapped back from the blow to her jaw. She heard something snap, and he hit her again and again and again. She was in a red haze of pain until there was nothing left at all.

Taylor shoved papers around on her desk, watched the clock, and wondered why Stone hadn't called yet. A tentative knock sounded on her door. "Come in."

Eva walked in and sat in the chair facing Taylor's desk. "I hope this isn't a bad time, but I need to talk to you."

"It's fine. How can I help you?"

Eva shifted in her chair. "I've been talking to my husband, and we want to give it another chance. He's committed to counseling."

"He put you in the hospital, Eva, and just last week you were terrified that he'd find out where you were staying. What changed?"

"He's stopped drinking and he's going to AA meetings regularly."

"You're sure? You're not frightened anymore?"

"He only hit me that one time and he was drunk. He was under a lot of pressure at work . . ."

Taylor just looked at her.

"I think I'm pregnant."

"All the more reason for you to ensure your safety, and a home free of violence for your child."

Eva looked off into the distance. "It's not that easy. My family is very traditional and have expectations that are hard to shed. I put a lot into this marriage, and especially now that I'm going to have a baby, I don't want to let it go that easily."

Taylor shook her head, but held her tongue. It wasn't her decision to make.

"I wanted to tell you personally. You've been so good to me. I'm ready to leave now."

She stood and embraced Eva. "Take care of yourself. You'll be in my prayers. And remember we're always here if you need us."

Eva walked out of her office without a backward glance. Taylor watched her go, worried. Prayers were the only thing left to give Eva, and the sad thing was, she'd probably need them.

TWENTY-ONE

At the head of the table, Marian shredded a napkin, an uncharacteristic and unconscious gesture of nervousness. "A major grant is coming up for renewal, and with the situation with the shelter as it is now, I don't need to tell you our situation is grave."

She looked at each face around the conference table. "If that grant doesn't come through, we're talking layoffs."

Silence.

Then Lily cleared her throat. "Why don't we start admitting clients to the shelter again? The police still have no firm evidence that the murders are connected with our shelter residents."

"Amber's leaving tomorrow for her mother's home. That leaves only two adults and three children in the shelter," Christine said.

"We have ten shelter staff on the payroll," Carol reminded everyone needlessly.

Marian nodded. "I'll speak to the detective on the murder cases about the feasibility of reopening the shelter to new admissions."

A spontaneous cheer went up.

Sandy, the office manager, stuck her head through the door. "Marian, you have a call. They say it's urgent."

A momentary look of irritation crossed her features. "Excuse me," she said. "I'll be right back."

"I can't afford to lose my job," Christine murmured after Marian left.

"Nobody can," Carol said.

Taylor shifted uneasily. The darkness she'd sensed since the murders hadn't lifted. She had the sense of a storm gathering, waiting to release its full fury.

"Once we reopen our shelter program, I don't see why that grant wouldn't be renewed. I think everything's going to be okay."

A murmur of assent went through the room. Marian walked slowly back in and sat down heavily. Her face was gray and drawn, and for once, she looked her age. "Christine, you need to bring Joan over here right away. The police need to meet with her. Her husband was just found. Someone doused him with gasoline and set him on fire."

Taylor let herself wearily into her apartment. It had been a rotten day, and Stone not calling was the icing on the cake. She glanced at her answering machine. No messages. Figured.

She walked into the kitchen and got a bag of potato chips for dinner. Tiffany had called and said she'd be out until late taking care of business in preparation for her upcoming move. She picked up the phone to call Kara and set it down again before dialing. She really wasn't in the mood to talk to anyone. Except that one person who hadn't bothered to call her.

She clicked on the TV and stared at it unseeingly. She thought about the shelters and the deaths and smacked into that black wall of clouds. She tried to force her mind away, but the thought of the murders came again and again. Then a whisper, the woman's voice. "Black magic."

The voice spoke to her through the black cloud. A sending, and a warning directly to her. For her. The murderer was a woman, and the woman had the gift also. Just like she did, maybe stronger; she was certainly more knowledgeable in manipulating the gift. Taylor didn't begin to know how to send a verbal message, or to block someone out.

Black magic, the woman had said. Black signified the absence of color and light: void, nothingness, death. Taylor shuddered. What did it mean? Murders took place in Atlanta every day. These murders had to be connected to her or her fate in some way, or she wouldn't have the precognition about them. Previously, women had stayed in the shelter, and been murdered by their abusers, with Taylor having no foresight.

She'd never met anyone like herself, although people claiming psychic powers abounded. They must be out there, people with the gift. There was so much she didn't know. She accepted the power as a part of her, much like people accept any talent, such as being able to draw or play the piano well.

She'd never taken any special note of it, or made any study of the occult, the hidden mysteries. A long time ago, when she was in college, she'd met a man, a much older man. He'd regarded her steadily, and said she needed a teacher. She knew immediately what he meant, and she asked him if he was that teacher. A tiny shake of his head. No, he wasn't her teacher, he'd said, then he spouted the old maxim, when the student is ready, a teacher will come.

She longed for that teacher now, anyone who could help her understand what in hell was going on. You're right about one thing, Taylor, she thought to herself, there's hell in whatever's going on.

The phone rang, and Taylor jumped. She dived across the coffee table to grab it, and took a deep breath to compose herself before she spoke. "Hello."

"Taylor, it's Stone. How are you doing?"

"I had a pretty rough day at work. How about you?"

"The same. You heard about Joan Spencer's husband?"

"Yes. I was just thinking about that."

"I know this is short notice, but I've been tied up today. What are you doing for dinner?"

Taylor looked at the open bag of potato chips. "Nothing. What do you have in mind?" she asked, her pulse quickening.

"Probably grab a bite out. I eat out so much I probably keep several fast food restaurants in business."

"Why don't you come over here? I'll cook something."

"Mmmmm, sounds great. How about in a hour?"

"That'll be fine." Taylor slowly replaced the receiver. Had she actually offered to cook? Cooking and her were a combination that never mixed. She bounded up and went into the kitchen, and stared in the refrigerator in despair. She couldn't serve Stone just a salad, she knew how he felt about tofu, and plain brown rice and beans were out of the question. Going back into the living room, she picked up the phone. She sure hoped Stone liked Chinese.

"Wendy!" George called for her. She swallowed hard and moved toward the den to meet him.

"Why didn't you answer me when I called you?"

Wendy lifted her chin. "I was on the way."

He approached her, and stood mere inches away. "Where were you when I tried to call you from work this afternoon?"

Wendy fixed her eyes on her feet, her former bravado failing her. "I didn't hear the phone."

"You didn't hear the phone. How unusual. May I ask what you were doing that prevented you from hearing the phone?"

"I was doing laundry. The phone must have rung during the spin cycle." She'd said she wasn't going to lie to him, she was going to stand her ground. He hadn't hit her since she'd come home, even though he'd gotten pretty mad. Somewhere between then and now, she'd lost the nerve. She took a step back.

"Where are you going?"

"May I sit down?"

"No, you may not. Was that sarcasm I detected? Hmmm?"

"No, George, I'm just tired."

"You got any reason to be tired? You sit on your ass all day around the house while I go out and earn our living. And that brings us back around to our discussion. What were you doing that you couldn't hear the phone?"

"I said I was doing the laundry—"

She wasn't prepared for the blow to her jaw that knocked her to the ground.

"You're a damn liar. I called you from my cell phone. I was pulling into the driveway, bitch, and you weren't here."

She tried to struggle to her feet. "George, I was scared to tell you that I went to the—"

Her words were cut off by a kick to her midsection. The pain robbed her of her breath. She fell to her knees.

"Who are you whoring with, slut? You think I should be happy you didn't bring him into our bed, huh?" he yelled, punctuating each word with a vicious kick.

She screamed in pain and anger, scrambled to her feet and attempted to run.

He grabbed her by her hair and threw her against a wall. She slid to the floor and curled into a fetal ball as he kicked her again and again.

His shouts receded into the background along with the pain. She fled to that place within her mind where he couldn't hurt her. She was barely conscious when George had finally tired himself out and stormed out of the room.

She tried to move, to get up and run out of the house. She'd never come back again, she vowed. Her muscles wouldn't obey. He'd hurt her bad this time. She opened her mouth to call for him to help her, but only a croak emerged. It was getting hard to breathe. She heard the television come on in his library. It didn't matter anyway. Who cared about what happened to her? She wasn't worth anything to anybody. She didn't fight it as her world darkened to shades of gray, then black.

TWENTY-TWO

Taylor rushed to the door at the sound of the doorbell, hoping the Chinese food delivery made it there before Stone did. But there he stood, looking luscious.

"May I come in?"

Taylor stood aside, embarrassed that he might have noticed her staring at him. "Of course. Have a seat." She gestured to the sofa. "Would you like something to drink?"

"That would be great, whatever you have is fine."

"Uh, the Chinese food will be here any minute."

Stone grinned. "Great. I love Chinese."

She went into the kitchen and got out two wine glasses. A little fortification sure wouldn't hurt. The doorbell rang, and by the time she got back to the living room, Stone was paying the deliveryman.

"You didn't have to do that. I'd said I would have dinner here."

"That's all right. Do you want to eat here or at the table?"

"Here is fine."

Going back to the kitchen to get their drinks and utensils, a tingle started behind her eyes, sort of like an itch. Oh, Lord, not with Stone in the next room, sexual awareness and interest lying thick between them, making her heart pound and her mouth dry. Not now. He'd think she was crazy. He already knows you're crazy, an inner voice whispered.

The vision rushed over her like a river. She was in a strange house, a kitchen. Her hands grasped the sink. Her hands. My God, they weren't hers. They were white and masculine. She was seeing through someone else's eyes, feeling through someone else's body.

A buzzing sounded in her ears and a tingling like electricity flowed through her body. A small sound behind her. A cough, a snuffle. The hairs rose at the back of her neck. Someone was behind her, someone who didn't belong in the house. She tried to scream, but nothing came out. Her muscles were immobilized by some strange force and locked in place, only her eyes could move.

"Hello, it's me, Black Magic," a woman's hoarse voice whispered behind her. "I know you're in there. He has earned this destiny, not you. I suggest you leave now, this isn't going to be pleasant. Not pleasant at all." The woman gave a dry chuckle.

Taylor strained to recognize the voice. There was something about it, something tantalizingly familiar . . . incredible pain exploded at her back. Again, and again, my God. A scream rose in her throat, and her knees tried to buckle in agony, but the unnatural force held the man's body locked into position.

The wet, sucking sound of tearing flesh. She couldn't bear the pain, the terrible pain. Searing fire ripping into her back. Oh, my God, she couldn't breathe—she was dying . . .

"Taylor! What's wrong?" Stone cradled her in his arms, alarm in his eyes. "Taylor, speak to me. I'm going to call 911."

"No, don't," she croaked. "I'm all right." She was herself again, safely ensconced in her own body, lying on her own kitchen floor. She tried to twist around to look at her back.

"What are you doing? Are you sure you're okay?"

"Are there any wounds on my back?"

"What?"

"Do I have any wounds on my back?"

Stone frowned, but lifted her up and peered at her back. "No. Should there be?"

"I had a vision."

"A vision?"

"I was in a white man's body while someone stabbed him to death from the back."

"Stabbed?"

"Would you stop repeating everything I say? Listen. A woman stabbed him, the same one that is sending to me. She paralyzed him in some way. That's how she's been able to overpower these men she's killed."

"You lost me way back."

"Where?"

"Somewhere around where you asked me if there were any wounds on your back. Taylor, did you fall and hit your head?"

She sucked on her teeth, exasperated. "I had a vision of something that is going to happen, is happening, or has happened."

It was hardly possible for Stone to look more concerned than he did already. "Do you have these visions often?"

"Every once in a while, but I'm not crazy."

"I didn't say you were."

"But you were wondering."

He didn't deny it. Taylor got to her feet. "I need to find out what's going on. Magic is involved." She grabbed her glass of wine and went to the living room. Stone followed.

Taylor paced. "I've been getting sendings about the killings almost since they started. Specific sendings for me. I wonder how I'm connected?"

"You work for the agency. And what do you mean by sendings?" Stone was looking through the cartons of Chinese food. He picked one and got a plastic fork and dug in. He seemed remarkably unconcerned, she thought, but that was Stone. She had a feeling a demon could materialize in the room, and he'd offer it some Chinese food.

"Someone is sending me psychic impressions about the murders. She calls herself Black Magic."

"She's a sister?"

"Not necessarily. In this instance, I feel black has the connotation of death."

"Hmmm. Do you have a Coke?"

"There's some ginger ale in the refrigerator." She looked at the wine glass in her hand. Empty. She needed a refill. "I'll get you a glass."

She filled a glass with ginger ale, her hands still shaking in reaction from her horrific experience. Starting to refill her wine glass, she reconsidered and grabbed the bottle and the empty glass. She returned to the living room, handed Stone his drink, refilled her glass, and carefully set the bottle of wine on the coffee table. Then she resumed pacing.

Stone discarded the empty carton of Chinese food, and picked up another. "Taylor, why don't you sit down and eat something?"

"I'm not hungry. I need to figure this out. I suppose the next victim will die by stabbing. We need to warn all the white male partners of shelter residents of the past month—"

"Whoa. C'mon and chill out. Sit down here and talk to me. Help me understand what's going on with you."

Taylor hesitated, then sank onto the couch next to him. She stared at her hands.

"Okay, sweetheart. Start at the beginning." Stone's voice was as gentle as a caress. Then to her utter dismay and disbelief, she burst into tears.

She never cried. Maybe she was losing her mind. She covered her face with her hands. Deep shuddery sobs racked her. Fighting to regain control, she couldn't.

He was rocking her. Her head was buried in his shoulder,

his shirt absorbing her tears. He smelled like pure essence of male and Ivory soap. His body was large and warm, with just the right degree of hardness to match her feminine softness. Perfection. She stilled, another emotion replacing her shock and delayed reaction. She drew away from him. "I don't know what came over me. I'm sorry."

He touched her lips with his finger. "There's nothing to be sorry about. You've obviously been through something that affected you deeply."

Not nearly as much as he was affecting her now. "I know it sounds crazy. But the killer has mental powers similar to mine. Except maybe stronger. I'm receiving . . . I don't know, messages, maybe?"

"I can't pretend to understand. But I believe you, if that means anything to you. If there's anything I can do to help you, I'll do it."

Taylor drew in a deep breath. He was telling the truth, with no ulterior motives. She could feel it. "Thank you," she replied, her voice soft and husky.

They looked into each other's eyes. When their lips touched, it was as if the heavens had opened up for Taylor. So right . . . the way things were meant to be. Stone deepened the kiss, drawing her closer to him. Their breath mingled and their tongues danced, imitating the primeval rhythm of what was to come. Her body strained, she needed to be closer to him. She needed . . .

Stone broke away from the kiss, and stood, holding out his hand to her. No words were needed. She reached out and put her hand in his. He started to pull her to him, and the door opened.

Tiffany stood in the doorway. She and Stone had turned their heads toward her, frozen in an odd tableau.

"Excuse me, I—" Tiffany started to say.

"Would you like some Chinese food?" Taylor asked, her voice a little too loud.

"No. I ate already. I'm going on to bed."

Tiffany never went to bed this early. The aura of frustrated lust and longing hung in the air, thick enough even for someone who wasn't psychic to detect.

"I was just leaving," Stone said.

Noooo, Taylor wanted to groan, but she said nothing. He dropped a light kiss on her lips. "I'll call you."

Right, she thought. Then like that, he was gone. Why did he run from her at the slightest excuse? Wasn't she the one who was reluctant? Wasn't she the one who should be running from him? Yet, she advanced, he retreated. For once, he'd drawn her to him. He'd wanted her as much as she wanted him. Why did he run? Taylor bit her lip in pure frustration.

"I didn't mean to chase him away," Tiffany said.

Taylor dropped back to the couch. "He wouldn't have left if he didn't want to go."

Tiffany raised an eyebrow. "So, you're resigned to dating the big, bad, Stone now? Do I detect the desire to do more than the nasty with him?"

"I can't even get to second base with the man. I don't know why he's holding out. I can tell he wants to."

"You two looked like you were well on your way to a home run when I walked in."

"I get the feeling that batting in all the home runs in a season wouldn't be enough to get him out of my system. Maybe it would be a mistake to go further."

"Taylor, you need to chill out and allow nature to take its course."

"That's the second time I've heard that I need to chill in the last hour."

"See, you know I'm right. He's perfect for you."

"He smokes."

"He's trying to quit."

"He's an incredible slob."

"If you move in with him, hire a cleaning lady."

"He makes me feel out of control."

"Ahhh. That's the root of the problem. It's the first time you've come close to surrendering control to a man, isn't it?"

Taylor stared at her, hating to admit she was right. Tiffany leaned close to her. "Let me tell you something, if he doesn't make you want not only to give up the sex, but to offer up your heart, soul, everything . . . he's not worth it. That's what you're scared of, isn't it? Stone makes you want to give it all up?"

Taylor looked away, unable to answer.

Tiffany patted her hand. "Surrender can be sweet, and with the right man, it's sublime," she said. "You'll see."

Taylor sighed. Once she'd believed that sex was all it would take to be free of her craving for Stone. Now, she realized that she'd never be satisfied with having any less than his heart, mind, body, and soul.

TWENTY-THREE

"Man, I was just protecting myself. That freak was going to kill me," the suspect said. Stone watched the interrogation behind the mirrored glass. Milton was charged with assault, and possibly murder if the victim, a transsexual and ex-shelter resident, died.

The first solid lead on the case of the shelter murders, Milton said Kay was the killer, and the detectives grabbed at it, anxious to close the case. But something about the situation left a bad taste in Stone's mouth. Milton's story was too pat.

"He's lying about something," Stone said to Charles.

The detective standing beside him shrugged. "He's not denying he almost beat Keith or 'Kay' Nichols to death. What motive would he have besides self-defense?"

Stone watched Milton thoughtfully. "I don't know, but I have the feeling something else is going on."

He was officially off the case, having dropped George McIntyre as a client, but he hated to leave threads untied. And the shelter murders weren't just a thread, they were a rapidly unraveling rope. Also, the murders were affecting Taylor profoundly, in ways he didn't understand.

"Thanks for letting me know what's going on," he said to Charles.

"No problem."

He'd stop by the mission and talk with Milton's girlfriend,

Quanita, an ex-shelter resident. Maybe she could shed some light on what was going on with her ex-boyfriend.

"Can I help you?" a security guard behind the desk asked when he got to the mission.

"I'm looking for Quanita Nelson."

The guard perused a clipboard. "She's gone."

Stone frowned. "Do you have any idea where?"

The security guard shook his head. Stone slipped him a twenty.

"She said she was going to live out in the suburbs with a friend whose husband just died. That's all I know."

"Thank you," Stone said. He took out his cellular phone, he wanted to talk to Taylor about Quanita. He had a feeling she could shed some light on what was going on.

Taylor looked up, surprised that Marian had walked into her office without knocking. "It's bad. It's very, very bad," Marian said, sinking into a chair next to Taylor's desk.

"What's going on?"

"Word has come down from the board. The shelter must close. Effective immediately."

"Oh, no!"

"I'm going to have to lay off all the shelter staff."

Taylor closed her eyes briefly. "My God, Marian. This is terrible."

"Fifteen years I've fought to establish this agency. Every grant I've wrung out, every volunteer I've cajoled . . . and now on the whim of some madman it's disintegrating before my eyes."

"Madwoman," Taylor corrected automatically.

"I can hardly credit a woman with overcoming three men."

"There's strangeness in the world. A woman can carry as much darkness in her heart as a man," Taylor murmured.

Marian rubbed her eyes. "I suppose that's true. But I can

hardly bear this. Christine has been with us for years, and Lily . . ."

"There's nothing we can do? Can we shift their responsibilities? The office is going to stay open isn't it?"

"Yes, but there simply isn't the money to pay them. The grant wasn't renewed. We'll have to lease the shelter house."

"When are you going to give everyone the news?"

"I have to do it today. Effective immediately, the board said. They made it clear it wasn't open for debate. The agency may not recover from the blow these murders and the accompanying publicity has given us. Everyone's calling us the agency of death. Taylor, this is confidential and FYI only, but I'm polishing up my résumé, and it might not hurt for you to do the same."

Taylor nodded. "Is there anything I can do to help you now?"

"No. I've got to do this myself. When I come back from the shelter, I want to take the afternoon off, go home, and eat Ben and Jerry's ice cream until I pop. Cover for me, will you?"

"Sure, Marian."

She sat there doodling on her desk pad after Marian had left. The agency's days were numbered because of the killer, her evil nullifying all the good work the agency would have done in the days to come.

The phone rang. Stone said, "Taylor, there's something I want to talk to you about. Can you take an hour off over lunch?"

Her heart leapt. "Sure," she said, trying to sound casual. "Where shall we meet?"

"How about the Red Beef Barn around noon?"

"All right." She hung up the phone, a warm glow enveloping her at the thought of seeing Stone. But the Red Beef Barn? Please.

She arrived at the Red Beef Barn a little early. The setup was a little unusual. You paid for your food and they gave you a tray and dishes and herded you through several buffet lines. At least it was fast.

There was enough food spread out to feed an entire third-world country, she thought. Taylor got a glass of ice tea and a salad, and settled down to wait for Stone.

There he was. Stone approached carrying a platter with a huge steak and a baked potato stuffed with sour cream, bacon, and cheese. Ice tea and apple pie topped off the feast. "Hello," he greeted her cheerily.

"Hello," she said, her voice lowered an octave. Someone once said her deep voice was irresistibly sexy.

"You have a cold?"

"No. I don't have a cold."

Stone sawed on his steak, which looked like it was charred to a cinder. He chewed on a piece and sighed in bliss. "Nothing's better than a good cut of steak."

"Is it tough? It looks overcooked."

"I like my meat well-done. Is that all you're going to eat?"

"Ummm. You want me to get you a salad?" Taylor surveyed the wealth of fat and cholesterol on Stone's tray. He could really use some more vegetables in his diet.

"I doubt that I'll have room."

"You wanted to talk to me?" He probably wanted to talk to her about their relationship. She supposed it was too early to declare any commitment, but he likely wanted to assure her exclusivity. Make sure his territory was marked in the way men liked to do.

"I wanted to ask you about Quanita Nelson," he mumbled around a piece of steak.

"What?" She wasn't sure she heard him right, certainly he wasn't asking her about Quanita. She had her on her mind, so she must have heard him wrong.

He finished chewing and took a sip of ice tea. "I wanted to ask you about Quanita Nelson and Keith Nichols."

"I thought you asked me here to talk about us. You could have asked me over the phone about Quanita and . . . Keith who?"

"You might know him as Kay. Talk about us? What's there to talk about?"

Taylor stared at him. She'd just about had enough of his rejection. She folded her napkin carefully and laid it by her plate. "I'm leaving." She rose and walked to the exit. There was an upside after all about having to pay for your food beforehand. She ignored Stone's shout after her.

In the bright noon sun, she took a deep breath and walked to her car. Stone Emerson was out of her life. She wasn't going to put herself out for him to hurt her anymore . . . a high pitched squeak emerged from her lips as she was spun around, none too gently.

Easygoing, ever affable, nothing-ever-got-to-him Stone looked quite irritated. "Why did you walk out on me like that?"

"I'm sick of you putting me down and hurting my feelings, and I'm not going to take it anymore!" she yelled.

Stone stepped back. "What are you talking about? I'd never hurt you."

"What do you call walking out, and rejecting me all the time? I thought you asked me out to spend some time with me, but you just wanted to pick my brain. I'll tell you what, I'll make it easy for you. Stay away from me from now on!"

She marched away from him. Her hand was on her car door when she gave a strangled scream. He'd picked her up like a bag of potatoes and thrown her over his shoulder. "Put me down. Put me down this instant!" She beat on his shoulders.

"Marital spat," Stone said to a group of fascinated bystanders. "Sometimes you need to take the little woman in hand."

"I'm not his little woman. Help me!"

Taylor watched the group's initial concern transform into amusement. Stone opened his car door and dumped her in the front seat. The next thing she realized, he pulled out on the street. She dived for the door handle. "I wouldn't advise it. You could get injured falling from a moving car."

"This is kidnapping."

"Woman napping."

"That's not funny. Take me back to my car right now."

"I don't think so. You made grave and unearned accusations. I'm not letting you go until we get to the bottom of them."

"Do you realize I'm a lawyer? That I'll press charges?"

Stone pulled up to his apartment. "Do I have to carry you in, or are you going to walk?"

"I'm not going anywhere but back to my car."

"It's up to you." He got out of the car and walked around to her side, he opened the door and picked her up and slung her across his shoulder again as easily as if she'd been a twenty-five-pound bag of dog food.

She howled.

"Not in my ear, Taylor. That hurts."

She howled louder and Stone shook his head. He opened his door with one hand. She was afraid to struggle, because if he dropped her it would probably be painful.

Ernie started to jump on them but subsided with one word from Stone. The dog cocked his head and watched them with an almost human interest. Taylor was getting no help from that quarter.

"Let me down, dammit!" she yelled.

"Okay," Stone strode into the bedroom and dumped her on his bed.

Taylor caught her breath and glared at him. He watched her, a slight smile on his face. "And what's going to happen next is even better. I'm going to join you. We'll talk later."

TWENTY-FOUR

Taylor looked so good sprawled out on his bed. He took off his shoes first and loosened his tie. When he took off his shirt, her eyes widened, but she didn't make a sound. He unbuckled his belt, and dropped his pants.

The apprehension in her eyes transformed to lust when she saw his readiness, and he almost lost it. Forcing himself to take his time, he took off his socks, then finally his briefs. He dropped to the bed on one knee, over her.

She moistened her lips, an unconscious gesture. He needed to kiss them, but not quite yet. "Now, your turn," he said. She didn't protest as he drew off one of her sandals, then another. She wore a white silk T-shirt, tucked into a short black skirt—simple, direct, and sexy as hell, like her.

He ran his hands up her silky brown legs to the hem of her skirt. He reached behind her, his hands molding her full buttocks. He couldn't resist drawing her to him, momentarily pressing himself against the soft vee of her femininity.

She gasped softly and her hips arched to him. He breathed harshly and drew back. Slowly. He unsnapped the button at the back of her skirt and drew it over her hips. He burned when he saw the white silk and lace panties that accentuated the crisp, dark, curls that covered what he wanted most in the world at that moment. He ran trembling fingers over her quivering mound, between her legs, pressing teasingly where he knew the pleasure was keenest. She moaned, her legs spreading, her panties soaked.

He pulled the T-shirt up over her head, trailing fingers over silken flesh. The nipples of her surprisingly full breasts strained against her matching lacy white bra. He kissed one then another through the sheer fabric, feeling them harden with desire.

Taylor's hips rotated under him. He was so hard, it almost hurt, but slowly, slowly. He unsnapped her bra and her breasts sprang free from their prison. He cupped them, swirling his tongue around her nipples. She moaned incoherently, and finally he kissed her. Savage passion too long withheld exploded between them. Their tongues thrust and danced with a hot anticipation. He slid down her body for the most intimate kiss of all.

"Please, please, now," Taylor's voice whispered, husky with passion. "I need you inside me."

She reached for him, her back arching, and his control snapped. With a growl he pulled off the tiny bit of fabric separating them and poised himself between her legs. At the entrance to his ultimate desire and need he paused, fighting for control. She gripped his hips, trying to draw him inside her.

Agonizingly slowly he slid his full length into her slick, velvet walls. So tight, she fitted him like snug handmade gloves. Then he withdrew as slowly, his breathing harsh.

"Give it all to me, now," Taylor begged.

He plunged into her again and again, the friction painfully sweet. She gasped and met him with equal vigor, wrapping her legs around his hips, bucking against him in a frenzy of ardor.

"Oh, God," she sobbed, and he felt her contractions within like waves cresting. She clutched his shoulders and stiffened, thrusting him over a precipice of his own. He groaned and sank himself deeper into her, feeling ecstasy work its way up and explode against her womb, in endless surges of bliss.

George sipped his bourbon as he watched the first World Series game. The Braves were so far ahead, it was hardly worth watching. He cracked his knuckles. If that Wendy came in here with her whining, he didn't know what he'd do. Kill her maybe.

But it wasn't worth doing time in prison for the sorry slut. George burned with self-righteous anger. He'd put off teaching her a well-earned lesson, gone to that stupid counseling class for her, and this was how she repaid him. Well, after the butt-whipping he'd given her, he bet she'd think twice before sneaking out of the house again.

A tingling started in his feet, like they were going to sleep. He set down his glass and wriggled his toes in his shoes. It got worse. He stamped his feet and held out his legs to make sure the circulation was unimpaired. Damndest thing, very uncomfortable. The tingling turned to pins and needles and he started to stand to walk it off. He couldn't move.

His eyes widened in alarm, and he struggled to get out of the chair to no avail. Unseen steel grips held every muscle in place. He could move his eyes and rolled them in fear as an indistinct black shape approached. A man-shaped haze hovered over him. He could make out no distinct features. He stared at the baseball bat the figure carried.

A woman's voice spoke from the haze, low and gravelly. "Strrrike one." The bat swung against his right knee and he heard it shatter and crack before the pain hit his nerve receptors.

Tears flowed from his eyes. He tried to scream, but nothing but a moan of pure agony emerged from his throat.

"Strrike two!" His left knee.

"Strrike three!" The bat struck his groin with vicious force. Indescribable pain. He wanted to die. He wanted to plead that she kill him with the next blow.

He was barely conscious when the bat rose high over his head. A voice that sounded just like Wendy's emerged from the figure. "How 'bout going for the home run, big boy?"

A deafening crunch, then blessed nothingness.

TWENTY-FIVE

Sated, Taylor and Stone melded together, limbs entangled, damp and still heated after several bouts of lovemaking. "I'd kill for a cigarette," he murmured.

"That's not very romantic."

"Sorry."

Taylor heard a snuffle in the doorway and lifted her head to see Ernie staring at them, head still cocked, eyes fixed and intent. "Did that dog watch us the whole time?"

"Probably. He's something of a voyeur, but don't worry, I've had him fixed."

"What does that have to do with it?"

A deep, rumbling laugh emerged from Stone. "This is not your usual romantic postcoital conversation."

"Stone, we're never going to be usual."

"I guess that's why I'm crazy about you." He nibbled at her lips and Taylor caressed his back.

He deepened his kiss, and their breathing quickened. He pulled her on top of him, his body hard and ready again. She sighed with pure contentment. She adored a man with a quick draw and a slow trigger. Loving couldn't get much better than this.

"I don't think we're going to get much sleep tonight," Stone whispered in her ear.

"Good. But get that dog out of here."

The trill of a cell phone cut through their rising passion. "Yours?"

Taylor shook her head no. "Yours."

Stone rolled off the bed and reached for his pants, pulling his cell phone out of the pocket. "Yeah?"

Taylor watched him. Geez, he was a beautiful man. Not only was he amply endowed in every way, but he knew how to use well every muscle the Lord blessed him with.

She noticed his face turn grim as he listened. He clicked off the cell phone with an abrupt movement and turned to Taylor frowning. "That was the detective on the shelter case. George has been murdered in his home."

Taylor gasped. "Was Wendy there?"

"Unfortunately so. She's been badly beaten, but she's alive. I'm going to the crime scene, you should come, too. Maybe you can pick up some impressions. Want to join me in a quick shower?"

Taylor hugged herself. She stood well away from the crime scene, where Stone was talking with some detectives. George's body hadn't been removed yet, and from the maroon stains seeping through the sheet that covered him in the chair, she didn't want to get any closer.

Stone approached her slowly. "Someone called 911, from the house, and left the phone off the hook. When a policeman came out to make a routine investigation, he found George like this, and Wendy lying unconscious in the hallway."

"Who called 911?"

"No idea, and no fingerprints on the phone. It's been wiped clean. But Wendy lucked out. She was bleeding internally. If she had lain there through the night, she probably would have died."

"Has any evidence been found?"

"What they can piece together is that George was watching

the game when someone approached him from the front with a baseball bat."

"And he just sat there?"

"That's the unusual thing. The killing blow to the head came last. He apparently sat through several excruciatingly painful blows. Both knees were crushed, and his genitals pulped. I wouldn't consider it humanly possible for a man to sit erect through that."

"Was he drugged?"

"We won't get toxicology results back for a while."

"So Wendy's not a suspect?"

"There's no way she could have assaulted George, the way she was beaten. She was kicked, and from a cursory inspection, it looks like it was him doing the kicking."

"How do you know?"

"Shoe imprints."

Taylor shuddered. "Black Magic," she whispered.

"What's that?"

"I feel the residue of power. It's like the smell and smoke that's left over after you explode fireworks, but intangible. Hard to describe."

"So you think someone came in here and bewitched him?"

"Someone created an illusion so strong it virtually paralyzed him. I experienced the same phenomenon in the vision I had yesterday when you were with me."

Stone raised an eyebrow.

"Remember when I asked if there were wounds on my back? I was in a white man's body, standing at a kitchen sink, grasping the edge. I could feel someone approaching me. What was interesting was that she knew I was in the man's body. She warned me to leave. Then, I couldn't move or scream, even when she plunged the knife in my back. Repeatedly. It was god-awful painful."

Stone frowned. "Nobody has been killed by stab wounds to the back."

"Yet," Taylor said.

"Do you want to go back to my place?"

Taylor shook her head. The recent revelations had left her pensive, moody.

"Tiffany's leaving tomorrow. I need to see her off. I'm taking the morning off." Suddenly Taylor gave a horrified gasp.

"I was supposed to cover for Marian at the office this afternoon. I didn't show up after lunch or call or anything. What time is it?"

"Almost nine."

Taylor bit off an expletive. "Marian's going to kill me."

"Tell her you had something come up."

Taylor shot a glance at him to see if he was kidding. He looked dead serious. A laugh bubbled up. "I suppose something did come up, in a big way."

"Why, thank you. I think something may come up again tonight. You seem to have that effect on me."

"I suppose I need to take care of all these pressing emergencies."

"Pressing is a good word."

"Maybe I'll have to stop by your place and calm things down before I go home."

Stone grinned. "I hoped you'd see things my way."

A light tap sounded on her bedroom door. Taylor groaned, then her eyes popped open and she stared at the red numbers on the clock next to her bed. Nine o'clock. Damn.

"Taylor?" Tiffany called.

"Come on in." Thank goodness she didn't have to go to work

this morning. She felt like that big dog of Stone's had chewed her up and spit her out.

Tiffany entered looking wide awake and cheerful. "You look like you tied one on, girl. I heard you coming in around five this morning. I was worried about you. I called Marian last night and she said she heard you went out to lunch with Stone. Stone's office said he'd called and said he'd be unavailable. We put two and two together. Did you have a good time?"

Taylor's face burned. "I can't believe I didn't call anyone to tell them I wouldn't be in. I'm sorry, Tiff."

"That's all right. I'm flattered you made it home to see me off. So how was Stone?" Tiffany asked, a little too casually.

"Somewhere in the region of darned near perfect. I feel like I died and went to heaven."

"Did it get him out of your system like you hoped?"

Taylor shook her head. "He's unbelievable. I'm addicted. A regular slut puppy."

"I thought so. That idea you had about loving and leaving him was pretty warped, I thought."

"You didn't say so."

"I could see that Stone wasn't the type of man you could simply walk away from, even assuming he'd let you. But you wouldn't have believed me."

"I'm a little stubborn, I guess."

"More like incredibly pigheaded."

"Pigheaded!" Taylor started to giggle, then subsided, looking sober. "I'm going to miss you so much, Tiff. Nobody tells me about myself better than you do, even Kara."

Tiffany hugged her. "You and Kara are like two more daughters I've adopted. It doesn't matter where we live. We're always going to be connected."

Taylor hugged her back fiercely. "It's not going to be as if you're going too far away. You're staying with my dad. He's had housekeepers and all, but that place sorely needs a woman's touch."

"Don't get your hopes up. I'm not going to your father's to 'touch' anything. I'll just be a temporary houseguest. Anyway, from what I hear, he's a confirmed bachelor."

"Yeah. But I never imagined he'd ask any woman shy of seventy-five to be a houseguest." Taylor stood. "I better get showered and dressed to get you to the airport by noon."

"Yes," Tiffany got up to leave, then turned by the door. "I'm glad you're giving Stone a chance. Let things unfold. He's a good man."

"Too good, it feels like he's going to swallow me up."

"In a relationship, you do lose some autonomy, but in a good relationship you grow. Giving yourself to the right man increases rather than diminishes you, because he gives himself to you also."

Taylor bit her lip, knowing that Tiffany was speaking the truth, but a small corner of herself still resisted being drawn into Stone's web. Not that it mattered, it was already too late. Her heart was entangled by his, thoroughly caught in his snare. "Thanks, Tiff," she said softly.

TWENTY-SIX

Taylor hurried into Helping Hands to apologize to Marian for her defection yesterday, but Marian's office was dark, her door closed.

"Taylor," Carol called, sticking her head out of her office.

"Marian said she wasn't coming in. I've got a message for you." She proffered a piece of paper. "This man really wants you to call him back."

A warm glow enveloped Taylor when she saw Stone's name.

"Thanks, Carol."

"Good thing you cleared out of here yesterday before all the drama."

"Drama?"

"People were pretty upset because of the layoffs."

"I feel terrible we lost our grant."

"I bet that's not the first one we lose if the police don't find the killer. I've been working all morning to relocate the residents still in the shelter. I checked seven counties. Every shelter is full, and even the mission is overflowing."

"What are you going to do?"

"Pray."

Taylor made her way back to her office, a germ of an idea forming. She dialed Stone's cellular phone number.

"Hello." The sound of his voice made her feel like a teenager with a crush. "I got your message."

"Hi. Thanks for getting back with me so soon. Do you want me to pick you up tonight? See, I'm already taking it for granted we're going to spend all our free time together. I hope you don't mind."

"I'd like to see you tonight, but sometimes I do have other plans."

"Ummm, I see that I'm going to have to work hard to earn that number one spot in your affections. I've been trying to locate Quanita Nelson. She's left the mission. I wondered if you had any leads."

"She's gone to stay with a friend of hers from the shelter, Joan Spencer."

"Wasn't her husband just killed?"

"Yes. She was able to move back home with her kids. She has a large house in Marietta, and Quanita was a good friend of hers."

"Interesting."

"Can I ask you why you wanted to know?"

"Kay is the lead suspect for the shelter murders because of Milton's testimony. I wanted to talk to Quanita about a few things relating to her ex-boyfriend."

"I thought you were off the case."

"Officially I am, but that doesn't mean I'm not still interested."

Taylor didn't know whether to feel relieved or nervous about that. Stone brought a reassuring presence to something that disturbed her greatly, but the killer was dangerous. She had the sense if Stone got deeper into the case, darkness would touch him.

"You want to go with me to talk to her?" he asked.

"It would be nice to see how Quanita and Joan are doing."

"Can you leave now?"

She looked at her schedule. No appointments. And this would be a good time to talk to Stone about the idea she had. "Sure."

* * *

Eva sipped a mug of coffee while Ben cooked dinner for them. When she got home, the house was spotlessly clean, and he'd greeted her with a kiss, and a cup of her favorite decaf. He was really trying to make their relationship work, she had to say that for him.

He'd actually cried when she'd told him she was pregnant, and vowed to be a better husband and a good father. She sipped her coffee, a warm glow filling her. Things had turned out so much better than she'd ever expected.

Their fight and the subsequent violence that erupted apparently caused Ben to examine himself and their relationship. He must have not liked what he saw, because he was making a real effort to change.

She was more in love with him than she'd ever been. She hated to admit it, but Ben's one-time loss of control and her flight that resulted was the best thing that ever happened to their marriage.

She sniffed the air. Something was burning. "Ben?" she called.

No answer. She sat her cup on the coffee table. "Ben?" Silence. Eva hurried into the kitchen. "Ben, where are you?" A saucepan of vegetables was burning on the stove, a curl of smoke rising. She turned off the burner.

"Ben?" she called, the first note of fear in her voice. She started to slip a little on the unexpected wetness under her feet. A dark liquid splattered the floor. Then she saw Ben lying face-down on the floor near the sink. Oh, God, his back. So much blood. She cradled his head, and felt the cold, clammy feel of death under her fingers. Then the scream rose up from the very depths of her being, and it seemed she'd never be able to stop.

Taylor couldn't help a spontaneous grin breaking out on her face when Stone pulled up in his old Chevy. She slid in next to him, and gave a little squeal of surprise when he pulled her to him. He nuzzled her neck. "You smell good," he murmured. Then he kissed her lips tenderly and thoroughly, drawing the very breath from her.

She felt as boneless as a rag doll when he finally drew away, and pulled into traffic. "I forgot what I was going to say."

He looked over at her. "I never worry about anything I forget. I figure if it was important, I would have remembered."

Taylor stared out of the window frowning, searching her memory. "Oh, I wanted to tell you I had a great idea. The shelter's closing—"

"That's major news. Sad, too. There are not enough shelter spaces as it is in the city."

"We lost a key grant. I'm hoping Marian will search around for other funding sources, but she's considering leasing the shelter until the murderer is caught."

"I apologize for cutting you off. It surprised me when you said the shelter was closing."

"That's all right. Anyway, we have two women and three children left at the shelter. Carol said she's having a terrible time finding a place for them to go. I thought I could let them stay with me."

Stone glanced at her. "Do you really think that's a good idea? Five people in your apartment is a lot of folks."

"I have the space. Tiffany's bedroom and her office makes two bedrooms free. Teensy's kids are little. I can put the oldest in the little alcove off the back entrance."

"There's a killer out there who is specifically targeting the men in these women's lives. I don't think it's a good idea."

"So you think one of these women is the killer?"

"Not necessarily. It could be any of the shelter residents."

"Why does it have to be one of the residents, the victims? Why couldn't it be somebody connected with them, or God forbid, somebody who works at the agency? This society always blames the victim first and foremost. Well, I don't buy it."

Stone shrugged. "I was simply stating a possibility. What about your money troubles? How are you going to pay the extra rent now that Tiffany's left, and feed five extra people also?"

"What do you know about my money troubles?" Taylor snapped.

"You were concerned about your car for one, and I see you still haven't replaced it. I also think—"

"I'd rather you keep your mind off the state of my finances, if you please."

"Fine. But I don't think letting the shelter residents stay with you is a good idea."

"Then it's a good thing it's not your decision."

They drove the rest of the way to Joan's house in silence. Taylor looked surreptitiously at Stone. Obviously deep in thought, a preoccupied look on his face, he tapped the steering wheel with a finger as he drove. It was nice he was concerned about her, but he really had no business commenting on her finances. Her stomach clenched a little. Even though he was right. But she'd find a way. She always did.

TWENTY-SEVEN

"Nice place," Stone murmured as they pulled into the driveway of Joan's house.

Taylor had barely gotten out of the car when Joan exploded out of the front door. She caught Taylor in an enthusiastic embrace. "I'm so happy to see you again. Everything's going really well for me."

Quanita followed Joan, more slowly, her daughter trailing. "Hey, Taylor. I hope it's all good with you."

Taylor nodded pleasantly.

"Come on in," Joan said, giving Stone a curious glance. He'd stood by the car observing their greetings.

"Joan, Quanita, this is Stone Emerson. He's investigating the shelter murder case."

"I'm not talking to no police," Quanita said flatly.

"I'm not with the APD. I'm a private investigator interested in the case."

"Who hired you?" Quanita demanded.

"Nobody, really. I'm dating Taylor, though."

Joan and Quanita swung curious glances at Taylor. She shrugged. Quanita eyed Stone, then gave a short laugh. "Taylor could have done worse. Let's go on in."

They entered a comfortable living area with soaring cathedral ceilings and a contemporary look. "Shamita, go play in your

room, I'll be up in a few minutes." Quanita's daughter obedi-
ently left the room.

"Is there anything I could get you to drink?" Joan asked.

"I'd like a Coke if you have it," Stone said.

"Taylor?"

She hesitated. "Herbal tea would be nice."

Joan hurried out of the room. Quanita leaned back on the
couch and looked at Stone through narrowed eyes. "What do
you want to know?"

"Do you realize Milton's in jail?" Stone asked.

"It doesn't surprise me. That's where he needs to be."

"And he beat Kay so badly, she's in intensive care at Grady."

Quanita sat up straighter. "He wanted me to go with him
back to the house. He said he had something to tell me. Then
he said he wanted to make up. I told him to kiss my behind.
That was just a couple of days ago."

"He beat Kay a couple days ago."

"That skank hates me. She, he, whatever it is, kept asking
me about Milton when we stayed at the shelter. She'd gone
through my things and found his picture. That was one reason
I beat her butt. I didn't know they knew each other, but I'm
not surprised."

"Why do you say that?" Stone asked.

"Milton was sniffing around the mission after I moved there.
Kay told me she had seen him, but I just said for her to keep
out of my face."

"Milton beat Kay up at your apartment."

"Oh, yeah? Well, I guess if he took Kay there it was because
he wanted some. Yeah, he'd whip her butt for sure when he
got down to the stuff and found out it was like his." Quanita
started to laugh.

"Have you ever noticed anything that would make you suspect that Milton or Kay might be doing away with the shelter
women's abusers?"

"Milton didn't have the balls to kill nobody close up like that. He'd blow someone away with a gun though. Joan's husband was set on fire, another one beat to death, and stuff like that. Nah, Milton didn't do it. But Kay—that thing is crazy. I wouldn't put anything past her."

"Joan's husband's death made a big difference. Didn't it?" Stone said quietly.

Joan came into the room with drinks on a tray. "I got Cokes for both of us, too, Quan." She turned to Stone. "His death was the best thing that ever happened to me. I got my kids back, I got money now. All my worries are gone."

Stone picked up his Coke and took a sip. "Pretty good thing for you, too," he said to Quanita, looking around the room. "Pretty nice setup you have here."

Quanita stood up. "I don't think I like where you're going with this."

"And where is that, Quanita?"

"That Joan or I had something to do with her husband's death. In fact, I don't like it at all. I apologize, Taylor, but I'm going to tell your man to get out of this house."

"I'm afraid I'm going to have to agree," Joan said. "The police put us through quite a bit, and there's no reason to rehash it. Taylor, you're welcome any time, and I hope you come back to visit us soon."

Taylor sighed and stood up. There was no point in continuing this. She understood how it might look to Stone, but she knew Quanita. She'd bet money that the girl wasn't capable of such sneaky, bloody murders. Not to mention black magic.

"Stone, let's go." He gave one long, last look at Quanita before he followed her out the door.

Stone dropped her back at work. She'd wanted to know what was his point, what made him think Quanita was the killer? He was uncharacteristically tight-lipped. Marian still wasn't in.

She walked to Carol's office and tapped on the door. "Come in," Carol called.

She was on the phone and motioned Taylor to sit by her desk. Carol laid the phone down with a heavy sigh. "No luck. There's no shelter beds available anywhere. Oh, Marian is not coming in."

Taylor nodded. "I wanted to talk to you about the shelter residents. My roommate moved out, and I have a big empty apartment."

Carol's eyes widened. "Are you kidding? You'd take Teensy and her kids and Mai Lin in? That would be fantastic."

Taylor laughed. "You make it sound as if it's my good turn for this lifetime."

"But it is! I really didn't know what I was going to do."

"Let's go over together and tell them. Maybe they can come over later and help me get things organized for their stay."

"Okay, give me a few minutes," Carol said.

Taylor went to the office to check her messages. She strongly suspected that Marian had some job interviews lined up already. She remembered what Stone had said about letting the shelter resident stay with her. He was being overprotective, and it got her back up. It reminded her unpleasantly of her father and her brothers. Nobody had the right to tell her what to do.

The phone rang, and she snatched it off its cradle.

"It's Stone. I wanted to tell you that Eva's husband has been killed. They questioned her as a suspect until her parents showed up with a high-powered lawyer." Stone paused a moment. "Eva's husband was stabbed in the back, multiple times."

TWENTY-EIGHT

Taylor looked up from her book, a murder mystery, at the soft tap on her door. "Come on in," she called.

Mai Lin stepped in the room. "I don't want to bother you," she said, looking at her feet and wringing her hands.

Taylor swung her feet over the bed and sat up. "No bother, what's going on?"

"I wanted to thank you from the bottom of my heart for opening your home to me. I had no place to go. My husband—I think he's got another woman."

"I wouldn't want you to go back with him anyway." She knew Carol was working to get benefits and job training for Mai Lin. She was also on a waiting list for public housing. It wasn't ideal, but at least it would be her own.

"No. Well, I want to thank you very much."

"No problem. Actually you and Teensy are helping me out, too. My roommate just moved out, and frankly I was dreading the thought of an empty apartment."

Mai Lin smiled a little. "Anything, I will do for you. One moment."

She disappeared out of the door and reappeared with a laundry basket full of clothes. Taylor peered in. Her clothes had been washed and folded neater than she'd ever managed to get them. "Mai, you don't have to do my laundry. I'm serious."

"But I want to do it. It makes me feel good."

Taylor was at a loss for words. "Thank you," she finally said.

Mai Lin broke out in a wide smile. "You're so welcome," she said with a dip of her head as she backed out the door.

Taylor closed the book with an exhalation of satisfaction. That had been one good story, it had kept her attention to the very end. The aroma of food reached her nostrils, and she realized that she was hungry.

Two of Teensy's children were sitting around the dining room table doing their homework, and a third was setting the table with plates and silverware. Teensy was in the kitchen, standing over the stove. Taylor saw the ground beef frying in the pan with dismay, the smell making her stomach roil a little. "Teensy, I don't know if I told you, but I'm a vegetarian."

"I know," Teensy said cheerfully. "I made you a veggie burger with this soybean mix I found." She gestured to a delicious looking patty on a plate. "I was going to ask if you wanted cheese?"

"No thanks." This arrangement was working out pretty well, she thought.

They settled down to dinner, which was casual but good, hamburgers, french fries, and salad. Afterward, Teensy checked her kids' homework, then they settled in front of the TV. Mai Lin worked on her needlework, and Taylor started to get out her deck of Tarot cards when the doorbell rang.

She pulled open the door and Stone stood in the doorway looking thoroughly pissed off. "I called your office and Carol told me you were home with the shelter residents. I thought we agreed that this wasn't a good idea."

Taylor looked toward the living room. "Lower your voice," she hissed. "Excuse me? I didn't agree with a thing," she whispered.

"Let's go. I want to talk to you. Privately," Stone said.

Taylor turned and saw Mai Lin regarding them solemnly. "I don't think I want to go anywhere tonight."

"Taylor, let's go," Stone repeated, a note of command in his voice.

"Are you okay, Taylor?" Mai Lin asked in a quavering voice.

"I'm all right. I'm going to leave. You have my beeper number if you need me." She stalked to her room and grabbed her purse. The only reason she was leaving with him was to avoid a scene that he'd probably be only too willing to make in front of these traumatized women.

"Bye everybody," she called as she walked past Stone out the door.

"You take care," Teensy said meaningfully.

"How could you embarrass me in front of those women?" Taylor said as soon as the door closed behind them.

"Embarrassing you was not my intention. I'm concerned. A serial killer is connected with these women somehow, and you invite them into your home. It makes no sense, Taylor."

"It makes perfect sense to me. These women were about to be homeless because of this killer, and I have plenty of space." They'd reached Stone's car, and Taylor slid in. Stone started the motor, shaking his head.

"I have a brainstorm," Taylor said. "Why don't you keep your opinion to yourself about my affairs, which includes my living situation, and I'll do the same for you."

"Why are you throwing up a wall, and trying to be so hard? You know I care about you."

She looked away, her face crumpling. "I'm always such a bitch with you, and you're always putting up with me. I'm sorry, Stone. I have problems with men telling me what to do about my life."

"I know. But I can't change who I am. I'm going to have opinions, especially about people who mean something to me, and I'm going to express them. I'm not a control freak, I'll always listen to you, but sometimes I'm going to have to have my way, too."

Taylor shook her head, not believing her ears. He was doing so good until he added on that last part. "Excuse me?"

"I'm a man, Taylor, and I'm not going to kowtow to your wishes all the time. Sometimes what I say will be what goes."

"What you say?"

"Exactly."

"Take me home."

"What?"

"Turn this car around and take me home right now."

Stone's lips tightened, but he turned a corner and headed back in the opposite direction. "It's best that you take time to cool down. So much is happening, and it's affecting your judgment."

"My judgment! You're the one who's talking like you've gone *stone* crazy. What you say goes. What kind of crap is that?"

"I'm worried about you."

"Then protect me. But I don't need any more masculine ego trips. I grew up with them."

He pulled up in front of her apartment building. "What if we go half and half?"

"What?"

"Half and half. Half the time what you say goes, and the other half it's what I say."

Taylor studied her fingernails, taken aback at his offer, this reasonable compromise. "Which half when?"

Stone laughed and drew her to him. "Life with you is never going to be boring." Then he kissed her, his lips soft and tender. Taylor exhaled against his mouth, melting against him as he deepened the kiss and his lips grew firmer. When they drew apart, they were both breathing hard.

Taylor looked deep in his eyes, wondering what she'd done

to deserve this kind, gentle man wanting her. She thought about love and swallowed hard. It was too soon for love. He made it clear he wanted her in his bed. He wanted to spend time with her, but love was another level entirely. He'd never mentioned love.

"No, being with you is never going to be boring," Taylor murmured.

TWENTY-NINE

"Taylor, phone," Teensy called. Taylor rolled over to the phone, and looked blearily at the clock at her bed. Seven thirty in the morning, who could it be?

"Taylor, it's Marian. I just got a call. Could you come in early this morning? We've got a situation developing at the agency."

Taylor assured her she'd hurry in to work, and stumbled to the shower with a groan. She really wasn't a morning person. When she got out, a steaming cup of coffee was waiting for her on the dresser. Mai Lin probably put it there. She was getting quite spoiled by all this pampering, she thought as she took a sip of the delicious coffee.

Taylor dressed in record time and grabbed a bagel on the way out of the door. When she arrived at the office, she stared at all the men in black standing around. She headed for Marian's office. She was deep in conversation with that older detective on the case, what was his name? Charles.

"What's going on?" Taylor asked.

Marian's mouth looked pinched, and dark circles haunted her eyes. "The FBI is on the case, and the police have a search warrant for the shelter house."

Taylor nodded, she was expecting this.

"They're going to search the offices also." Taylor's eyebrows shot up. This is something she wasn't expecting.

"They said none of us could be present. In case someone tampered with evidence, or something like that."

"They're afraid that someone would run and hide the bloody knives," Taylor quipped.

"God. I pray they don't find anything. If they do, you realize that it's over. Period. We'll have to close completely. I've called everybody and told them to take the day off. I wanted you to be here with me, in case something came up and we needed your legal expertise."

Taylor didn't have much expertise in FBI or police investigations of serial killings, but she nodded again.

"They've already started. How about we go to breakfast?"

"Sounds like a good idea. I could sure use another cup of coffee."

The police searched them before they left the building.

When they arrived at the small French restaurant, for the first time Taylor saw Marian look her age. She reached out and touched her hand as they looked at their menus. "It'll be all right. It has to be."

Marian sighed deeply. "I don't know what to think. Five men dead, our shelter house closed down, grants lost. Now the search. They really must believe someone who works in the agency is a suspect."

"Or someone who lived in the shelter."

A perky waitress came by and asked for their orders. "I only want coffee," Marian said, handing her the menu.

"The same," Taylor added, her appetite gone.

"There's no point in going back really. They said the search will go on all day, and they don't want us present. I have a feeling that this is it. It's really all over."

Taylor had the same feeling, but she didn't want to say so.

"Thanks for getting here so quickly this morning. I needed your moral support."

"Maybe we can hang out together," Taylor said. She didn't want Marian to be alone.

"Thanks, but I think I'll go out and visit my daughter and grandbaby. I've been so busy with work lately, I haven't seen my little darling as much as I'd like."

Marian waved goodbye as she climbed into her car after they'd left the restaurant, and it was Taylor who felt at loose ends. She sat in the car, thinking about going home, but ruling it out. Teensy would be at work, but she didn't feel like explaining to Mai Lin why she was back home so soon.

And always, as always, she thought of Stone. She'd wanted to feel his hands on her body last night. Making love with him had done nothing to relieve her craving for him, only intensified it.

He was interested in her sexually now, but how long would that last? Her relationships never lasted. The rule was to hit it and quit it. She followed her motto and never cared too much that her lover's motto might be the same. Then again, she'd never wanted to belong to anyone before. She had to face the fact she wanted to belong to Stone.

The thought started a tingling at the back of her neck. She started to turn the ignition, but something made her stop and listen intently. The tingling deepened.

Whispers echoed within the car, hushed voices sounding as if they were far away. The hairs rose at the back of her neck. A black, smoky haze began to form, and the whispers intensified.

Feet don't fail me now, she thought, as she quickly stepped out of the car into the bright morning sunshine. She never would have made a horror movie heroine, sticking around for whatever freaky thing was going to happen next. She took off at a brisk pace down the city street. She'd have that car towed and sell it in a hot second if that whispering foggy stuff didn't quit.

"Taylor," a husky female voice behind her whispered. She

wheeled around, but there was no one there. A low chuckle. "You can run, but you can't hide."

She'd be damned if she was going to walk around hearing voices. She'd go to a psychiatrist and get on major tranquilizers before she'd put up with this.

"That wouldn't help, because you're not crazy."

"Who is this?" Taylor stopped in the middle of the street and demanded. Two women in business suits stared at her and scurried away.

A giggle. "Righteous judgment and justice. Women's liberation. Magic . . . powerful magic, of course."

The words were coming from behind her, on her left. She whirled, and no one was there. Taylor sank onto a park bench and buried her face in her hands. What do you want from me, she thought.

"I can't hear your thoughts."

"What do you want from me?" she whispered into her hands, trying not to cry.

"Understanding, that's all, just a little understanding."

Then the tingling was gone, cut off like a switch. The atmosphere cleared and the presence was no longer there.

Taylor shuddered in reaction, breathing in ragged gasps. What had happened was far beyond her experience. Someone talked to her and heard her from afar. Were they sending their presence, their astral body? She needed answers, and she needed them now. She also needed to throw up. Taylor stumbled into a nearby office building in search of a bathroom.

Thankful the restroom was empty, she rinsed out her mouth when she was done. She walked into the office suite adjacent to the bathrooms. "May I see your phone book?" she asked politely. "The yellow pages."

After the receptionist handed her the heavy volume, she sat in one of the chairs in the waiting area. She pulled out her small calendar book and started copying addresses. The yellow

pages were as good a place to start as any when you were desperate for answers.

Taylor pulled up to a little shotgun-shack-looking house near
Atlanta University. An old weathered sign was stuck in the front
yard, an open hand and a crescent moon painted on it. FIND
OUT YOUR FUTURE HERE, the sign read.

Taylor knocked on the door. An African-American woman
who looked like she'd reached her forties opened the door. She
was heavy and wore a faded housedress and open-toed house
shoes. Her head was wrapped with a scarf.

"Can I help you?" the woman asked. Kids screamed and
played and from within, Taylor heard the blare of a TV.

"I got your address from the yellow pages. Are you a psychic?"

The woman visibly relaxed. "Yes, I'm the psychic. You want
a reading? Come in." She swiveled her head. "Turn off that
TV and go outside and play," she suddenly yelled at the children, causing Taylor to jump, startled.

The two children wailed in protest, but she quelled them with
a look. "My grandchildren," she said to Taylor. "Sit down."

Taylor sat on the edge of the stained beige sofa. The house
was hot, and a stale, rank smell hung in the room. The whir
of the square window fan did little to stir the air.

"My fee is thirty dollars up front for half an hour."

"Will you take a check?" Taylor asked.

The woman just looked at her. Taylor dug through her wallet.
"I only have twenty-two dollars in cash," she said, holding it
in her hand.

She snatched the money and folded it in the pocket of her
housedress. "That'll do."

"I don't really want a reading," Taylor said. "I want to ask
you some questions."

The woman squinted at her, looking guarded.

"I'm doing research."

"It's your money," she said, shrugging.

"When did you first know you had the gift? Did you have dreams, see visions, or hear voices?"

The woman laughed, then sobered, darting a nervous glance at her. "I first knew I was psychic when . . . when I knew what was going to happen to people."

"When was that? And how? How does the information come to you?"

The woman shrugged. "It comes when I get my thirty dollars." The children had started squabbling noisily from the backyard. She looked toward the back door, frowning. "Are you done?"

Taylor bit her lip. "Yes, I guess I'm done."

"I hope you don't mind letting yourself out," she said, striding to the back door. "I'm going to put a hurting on those kids."

Taylor walked slowly to her car, her heart heavy. This was going to be harder than she'd thought.

THIRTY

The sun had sunk in the sky and the day had deepened to blue when Taylor pulled up to Stone's apartment, exhausted. She'd run all over town, trying to get some information from the people who'd styled themselves as psychics. It had been an expensive undertaking, and she hadn't found one psychic she believed was authentic. The whole psychic thing was nothing but a scam.

She'd never really thought about the fortune telling industry before. Taylor knew that while she was truly psychic, she couldn't tell anyone's future on demand. It didn't work like that. The gift was like an occasional glimpse through a blowing curtain. The curtain constantly shifted, and never lifted predictably. You hardly ever saw what you needed when you wanted it. The gift was as capricious as the wind, and as easily captured.

Was she the only true psychic in the area? Surely not. The gift was rare, but not that rare. Taylor knew that with study and application, the wind could blow harder, and the glimpses could become more frequent for anyone.

She wanted to find someone who could help her protect herself and explain what was going on. For the first time in her life, Taylor prayed for someone to help her with her gift.

Her eyes flew open when she heard a tap on the glass. Stone stood on the sidewalk outside her passenger door watching her quizzically. She got out of the car and walked around to join him.

"I saw your car in front of the house. I waited and you didn't get out. I wondered what was going on."

"I was thinking. It's been an eventful day."

Stone reached out and rubbed the back of her neck. "Let's go in and relax. You can tell me all about it."

Ernie started to lunge at her when they walked into Stone's apartment, but settled down with a sharp word from his master.

"Are you hungry?" Stone asked.

"Starving."

He went into the kitchen. "Uh, what sort of frozen dinner would you like?"

Taylor smiled to herself. The man certainly wasn't domestic. His living room was decorated with laundry baskets and heaps of clothing. "Doesn't matter as long as it's vegetarian."

"Macaroni and cheese?"

She usually didn't eat dairy products, but what the hell. "That's fine."

She heard the beep of the microwave, and Stone reentered the room. "It'll be a few minutes." He looked uneasily at the clothes scattered all over. "Sorry about the mess, I just did my laundry."

She slipped off her sandals and stretched out on the sofa. He sat down beside her and laid her feet in his lap. He started rubbing them with firm, deep strokes, and it felt so good that Taylor couldn't hold back a groan. "And I'm just getting started," Stone said with a grin. "Tell me about your day."

Taylor groaned again, only this time not with pleasure. "I've been running all over town trying to interview so-called psychics."

"Why?"

"The agency is being searched by the FBI."

Stone raised an eyebrow. "What does that have to do with psychics?"

"Nothing, except I didn't have to work today. I had a very strange experience this morning. The killer has some sort of powers, and she's interested in me. She's been sending."

"Sending what?"

"Sounds, sights, sensations."

Stone's hands stopped their caressing for a moment, then continued. "So, you want to talk to another psychic and get advice on this phenomenon," he said.

"Exactly. But I can't find any real ones."

"Relax. When the student is ready, the teacher will come." Taylor cut a sharp glance at him. How could he possibly know what was on her mind?

With a quick, smooth movement, Stone covered her body with his own. "Taylor, you need to take things easy and let them unfold. If you've been doing right, everything will work out." Then he covered her lips with his own, and all thought fled from her mind.

"Don't forget to water my plants, okay," Taylor told Teensy. "The sprayer is on the top shelf in the living room."

Stone propped himself on an elbow in the bed and watched her replace the receiver in its cradle. "How are your new roommates doing?"

"They're fine. When I'm home, they spoil me outrageously, cooking for me, cleaning, doing my laundry." It was Saturday night, and she'd spent the last twenty-four hours in Stone's arms and bed. She ignored the mess, happily ate the vegetables out of numerous frozen dinners, put on an old T-shirt of his to ward off the air-conditioned chill the brief times she was out of bed, used a new toothbrush Stone happened to have on hand, and she was in utter bliss.

"I hope I'm spoiling you, too."

"Outrageously," she said, moving over him, her breasts brushing his lightly furred chest. "Now it's your turn."

She kissed his lips lightly, trailing kisses down his neck, kneading her hands over his shoulders. She licked his nipples, then blew, watching them harden. She tasted his flat abdomen working her way south, curling her tongue in his belly button. He shivered and she smiled, loving the way he lay acquiescent under her fingers, his flesh firm and responsive. Finally, she focused on the object of her desire.

Stone drew in his breath sharply as her mouth caressed him. His fingers curled in her locks. The moment before his release she lifted her head, eluding his grasp as he reached for her. She slid up his body and impaled herself on him. She moved deliberately and slowly, fully in control, sensuously savoring the fullness of him. He grasped her hips and tried to quicken the pace. She resisted.

"Taylor, yes, now," he whispered, rolling her over, not withdrawing himself from within her, driving hard, smooth strokes into her. Forceful and fluid, raising the heat within her, and with a sound like a sob, she surrendered completely to his rhythm. He never broke stroke, never caused her to lose his beat, and her quivering tremors rose to a quaking crescendo. At the perfect moment, just when she came back to herself, he stiffened and deep within her she felt his warm explosion.

He relaxed over her, burying his face in her neck; they subsided together. Holding each other and settling into a mellow afterglow. Lord, the man was good. Every time she tried to take control, he took it back, and played her like she was an instrument and he was a virtuoso. And damned if she, Taylor Cates, didn't love every movement of his symphony.

THIRTY-ONE

"Get your behinds up out of bed!" The guard noisily ran his baton over the metal bars of the jail cell. What did they think this was, a resort? The man on the top bunk sat up and slowly climbed down. The guard slid one of the breakfast trays through the slot between the floor and the door. The man ignored it and urinated in the open latrine.

The man on the bottom bunk still lay there, unmoving. "I said get your ass up!" The guard angrily beat the cell bars with the baton. The man didn't move. "You don't want to make me come in there, nigga."

The other inmate picked up his tray, retreated to the corner, and started eating. "All right, you gonna regret this," the guard said to the unmoving man on the bed. "Come on down here, Jimmy," he called down the hall. "We got a problem here."

He opened the cell, and approached the bottom bunk, baton at ready. The man was motionless as a statue, his face turned to the wall. The guard poked him with the baton. The man's flesh rippled like a slab of beef.

He bent to examine the man closer. "Shit," the guard muttered, putting the baton away. He rolled the inmate over, and the man's head came apart, half of the head continuing to face the wall.

The guard jumped back with a squeal, and the other inmate

looked up. "Well, I'll be gawdd__," the guard said again. This meant he'd have to spend the whole damn day doing paperwork.

Sunday afternoon, about an hour before the funeral for Eva's husband, Taylor stood in front of her closet trying to decide what to put on. Stone waited in the living room. He'd offered to drive everyone to the funeral, and Taylor had shoveled out his car for the occasion.

She laid her hand on a short, cool, black rayon dress then withdrew it, too slinky for a funeral. She sighed and pulled out a black shantung silk suit. The suit was hotter than she wanted to wear during the outdoor graveside ceremony with the temperature in the high nineties, but it would have to do.

She slipped on a cream silk blouse and put gold earrings in her ears. Everybody would be there, Eva had said. Everybody from the original eight women who were in the shelter when their men started dying. Except Wendy. Wendy was still in the hospital, recovering from her beating and subsequent surgery.

Taylor zipped up the back of the skirt and drew the jacket on. She paused to examine herself one last time in the mirror before she went to join Stone.

"You look good," he said, taking his eyes off ESPN and the TV to admire her. Teensy's children were sitting lined up on the couch, all shined and polished. Mai Lin sat in a chair, wearing a long black skirt and Peter Pan white blouse.

"Mama said she'd be out in a minute," Teensy's oldest daughter volunteered.

"All right. Has everybody gone to the bathroom? We're going to be outside," Taylor said.

All the children nodded, but Stone sheepishly got up. "Thanks for reminding me."

Teensy swept in, looking good in a simple navy blue dress. "Is everybody ready?" she asked.

"As soon as Stone gets out of the bathroom, we're ready to roll," Taylor said.

Even with the heat, a lot of people turned out to mourn Ben and support Eva. The ex-shelter residents gravitated together. Taylor greeted Denise, genuinely happy to see her. She looked much less tense than the last time Taylor talked to her. Bea waved to her, a woman who was obviously her daughter beside her. Joan and Quanita sat together. They'd spoken to Taylor, but pointedly ignored Stone.

Amber entered, her baby in tow, with a faded-looking woman, her mother probably. Teensy was settling her kids down, and Mai Lin was sitting a little off to herself, her hands serenely folded in her lap. Eva sat in the front, her face a mask of grief, flanked by her family.

Of the original eight women who were in the shelter when the murders started, seven were present with five of their abusers dead, and those women's lives were profoundly changed . . . Taylor felt the now familiar tingling at the back of her neck, and drew her breath in, held it.

"Their lives changed for the better."

Taylor sucked in her breath and looked around wildly. She'd heard the husky voice of the woman.

"What's wrong?" Stone asked.

"I'll tell you later."

The pallbearers walked with the casket from the hearse. The mourners stood quietly and respectfully as the body made its way toward its final resting place. A woman's beautiful voice rose to sing a haunting song a cappella.

A low chuckle. "Normally, I couldn't hang out here, but my master shows me how to do new things every day."

Her master? A thrill of alarm went through Taylor. "What do you want from me?" Taylor whispered, as low as possible.

Stone looked over at her quizzically. "What did you say?" he whispered back. Taylor shook her head, frustrated.

"We should understand each other. We're the same sort."

"I'm nothing like you," Taylor whispered furiously in retort. Stone was staring at her, frowning, and Taylor felt her cheeks heat.

"You are me, only with a different view. Five gone, the rest to go." Taylor felt the mental contact broken like a light switch flicked off. She leaned forward in the metal folding chair and touched her temple.

"Taylor, tell me what's the matter. Do you need to leave?"

"She was talking to me. God, Stone, I know she's here somewhere." Taylor twisted around to scan the faces near her. People were giving them irritated glances. She turned back and tried to focus on the service. A priest was speaking. All her senses were heightened, including her gift. Magic hung and shimmered in the air around the gathering. Silver in color, almost transparent, diffuse, but concentrated around the priest.

His aura was tinged with the color of a mystic. A slight purple glow emanated from him. The priest was a truly holy man, one of few that Taylor had ever seen. There was no way that color could emanate from a killer. She looked around surreptitiously to see if she could see any other concentrations of power, or any of the black or red of chaos, death and violence. Nothing.

Taylor felt the woman's going and coming with clear definition. Her lips tightened. She felt invaded. It was a sense akin to rape. The woman had taken the liberty of the ultimate intimacy, she'd violated her mind. There had to be a way to block her.

The woman spoke of her master. She shivered, not even wanting to go there. Somebody was training her, raising her power quickly, exponentially. Or something was. Taylor had a feeling no human agency was capable of such a feat.

The coffin was lowered into the earth. Eva threw the first clod of dirt. Then a prayer was said. The silver shimmer increased, then faded as Taylor's acute awareness faded.

"The funeral was an ordeal for you," Stone said, after the service was over.

"You have no idea."

THIRTY-TWO

After giving condolences to Eva, the ex-shelter residents drifted into a protective knot. Nobody had much to say, but they were loathe to leave each other's presence. Expectant stillness hung over them, like something was going to happen that nobody was sure was going to be good.

"I have an idea, everybody," Taylor said. "Let's go to my place. We'll have pizza, my treat. It'll be a reunion." She couldn't really afford it, but these women obviously all needed to talk about what was happening.

A murmur of assent immediately rose. When Stone pulled out of the cemetery, Taylor used her cellular phone to call for the pizza delivery. She stared out of the window, lost in thought. What could she do? The threatening black cloud was building, containing its fury inside its billowing mass. Despite all the deaths, the feeling lingered that the storm hadn't yet begun.

"You know what would be perfect right now?" Bea asked, picking up another slice of pizza. "Watermelon."

Joan nodded. "Watermelon would be good."

Stone stood. "Your wish is my pleasure. I'll be back carrying an ice-cold watermelon."

"He's so sweet, Taylor. You're awful lucky," Amber said after Stone left.

Quanita snorted.

"Stone did not start on Quanita's good side," Taylor explained.

"Quanita has a good side?" Teensy asked.

Quanita threw a small pillow on the sofa at her with a smile. "Every side I got looks better than any of yours."

"All right, now," Teensy said without rancor.

"Have you heard from that man of yours?" Denise asked her.

"No I haven't, thank the Lord." Teensy cast a nervous glance at Taylor. "Not that I think he's dead or anything. Or that I want him dead . . ."

"I hope you took out insurance," Bea said.

Teensy looked embarrassed.

"You did take out insurance on his sorry hind end!" Quanita said. Amber burst out laughing, and even Mai Lin smiled.

"Half a million dollars," Teensy said. "I increased the benefits on my family life insurance coverage at my job."

"Damn. I'm going to take out a policy on Milton tomorrow."

"I'm so happy Jerry had good insurance from his job. I'm set," Denise said.

"If you take out insurance and something happens to that man right after, I hope you realize they're coming after you," Joan said.

"If I didn't kill him, they can come all they want. It's worth it," Teensy said. "I'm already planning how I'm going to spend the money. I'm going to get a house . . ."

"I took out insurance on Billy, too," Amber said. She rocked her sleeping baby in his carrier. "His mother made him take the AIDS test. If something happens to his daddy, my baby deserves to have something. I could only afford a hundred thousand though."

Taylor looked around at the women in disbelief. "You all are planning that your men get killed?"

"Honey, they're not planning anything, just being smart. If you were in the shelter with us, you'd be a fool not to take out a policy on your man. Look at the odds. We're over fifty percent," Bea said.

"Maybe you should take out an insurance policy on your new boyfriend," Mai Lin said to Taylor.

After Stone returned with the watermelon, nobody brought up the subject of the murders again. They talked for another hour, catching up on the details of each other's lives. Taylor was impressed with how well the women were doing, especially Bea, Joan, and Denise. They'd all said they felt happier than they'd ever felt in their lives. The unspoken reason: Their husbands were dead.

She lay against Stone's shoulder in front of the TV. Mai Lin bustled around cleaning, and Teensy washed the dishes in the kitchen. They'd both insisted that Taylor not help.

"Tell me what happened at the funeral," Stone asked.

Taylor shifted, not wanting to talk about it and lose her mellow mood. "Later."

He kissed the tip of her nose. "Are you about ready to leave?"

She'd been wondering how the evening was going to end. She'd contemplated going to bed, alone, to get rested for what was sure to be a trying Monday. She'd thought about it for a second or two. Still profoundly unsettled by the experience at the funeral, she didn't want to be alone. Perturbing also was how much she needed to be with Stone. She'd always been so independent, liking sex, but preferring to sleep alone.

Now, suddenly everything had changed. She was used to his warm body next to hers through the night already. Worse, she would miss him terribly when he was gone. *When.* It always came to that. He would eventually leave her like they always eventually did. Thrown off balance and resentful of her growing attraction, she was doing nothing to hold him. She was her natural snippy, smart-ass self, only more so with him. For the first time in her life she worried about what a guy thought of her, and it wasn't a pleasant experience.

"Yes, I'm ready to go. Let me go get some clothes."

They raced to Stone's front door. Stone fumbled with the key, and they fell into the room, tearing at each other's clothes. Ernie watched them quizzically and they didn't even make it to the bedroom, making fast and furious love on a pile of clothes. They laid in a sweaty tangle of clothes and limbs recovering from the intensity of their passion.

"You know I'm going to have to wash these clothes again. I don't like doing laundry."

Taylor turned her head to focus on Stone. "Send them out. They'll come back folded and you just have to stick them into your drawers."

"That's a good idea."

Ernie scooted over to them and breathed on them with doggy meat breath. "You're going to have to do something about that dog watching us. It bugs me."

"But Ernie's only pleasure is vicarious. I still feel guilty for neutering him."

"You're sick, you know that."

Stone chuckled and rolled over. He propped himself up on one elbow and leaned over to kiss her shoulder. "It seems like I should be making some romantic declaration right now."

"That's not our style."

Stone cocked his head, regarding her. "Once I thought it was, but you're right, it's not. I'd rather listen to you griping about my dog's voyeurism than having anyone else extol my manly and masterful sexual skills."

"Are you making fun of me?"

"Of course not."

"Do you want me to extol your manly and masterful sexual skills? I can if you want me to."

"Nah. I know I'm up there in the top percentile."

"Stone?" Taylor hesitated. "I hope I don't get on your nerves too much. My brothers say I'm evil and grouchy."

"Nothing I love more than an evil black woman. Y'all tell it how it is so . . . quaintly. I like that hand-on-the-hip neck roll thing, too." Stone rubbed his hand over his hair and closed his eyes. "That reminds me. I completely forgot. My mother wanted me to bring you over for dinner this evening. My two sisters were going to be there, too. I'll have to call them."

"The evil black woman thing reminds you of your mother and sisters?" Taylor asked, pleased that he'd planned to take her to meet his family, and worried that his folks were so evil he was afraid to give her advance notice before she met them.

"Uh-huh. And I love 'em to death."

Well, when a man loves and respects his mother it is supposed to be a good sign that he'd be good in a relationship. As long as it wasn't freaky, like he lived with her or talked on the phone with her three times a day, Taylor thought.

"Are you her favorite?"

"I don't think she really has favorites. Though my oldest sister and her are like best friends."

"You get along with your sisters coming up?"

"Are you kidding? I'm the oldest child, and the only boy. They drove me crazy."

"Sounds pretty normal. Though since I was the only girl in the house and the youngest, my father would jump any of my brothers who dogged me."

"I figured that you were spoiled rotten."

Taylor frowned at him.

"Don't worry, haven't you read any of those birth order books? As the oldest son from an all-female household, I think we're perfect for each other."

Taylor stared up at the ceiling and Ernie stretched out next to her and yawned. "Are you sure this dog doesn't have fleas?"

"If he did, you'd have 'em, too, by now. Tell me what happened at the funeral."

"It was awful. The woman was whispering to me, invading my privacy in addition to being plain spooky. She said she was getting more powerful, she had a master who helped her."

Stone propped himself up on an elbow again and stared down at her, a look of concern on his face.

"If you tell me I need therapy, I swear I'll kill you," she said.

He laid back down. "No. Now, medication, maybe."

"Arrgh." Taylor got up and hit him on the head with a pillow. Then she stalked to the bathroom and got into the shower. It wasn't a good minute until he'd joined her.

"Let me wash your back."

Taylor turned her back to him, determined not to speak to him first. He soaped up a washcloth and massaged her back with long, firm strokes. "I don't think you're crazy, Taylor. I believe that there are things in this world beyond our senses that I don't understand. But this sounds so . . . I don't know, implausible. Are you sure some kind of ghost whispers to you?"

Taylor sighed impatiently. "Not some kind of ghost. The killer. The berserk maniac who is killing all these men."

"I still find it hard to believe that one woman is doing these murders."

"Believe it. With magic you can do improbable things. If you're gifted, good enough, and have some sort of assistance."

"So you can do all sorts of improbable things? Like materialize inside of the vaults at Federal National Bank?"

"Please. Anyway, I'm just one out of three, naturally gifted. I've never made a study of the magical arts, and I certainly don't have any assistance."

"A man can hope. So you think this woman has assistance?"

"That's what scares me."

"You think she's part of some coven or something."

Taylor met his eyes. "Worse."

"What's worse than that?" Stone started to soap her back in long, smooth strokes.

"Forces from the other side. Dark forces."

"You're joking," he said.

"I wish I were."

"I hate to say I'm a skeptic. I'm going to have to see it to believe it."

"Then I hope you never see it. I really do."

"Mmmmm." Stone grasped her hips and drew her to him. And what was poking into her back wasn't a bar of soap. Taylor leaned into him and sighed with pleasure.

"I see that I need to take your mind off this magic stuff. And how do you think is the best way to do that?"

Taylor proceeded to show him, not tell him.

They didn't make it out of that shower until the water turned cold.

THIRTY-THREE

Taylor woke up and stretched. She smiled, feeling a flush of optimism and well-being. She reached over to touch Stone, and he wasn't there. "Stone?" she called. She got up to go to the bathroom. Surely he was in the kitchen fixing something for them to eat. He wouldn't leave without saying goodbye.

"Stone?" she called, as she went toward the kitchen. He'd left. She could find no note. She knew it was unreasonable of her to expect him to say goodbye to her on a Monday morning. He had a demanding job. He had employees and responsibility. She turned to go back to the bedroom and dress for work. A bereft feeling swept over her, and the morning's initial good mood evaporated.

When Taylor got to work, Helping Hands' door was locked. She looked at her watch, 9:15 A.M. Something was very wrong. She used her key.

Marian sat at the receptionist desk. She looked at Taylor then continued her regard of the computer screen, frowning. "Taylor, could you give me a hand? I'm trying to get this sign done in this stupid graphics program, and I can't figure it out."

"What's going on, Marian? Why is the door locked and where is everybody?"

Marian sighed and turned to Taylor. "Mai Lin said you were out yesterday evening. I didn't beep you because . . . well, I didn't want to bother you."

"And?"

"The agency is closing. A few people are here cleaning out their offices. I take it you didn't see the Sunday paper?"

"No, I didn't get a chance. With Eva's funeral and all, it was a busy day."

"It's over there," Marian said, gesturing toward a table.

Taylor went over and picked up the paper and gasped. A headline on the front page, top fold read, BATTERED WOMEN'S AGENCY INVOLVED IN SERIAL HUSBAND MURDERS.

"I got a call yesterday. Helping Hands is closed until further notice."

"I wonder why nobody mentioned this to me yesterday?"

Marian shrugged. "Maybe they didn't get a chance to see the paper either. Obviously it was a slow news day. I'm working on a sign to post on the door. I want to list some alternative agencies women can go to."

Taylor turned toward her office. "So I don't have a job? I'm off the payroll?"

"Two weeks pay after all accrued vacation and sick days are used, then indefinite leave. Of course, the board is saying that all this will be cleared up by then, and the agency reopened, but I'd apply for unemployment now."

Unemployment won't pay my bills, Taylor thought. "I'm sorry, Marian."

She gazed at Marian and the new dark circles etched under her eyes. It was infinitely worse for her. She'd built the agency up from scratch, and now for it to be gone so suddenly must be nearly unbearable. "I'm sorry, too," Marian said. softly. "You haven't heard the worst. Apparently something was found in the shelter implicating that the killer had been there."

"What?"

"I don't know. All of a sudden getting information is nearly impossible. Even Charles has clammed up."

Taylor packed up a few personal things, forwarded her calls, and went home. There was not much point in staying. The offices already felt abandoned.

Mai Lin looked up as Taylor came in. "Why are you home so soon?"

"Bad news. The agency is closed indefinitely."

"Oh no! So you don't have a job?"

"Marian said the agency is only temporarily closed, but in effect, no."

"This is awful." Mai Lin wrung her hands, seeming at a loss about what to do next. "I'll make you some tea," she said, disappearing into the kitchen.

Taylor rubbed the back of her neck, and sat down at her little desk in the living room. She picked up a stack of bills and shuffled through them. What was she going to do? Most of her credit cards were maxed out as it was.

"Mai, did you see the Sunday paper?"

"It's in the basket by the fireplace."

The paper was still rolled up. Taylor opened it up and shook her head at the offending headline. She read the accompanying article carefully. There was no mention of finding any evidence in the shelter. She wondered what had been found, and what was going on with the investigation. Now, apparently the big guns had been turned loose on the case.

Taylor turned to the want ads with resignation. Mai Lin entered with a steaming cup of tea. "Thank you, that's wonderful." Taylor took the herbal tea and gratefully took a sip.

"Oh, I forgot to say. Someone called shortly after you left. I let the machine answer."

Taylor looked at the ads and circled a few likely ones before she went to the phone to check her messages. Benita had called, she was still in town and wanted to get together with her for lunch. Taylor punched in the numbers to call her back. It would be a welcome diversion from her worries.

They decided to get together Wednesday. Taylor started to

pick up the paper again but laid it down and stretched out on the sofa instead. She should get up and redo her résumé. She should be calling around touching base with old contacts. Brent would certainly help her out.

She picked up the portable phone and called Stone's office. His secretary put her right through.

"They closed the agency," Taylor said, getting right to the point.

"I'm sorry. I can't get together with you for lunch today, I've got an appointment."

"That's all right." What a bummer, she thought.

"I had a key made for you. I'll leave it with Irene if you want to swing by."

He was giving her a key to his apartment. Taylor couldn't suppress a grin. That meant an exclusive commitment time. A man never gave you the key to his apartment unless he was sure you were the real deal. He wasn't about to risk his woman walking in on him while he was engaged in other amatory pursuits. "I'll be by and pick it up. What would you like for dinner?"

"I hoped you'd have that idea. Anything you decide will be okay. Bye, sweetheart, I've got to run."

She hung up, her mood lightened considerably. It all would work out. Everything happened for a reason.

Ernie greeted her happily, but remembered not to jump on her. She scratched the dog's head as she surveyed Stone's apartment. What was with that man? He seemed like he'd put nothing away if it was possible to throw it on the floor. She couldn't have tolerated it if he wasn't basically clean. He didn't have nasty habits, and his bathroom and kitchen were always relatively clean though cluttered. Clutter filled every nook and cranny of his entire apartment. An organizing system, that's what he needed. Taylor rolled up her sleeves and got to work.

An hour or so later, she heard a key in the door and looked at her watch in alarm, it wasn't even noon yet. Then she gave a little shriek of alarm. A young white man stood in the doorway. Ernie bounded to him with joy and jumped on him licking his face. Taylor relaxed, the dog obviously knew the man.

"I'm Jim. I walk the dog," he said.

"Great." Taylor had been dreading taking Ernie out. He was so big and enthusiastic.

"I'll be back in an hour, hour and a half. We take long walks because Ernie needs a lot of exercise."

It sounded good to her, besides that dog followed her everywhere, panting and always watching her with loving doggy eyes. It gave her the creeps.

"Keep him as long as you like."

Hours later, Ernie long back from his walk, she wiped her brow and looked at her watch with alarm. It was past time for Stone to be home and she hadn't done a thing about food. She got the phone book out. She knew a good Indian restaurant that delivered. She made her order and surveyed Stone's place with satisfaction. It looked good, awfully good, and if he followed her system, he could keep it like this easily. He was going to be so pleased.

"What have you done?" Stone stood stock still and looked around with astonishment.

Taylor embraced him with a grin. "Isn't it great?"

He set her aside absently, and prowled his apartment. "Where is everything?"

"I put it all up."

"But where? How am I going to find anything?"

"You heard of drawers, closets, and cabinets?" Taylor was disappointed. Obviously he wasn't as ecstatic as she thought he'd be.

Stone didn't say anything.

"Are you upset I cleaned up your place?"

"Well, I wish we'd talked about it or done it together. I'm not going to be able to find anything. That drives me nuts."

Taylor bit her lip to keep from saying the smart retort on the tip of her tongue. "I ordered Indian food for dinner."

"I thought you were going to cook."

"There was nothing to cook but a monstrous assortment of frozen dinners and convenience snacks. Do you realize that you have five types of potato chips on hand?"

"I'm going to change." Stone disappeared into the bedroom.

Taylor exhaled, the depressed feeling that had plagued her that morning returning in full force.

"Where's my gray sweatpants? A T-shirt?" Taylor sighed again, and went to the bedroom to show him. She'd put his clothes in the drawers of his chest and dresser, probably the first time since he bought them they'd ever been off the floor if he didn't have them on.

She'd set the table, and set out the Indian food in dishes. Stone eyed the food. "You're ready to eat?" Taylor asked.

"I'm starving. But I hope you don't mind if I throw a dinner in the microwave. I don't care for Indian food much."

It was one of her favorites. "All right," she said, deflated. "Do you want me to put one in for you."

"No trouble. I'll do it myself."

In a few minutes Stone returned. "I can't believe what you did with the frozen dinners in the freezer."

"Isn't it great? I alphabetized them, too, so you could find the one you want easily."

He just looked at her. The microwave beeped and he went to get his food, while Taylor dished up a good sized portion of curry. They started eating in silence.

"I have a surprise for you, too," Stone said.

"Oh?" Taylor hoped she liked it better than he apparently liked his surprise.

"I paid all your bills for this month. I had Mai Lin give me the account numbers, addresses, and amounts from the pile on your desk."

Taylor laid down her fork, her appetite gone. "You paid all my bills," she repeated.

"Yes, I paid off the balances on a few of your higher interest credit cards. It's not smart to carry high-interest debt like that."

"How much do I owe you?" she asked, her lips barely moving.

Stone frowned. "You don't owe me anything. It was a gift."

"Several thousand dollars is a gift? I don't think so. It feels like a payment."

"Taylor . . ."

"I am not one of your hoochie mama girlfriends that you have to buy. No man has ever paid my bills since I've been grown, not even my father. You don't own me. Nobody does." Taylor pushed back the chair and stood up. "I'm out of here."

He caught her on the way to the door.

"Take your hands off me."

"We've got to talk. I'm not going to let you storm out of here and cut off communication. That's not the way I do it."

"That's the way I do. Now you'd best take your hands off me."

"You act just like my little sister Vanessa. We're just having a disagreement."

"I'm not your little sister."

"Let's be adult and talk about this." He tilted up her chin and made her look at him. "Taylor?"

Taylor took a deep breath, then another. "Okay."

"You flare up so easily and die down just as fast. Come over here and let's sit down on my clean couch that for the first time isn't covered by anything, and we'll talk."

Taylor followed him over and sat down. She felt like she'd been knocked down and dragged by a truck. The day had been very trying.

"So what upsets you so much about me paying a few bills for you. I have the money, and you told me you lost your job."

She briefly closed her eyes. "I really liked that job."

"You're just upset with all that's going on?"

"That and the thought of you paying my bills seems so paternal and controlling. Just what I've been trying to escape all my life."

Stone nodded. "I know how you feel. When I came into my apartment and saw you'd cleaned it up, it really irritated me. It was like a flashback to what my sisters and mother would do. I used to hate it when they cleaned my room."

Taylor started to giggle. Stone raised an eyebrow. "I'm sorry," she said. "But I just wondered what people who've had real trauma in their childhoods do? Here we are still hung up over our bossy-but-loving parents and siblings."

Stone smiled and gathered her in his arms. "Yeah, we both had it pretty good. I doubt if we need therapy to get over excessive room cleaning and money giving."

"I don't think it's that they did stuff for us, it's all the bitching, expectations, and obligations that went with it."

"You're right about that." He nuzzled her neck. "Wanna go make up?"

"After I eat, suddenly I'm starving again."

THIRTY-FOUR

The bedroom door was firmly shut, Ernie banned from the room. Stone held Taylor, and she stroked his arm, in the quiet moments after the lovemaking. "I never wanted a cigarette so bad as I did when you started to walk out on me this evening," Stone said.

"How's the quitting going?"

"It's going. I haven't had a cigarette for a while, but damn, do I want one."

"Arguments and after meals?"

"How did you know?"

"Psychic," she said.

"You're full of it."

"As long as you still love me."

Silence. The L word dropped, bounced a little, and rolled off the bed. Nobody moved to pick it up.

Taylor bit her lip, feeling unaccountably shaken.

"I forgot to tell you something," Stone said. "Milton is dead. He was shot in his head in his locked jail cell."

Taylor turned her head and stared at him. "You're kidding."

"I wish I were."

"How could someone get in to kill him in jail like that?"

"That's the problem. They were thoroughly searched before they went in. The cell is routinely gone over for stashed contraband. And his cellmate heard nothing, which is pretty strange in itself."

"Mulder and Scully should turn up to investigate these murders."

"This would certainly be an X-File. But you'd be surprised how much weird stuff really goes on."

Taylor shook her head. "No, I wouldn't."

Taylor noticed the red light flashing when she got home late the next morning. "I let the machine answer the calls," Mai Lin said shyly.

Taylor nodded and hit the button. "The police are all over me," Quanita's voice echoed from the machine. "Can you help me out?"

"Amber here. My boyfriend has been missing for over twenty-four hours, so do you think it's too soon to go get my insurance money?"

"This is Marian. Give me a call."

"Please call 1-800-555-3842, as soon as possible." That likely was a bill collector.

She called Quanita back first. "It's just like that MF to go get himself killed before I got an insurance policy out on him."

"He probably would have had to cooperate with at least an AIDS test anyway. You called to ask me about the police?"

"They been over and took me down for questioning, they even talked to Joan again. But I decided I wasn't going to sweat it. I didn't do nothing, so they can't prove nothing. Joan wants to know if you'd be our lawyer though."

"I'm not a criminal lawyer. I think you and Joan would be better served by a criminal lawyer."

Quanita griped a little, but Taylor didn't feel guilty after she got off the phone. Joan had the money to afford a good lawyer for herself and Quanita.

She picked up the phone to call Amber and tell her, yes, it

was premature to file for the life insurance benefits on her boyfriend. She didn't feel up to talking to Marian right now, and she was going to ignore the bill collector.

She'd hung up the phone when the room suddenly darkened. The sunlight faded away and dissipated. A brooding, angry atmosphere descended. Taylor sank into a chair and stared at the phone. She had a feeling it wouldn't do any good to call 911.

A black haze filled the room and Stone's face formed in the blackness. He was banging frantically on a wall that looked as if it was made of dark metal—iron, maybe. Then the perspective of the vision changed, and she was looking in his face. He stared at her, his mouth moving, beseeching her to help him, his eyes wild and staring, fixed on something in the distance. Something that was coming for him.

Then his face transformed into a mask of pain. Oh, God, what was happening to him? Was he dying? Suddenly, he fell to the ground, arms flailing, flopping like a dying fish.

A sob caught in her throat. She was helpless to save him, to stop his suffering. Then the vision faded, and late morning sunlight filled the room again.

"Are you all right?" Mai Lin stood in front of her, looking at her with concern.

Taylor's face was wet with tears, and she was clutching the phone so tightly her hand hurt. "I'm okay," she said, replacing the phone on the cradle.

"You don't look okay." Mai handed her a tissue.

Taylor wiped her eyes. "I'm going to go lie down. I don't want to talk to anybody on the phone. Unless Stone calls."

She curled up on her bed in a fetal position. That wasn't a sending. This had all the earmarks of one of her visions. One of the ones that always came true. She closed her eyes and sobs shook her body. She didn't think she could bear it if

Stone . . . it had to be a warning, there had to be a way to change that reality. There had to be a way.

Kara frowned slightly and sipped her tea. Taylor had just poured her heart out to her about the troubling visions and "sendings" she'd received. Including the one where Stone . . .

"You couldn't find one real psychic to question about what's going on?" Kara asked.

"Nobody. I'm going to research the phenomena I experienced. I'll start out at the library and maybe do an Internet search. If it's happened before, somebody has had to have written about it."

"That's a great idea, Taylor." Kara peeked up at her from under her eyelashes. "Brent tells me you and Stone are going at it hot and heavy."

"How would he know?" Taylor asked, indignant.

Kara hid her smile with a sip of tea. "I suppose men talk just like we do. And we haven't talked enough lately. So tell me, what gives?"

"You're going to tell Brent, then he'll tell Stone."

"Not if you ask me not to."

"All right, I'm madly in love and if you tell Brent I said so, I'll kill you."

Kara choked on her tea. "I thought I'd never, ever hear those words, madly in love, from Taylor Cates. I can hardly believe it."

"Believe it, I'm miserable."

"Whatever for? Stone's crazy about you."

"Maybe in bed, maybe for a hot affair, but I don't think he's serious."

"What? A couple of weeks ago, you told me that if you got involved with him, you'd had a premonition that you two would probably be married. Mrs. Stone Emerson is how you put it. And you weren't all that happy with the notion."

Taylor looked even more miserable. "I practically asked him if he loved me the other night, and he didn't say anything."

Kara drew back, and stared at her. "Wonders aren't ceasing. If someone had told me Taylor Cates would be sitting here in my kitchen being insecure over a man, I swear I would have told them they'd lost their mind."

"You're right about one thing. I'm not cut out for this love stuff. I'm going to break up with him and get it over with before he dumps me."

"Whoa. Calm down, girl. Get a hold of yourself. Take a deep breath. Now repeat after me—"

"Kara—"

"Hush up. Repeat after me. I am in a good relationship with a good man and I am not going to do anything to screw it up."

"That's silly."

"C'mon, let's say it together . . ."

"Okay, okay, I get you."

"You're going too fast. I know for a fact Stone cares for you. Why else would he put up with your evil butt? Slow down, give him time."

"I am not evil."

"Well, testy then. I wouldn't put a whole lot of stock in what you saw happen to Stone. You said yourself, you're not always right."

"My seeings are always accurate."

"Depending on how you interpret them? Your emotions are so embroiled in this. I don't think you're thinking clearly in regard to Stone."

"I hope you're right."

"And don't worry about a job. I'm sure Brent will hook you up." Kara paused, a mischievous smile forming. "Whoohoo, Taylor's in L-O-V-E, and tripping about it, too. This is too good not to tell somebody."

Taylor cut her eyes at her.

"But, since I am your very good friend, I will contain myself. It's gonna be hard though," Kara said with a giggle.

Taylor took a sip of her tea. She felt a little better. Now, instead of feeling like killing herself, she felt like killing Kara.

THIRTY-FIVE

Taylor flipped the channels to the station that showed the time, to check it for the umpteenth time. Eleven fourteen at night, and she hadn't heard a word from Stone all evening. His secretary said he was out earlier. Why hadn't he called? Memories of her vision rose to choke her with fear. What if . . . no. She simply had to stop imagining worst-case scenarios.

The one where he was at home watching the game, tired of her presence already was pretty bad, but the scenario where he was out with another woman who wouldn't reorganize his apartment without permission or have crazy visions was the worst.

She heaved a long, deep sigh. This love stuff was hell, and she wished she'd get over it. She clicked off the TV and dragged herself into her bedroom. Brushing her teeth automatically and pulling a T-shirt over her head, she got in the bed and turned off the light. She sighed again and stared unseeingly in the dark. Depression crashed down on her. She'd better face that it was over between her and Stone. He'd gotten sick of her and deservedly so. She wanted to dig a large, deep hole and jump—

The phone rang, thankfully interrupting her melancholy reverie. She dived to the other side of the bed to reach for it, knocking the lamp and the phone off the end table. She scrabbled around on the floor to get the receiver. "Hel-Hello?" she finally said.

"Taylor, it's me. Are you all right? I heard a lot of banging."

Thank you, God, she said to herself. "I just dropped the phone."

"I'm sorry I didn't catch up with you today, but I had to drive to Birmingham to take care of some business on a case. I'm just now getting in."

"Oh. Well. I guess you're tired."

"I'm beat. I'm going to hit the sack. But tomorrow evening, let's go out to eat. How about that jazz club with the fondue? I can't think of the name, but you know the one."

"It sounds great. And Stone . . ."

"Uh-huh?"

"Thanks for calling. I was worried about you."

"You sleep well, baby."

She hung up, and reached for the lamp to put it back in its place. Suddenly, with one call, all was right with her world. She hadn't been this gone since high school. Geez.

Taylor spent the morning polishing her résumé and puttering around the apartment with Mai Lin. She was pleasant, undemanding company, and Taylor hoped everything would soon fall into place and she'd be able to get her own apartment. Mai had said with wistful longing one day that she'd never had a place of her own.

They repotted some plants. Mai seemed to love her plants almost as much as she did, and Taylor planned to give her plenty of cuttings.

She stopped to shower and dress for her lunch date with her brother's fiancée. She'd come to grips with her initial shock, and was looking forward to getting to know Bennie. She put on a brightly colored cotton shift and tied her locks back with a matching scarf.

Taylor got to the restaurant a little early. It was one of those trendy places that catered to the yuppie crowd. Taylor almost felt out of place with her unemployed self. She ordered a glass of red wine and settled in to watch the people and wait.

She'd just finished one glass of wine and ordered another when Bennie approached with a man in tow. Taylor took sip of her wine and wondered what was up. The man looked well into his forties, possibly his fifties. He was white, with a shock of premature white hair, and piercing blue eyes. Not bad looking if you liked the type.

"Hello, Taylor. It's good to see you again," Bennie said. She cast a nervous glance at the man. "Uh. This is Samuel."

That was a pretty laconic introduction for a man her brother's fiancée was bringing to a let's-get-to-know-one-another-better luncheon. Taylor smiled, and introduced herself to Samuel. "Please, sit," she said, gesturing.

The waiter approached and they ordered. Taylor noticed that Samuel ordered a vegetarian entree, also. "How are all the wedding preparations going?" She asked Bennie casually as she buttered a homemade whole-wheat roll.

"As well as can be expected. There's a hitch with getting the place we planned to hold the reception. Apparently the manager did a major screw up and double booked another event."

"That's awful."

"Even if he straightens it out, I think I'm going to try to find somewhere else."

Taylor nodded and cast a curious glance at Samuel, who sipped his water and observed them, but hadn't said a word. She decided to take the direct route. "What brings you to lunch with us, Samuel?"

"I wanted to meet you," he said.

"Oh? Have I met you somewhere?"

"Not really."

Bennie looked distinctly uncomfortable. "I stopped by the florist's to check out some alternate arrangements and Samuel was there."

Taylor waited for her to say more, but Bennie had taken a roll and was busily tearing it into little pieces.

"And?"

"He wanted to come to lunch with me so I brought him."

Taylor was starting to wonder about this girl her brother was going to marry. She turned to Samuel. "Why did you want to meet me?"

"I felt drawn toward you."

"Do you mind elaborating on that? Have you seen me somewhere?"

"No." He leaned toward her, his intense blue eyes piercing hers. "I had a strong feeling, almost a compulsion, to take this nice young woman to lunch, and she had a compulsion to comply. I realized right away it wasn't her I was drawn to, it was someone else I was to meet. You."

Taylor took a sip of her wine and regarded him. She was the last one to be skeptical of crazy stories and bizarre coincidences.

"Do you often go along with what strange men ask you to do?" she asked Bennie, not taking her eyes off the man.

"Not at all. I don't know what came over me."

"Lots of compulsions and impulses going on here. Just doesn't seem right, although I'm one to talk."

Samuel cleared his throat. "Taylor, that's your name right? You have certain gifts, may I ask?"

He already had, but she nodded, fascinated.

"So do I," he said.

When the student is ready the teacher will come. The words flashed across her mind, unbidden.

Taylor met his eyes. "Why don't you tell me more about yourself?"

"Sometimes I know, simply know, that things are going to happen, sometimes I see the future or the past. Sometimes I see glimpses into the other side, and perceive things other people can't."

Taylor nodded, feeling excited. This man felt authentic. He must be the real thing. "Are there many like us?"

"Probably more than you'd think. You won't find a true seer advertising their services, though."

Taylor grimaced, remembering her trek all over Atlanta. "I've figured that out."

"Have you also figured out the mark of a true seer?"

"Uh, no."

"We're never, ever wrong."

Taylor blinked at him rapidly. Not knowing what to say, then thinking of her awful vision of Stone.

Bennie cleared her throat, and pushed back her chair. "It seems that you two have a lot to talk about. I think I'm going to go."

Taylor focused her attention on her. "Thank you for bringing him, Bennie. I wish I could tell you how much. I'll call you and we'll reschedule, all right?"

"All right." Bennie gave them one last wondering look before she fled.

"All the visions I have come true, in one way or another. I've recently had a seeing that disturbs me greatly. I'd do anything to prevent what I saw from happening. You're saying it's inevitable?"

Samuel nodded sadly. "The actual vision will happen, but your interpretation could be awry. Generally it's only a very narrow window that you see through, only a glimpse. Your interpretation could very well be inaccurate. The vision, if you're a true psychic, never."

"There is this woman. This woman whom I believe is killing. She blocks me somehow, yet she sends her words to me, visions, too, whenever she chooses. She mentioned a master."

Samuel looked into the distance. "I've sensed great darkness loosed nearby, probably by a devotee of the left-hand path. Somehow you're involved, and under direct psychic attack."

"The left-hand path?"

"As in opposite from the right path. The sinister way. There are many branches to this path, but when you told me she referred to her master, the thought crossed my mind that she may have cohorts."

"In the murders?"

"Not necessarily. In the magic."

"I suppose she has a teacher or a group she's involved with," Taylor murmured, hopefully.

"I get a strong feeling, and I never discount my feelings, that she may have superhuman assistance. Possibly you've felt the same?"

Taylor nodded miserably. "You mean like a spirit or a demon or something?"

"Something like that."

"That's more than I want to handle. You mean that people actually draw circles, say mumbo jumbo, and conjure up demons?"

"It's very dangerous, but some do."

Taylor motioned to the waiter, and gestured at her empty wine glass. She needed some fortification.

"One of the reasons your gifts aren't more reliable is because you drink alcohol," Samuel said.

"I'm just a social drinker, and I never get drunk."

"It's that you drink alcohol, period. It dulls your senses. Especially your subtle senses. It's actually worse for that than eating meat. If you didn't drink alcohol, I bet you could perceive auric colors far more frequently than you do now."

The waiter brought her a new glass of wine and she stared at it morosely.

"But is there any way to protect myself from this demon or whatever?" Taylor asked, feeling anxious.

"There is a way to block negative emanations and psychic assaults. From what you told me, you were trying to thrust her out of your mind and ward off the assault by sheer power of will. That's not the way to approach the problem. It starts with visualization . . ."

Taylor and Samuel stood outside the restaurant. "Feel free to call me," Samuel said.

She caught his hand. "I can't say how grateful I am that you've taken the time to tell me all this. It's makes such a difference, not feeling so helpless."

"Most, you knew already. I just gave you a refresher. Remember fear is your enemy, Taylor, never waver, never doubt. This is your battle, not mine, but I have a feeling you will prevail." He squeezed her hand, then turned and strode away.

She watched him go. She wished she could be so sure. Still, he'd restored her hope and faith in herself. And she directed a little prayer up to the One who'd sent him to her.

THIRTY-SIX

Kay pressed the call light again with a muttered curse. Damn nurses. They sure took their sweet time coming to help her. They treated her like crap. Insisting on calling her Keith, looking at her like she was some freak. It was fifteen minutes beyond the time she was supposed to get her pain shot. They kept saying she'd have to ask for it, that it was "as needed." Lying heifers. Her doctor said she could have it every four hours, and she expected them to be standing in her doorway, needle in hand on the minute.

She spied something out of the corner of her eye. It looked like a black cloud approaching, a cloud roughly in the shape of a person. She blinked rapidly. Maybe she had been taking too many painkillers after all. The cloud came closer. Kay opened her mouth to scream, to get her roommate's attention, but no sound came forth. She tried to jump out of the bed, and she couldn't move.

She watched with horror as a hypodermic needle appeared out of thin air. "Time for your shot," a voice whispered. It sounded like Quanita. "A somewhat different brew than what you're used to. This will kill your pain, that's for sure." A low chuckle.

The needle hovered over the vein in the bend of her elbow. She frantically tried to move her arm, but couldn't. Her entire body tingled as if it had gone to sleep, and felt leaden. A drop of blood appeared as the needle effortlessly slipped in her vein.

She was going to die. She understood that clearly. And she really didn't care much. She'd screwed up this life; she'd been given past redemption. Maybe in the next one she'd have a better chance.

She watched the plunger depress, felt the cold, burning liquid as it flowed into her vein. Her blood carried death with each beat of her heart to her brain. A done deal. Her last thought welcomed the blackness that descended to take her away.

Taylor chewed her nails, a bad habit she'd thought she'd broken ten years ago. She sat in front of her computer monitor, scanning the screen rapidly—learning about demons, and trying to fight nausea. No way could she handle this. God better call in some reinforcements, some angels or something. She was opting out.

The doorbell rang and she flew out of her chair and landed on the floor. Lord have mercy. Forcing herself to walk slowly to the door, she shook her head at the level of her anxiety.

Her eyes widened with surprise when she pulled open the door and not only Stone was standing there. That older detective, Charles Redmon, stood by his side and they both looked grim.

"Are you saying that I'm a suspect now?" Taylor demanded. The detective pulled out a cigarette and Stone looked at the floor.

"Don't light that in here," Taylor snapped.

"Let's say we're exhausting all possibilities."

"Well, as you see, I don't have an alibi for the time of Kay's death. After I left lunch with Samuel, I walked for over an hour. I had a lot to think about."

"Who's Samuel?" Stone asked.

The detective snapped his pad shut. "You know the drill, Ms. Cates. You can't leave the city."

Taylor felt the blood drain from her face and she sank into a chair. She couldn't believe this was happening. She was a suspect.

Stone let the detective out. "Are you okay?" he asked when he returned.

Taylor shook her head.

"Can I get you anything?"

"No. No, I'm fine," she said, knowing she was lying.

"Where is everybody?"

"Teensy took the kids to a movie, and I think Mai went to the store."

Stone crouched down in front of her and lifted her chin. "It's going to be all right, baby. I promise you."

"Why all of a sudden, am I a suspect?"

Stone shook his head. "Charles and some of the other guys in homicide have become close-lipped now that they know I'm involved with you. I think it's something to do with some evidence they found, but I'm not sure."

"They've been so secretive about this investigation."

"Probably because they don't have much. Charles said they were baffled. Some of the killings seem like they would have been impossible to pull off. It's like a ghost materialized, killed, and disappeared, all without a trace."

Taylor shivered. "That may not be as far off track as you believe. Samuel said black magic is probably involved."

"Yeah, I've been meaning to ask, who the heck is Samuel?"

"This man who Bennie brought to lunch. He's a true psychic, and he told me so much."

"Black magic?"

Taylor nodded and bit her lip. "Demons, evil spirits, the works. I'm scared, Stone. Whoever is doing the murders is directing psychic attacks at me."

"You have no idea who?"

Taylor shook her head. "It could be anybody. But it's probably one of the ex-shelter residents or staff. All this is connected with the shelter."

"It's somebody with a big beef against abusers, that's for sure." Stone covered her hand with his. "Do you still want to go out?"

"No, I don't feel up to it now."

"Let's go to my place."

That sounded wonderful. Her apartment was starting to feel like it was suffocating her. She stood. "I'm ready to go."

Taylor gasped as she followed Stone into his apartment. She looked around her, eyes wide. "My God, it's . . . it's clean."

Stone looked around smugly. "Looks great, huh?"

"I'm flabbergasted. When did you find time to do this?" she asked, knowing Stone had already trashed the apartment from her previous cleaning.

"I didn't. I hired a cleaning lady. She's going to come three times a week."

"I thought you hated people cleaning up after you."

"I think I can learn to deal with it. I let my secretary tackle my office, too. She's thrilled, she's been begging me for years."

Taylor wrapped her arms around his waist. "Maybe we can work on you picking up after yourself next."

"Now, don't get carried away," he said with a chuckle.

"What are we going to do for food?" Taylor wondered.

"Order pizza, of course."

After they ate, they made slow, sweet love. Afterward, she laid in his arms and told him what Samuel had said. "I've never been so terrified in my life," Taylor said. Although now she felt safe, cradled in Stone's arms after his usual exemplary love-making. To be honest, the man could never pick up a towel, or put a dish in the sink, for the rest of his life. She'd either do it herself or pay somebody. His compensating qualities were extraordinary.

"So this guy says there is something you can do about these attacks?"

"Yes, and actually it's quite simple, you can do it yourself. I knew the technique, but I'd never associated using it with attacks of this magnitude. You start with visualizing a sheet of white light. Wrap the light around you using physical motions to reinforce the reality. Then ask God and specific angels for protection, using their names. You don't necessarily have to use Christian angels, but be sure you're calling on somebody on the right side."

"So how is imagining all this supposed to protect you from real psychic attacks?"

"Thought creates reality. Everything real first began as a thought."

"Still seems rather bizarre, why do you have to ask for protection? And why do you have to call on God and the angels by name? Isn't God's name God?"

"You don't get anything, good or bad, without asking for it. It's a law. God's name is I AM. Yahweh and Jehovah is this name in different languages and variations. God told Moses his name was I AM, that I AM."

"Oh."

"Most people don't realize that their thoughts are real. They go around thinking anything about themselves and their world, never realizing that they are creating their own reality. Then on top of it they voice negatives, saying things like, I am broke, or I am stupid, never realizing they are making their declarations real."

"Okay, picture this. This woman conjures up a big monstrous demon to come after your butt. You stand there and visualize a white light surrounding you. I suppose calling on God, angels, and anybody else you can think of isn't far-fetched at this point. But you're saying that this is actually going to protect you?"

"While I seriously doubt any attack would be that unsubtle and physical, yes, that would protect you."

"Uh-huh."

"It would protect you up to the extent of your faith, your surety that it would. Any doubt or fear would cause your shield to waver."

"I'm toast then, because if I see some monster demon coming after me, I'm hauling ass."

Taylor looked at him. "Stone, this is no joke. The best thing you could do for yourself is to practice this technique. Samuel did it in a sitting position in a crowded restaurant, without motions or audible words to cement the intention, and I actually saw a shield of protection form around him."

Stone propped himself up on an elbow, his finger tracing a lazy passage around one nipple, then another.

"I think we really should practice now," Taylor said.

Stone dropped a kiss on her nipple, his tongue teasing it into a hard peak. Taylor shivered in response.

"Tell you what. I'll count on you to protect me from mysterious forces, demons, and things like that. Because I can think of better things I'd like to practice right now."

And Taylor, as much as she thought otherwise, couldn't bring herself to disagree.

THIRTY-SEVEN

Brent said she could start at his office tomorrow. He'd been made partner last year, and apparently there was an opening in the firm for a part-time associate. She'd make twice the money working half the hours as she did in her old job. No elation filled her. She wasn't looking forward to doing the fat-cat corporate work Brent's firm specialized in. She missed Helping Hands already.

Mai's application for housing had been approved. She'd be moving out next week. And when Teensy got her next paycheck, she said she'd be able to finally get her own apartment. Taylor would miss them, and dreaded living by herself. She'd gotten spoiled with the luxury of having friends around her all the time. She'd lost the art of being alone.

She got in her car and started it up. Turning in the direction of her home, she wondered what she really wanted. An easy answer, Stone Emerson. Falling in love was hell, she'd rather . . . The bad thing was she could think of nothing she'd rather do.

Her apartment was bigger and far nicer than his. She wished he'd move in with her. They'd get the housekeeper to come every day, maybe cook dinner, too, it would be ideal.

She'd forgotten about Ernie. No way Stone was going to get rid of that dog. For Stone she'd put up with Ernie. She was getting sort of attached to that big mutt anyway. But Stone seemed perfectly content with the way things were, good companionship, good sex, and no real commitment.

Kara said she was moving too fast. Maybe she was, but with all that was going on she was frightened. She didn't want to be alone, and the only person she wanted to be with was Stone. The vision she'd had about him nagged at the back of her mind. She couldn't bear losing him.

The best approach was the direct one. Tonight, she'd actually cook for him for once, then she'd make a casual suggestion and see how he responded.

Stone leaned back in his chair, replete. "Baby, I thought you couldn't cook, but when you put your mind to it, you put your foot in some food." Taylor lazily ran her finger around the edge of her wine glass, now filled with juice, and wondered how best to approach him. "I noticed you didn't drink any wine."

"I'm not drinking alcohol anymore. Stone, you know Mai and Teensy are going to be leaving soon, and I'm going to be all alone in that big apartment."

"Are you worried about rent? I said I could spot you the money . . ."

"No, it's not the rent. I'll be making plenty working with Brent to catch up with all my bills. It's just that . . . I don't want to be alone."

Silence.

"You're a grown woman, Taylor, surely you've come to grips with the necessity of spending time in your own company occasionally."

She squeezed the stem of the glass. "You misunderstand me. I think it's time we move to the next level."

Stone's eyes widened and he reached for her hand.

"I think it's time we moved in together," Taylor finished in a rush. He withdrew his hand.

He leaned away from her and crossed his hands across his chest. "What if that's not something I want to do?"

Taylor's vision blurred and her eyes burned with unshed tears. She rose and turned away from him, reaching for her purse. "I need to go. I have to think this over and I can't do it with you," she said in a strangled voice.

"Taylor—" he started to say.

"No. Let me go. I'll . . . I'll call you later."

She walked out of his door before he could see her tears fall.

"Y'all wait in the car. I'll be right back," Teensy said to her children. She knocked on the door of the small, neat house she'd invested most of her life and money. The loss of the house was worth the freedom from the misery she'd suffered in it.

After a few minutes, she bit back an oath. That man knew she was coming to get the check. His car was in the driveway and the lights were on. He was obviously home. Maybe he was asleep over a bottle. That would be typical. She walked around to the back. The sliding patio door was standing open and Teensy felt the first twinges of alarm. She hesitated, then walked in.

The first thing that struck her was the smell. The smell of loose bowels. Then she saw him. He sat at the table, an incredible litter of liquor bottles around him. His head down, asleep. Her nose twitched. He'd soiled himself. She touched his shoulder and withdrew her hand as she felt the cold clamminess of his skin.

Then she looked closer. His legs were tied together with wire, and wire was wrapped around his waist to secure him in the chair. Her hand covered her mouth. Finally, the SOB was dead.

* * *

About three blocks from Stone's apartment, Taylor pulled over and parked. She gave herself over to the sobs that racked her. She'd played her card, she'd asked him point-blank, if he would move in with her. And just as point-blank, he'd turned her down. It was his right. She had no call to be angry. But the hurt stabbed her very soul.

What could she do now? Be satisfied with what he offered? Enjoy the sex. That was what she'd wanted in the beginning, wasn't it? Just to kick it with him, to have a good time and get him out of her system. That was all he seemed to want from her.

Well, he'd given her plenty of good times, and it wasn't enough. She blew her nose noisily; a sick emptiness was left from her storm of weeping. What could she do next? Be satisfied with what he had to offer? At least until he saw something better, she thought bitterly. Would he even want her around now that she'd played her hand so boldly?

A whimper rose from her throat as the familiar tingle rose on the back of her neck. She tried to raise her defenses, but her emotions were too tangled, her mind too unfocused.

"I'm almost finished here," the husky feminine voice announced.

"Why am I not seeing a black haze like last time?" Taylor whispered through stiff lips.

"Too much trouble."

"Oh."

"What's wrong with you?" the disembodied voice asked almost conversationally.

Taylor choked back an hysterical giggle. "Man trouble."

"Ahhh. Way more trouble than they're worth. Don't worry, I have plans."

Then, the tingling sensation was gone, the presence departed. Taylor started the car again and she was several blocks away when the implication of what the voice said finally sank in.

* * *

He writhed in the grips of the force that pinned him against the wall of the metal box he was jailed in. He felt it rip the very life force from his cells. Burning, stabbing anguish. He screamed in agony. Then it dropped him to the floor, finished with him. For now. Soon, he would have no more life left to give.

It didn't care how much he screamed, cursed, or raged. In fact it seemed to take pleasure in his emotional pain. Nobody would hear him. He once had hopes of someone coming and saving him. No more.

Sometimes she'd watch the thing feed on him impassively, indifferent to his suffering. He'd learned not to curse at her. He'd learned that the pain the force would cause him was minor compared to what she'd do to him. His scars had barely healed from the last time he'd angered her.

Once, right after it started, he'd been bold enough to ask her how she'd gained such power. "Hate," she'd said. "I hated so much, my hate became real."

Every so often she'd enter, while the force pinned him against the metal wall of the cell she'd imprisoned him in. She'd hose out his wastes, refill his water jar, and leave a tray with several days of food.

The passage of time had become meaningless. He could feel that he didn't have many days left and that was his only comfort, the peace of death would be a mercy.

THIRTY-EIGHT

When she got home, Mai Lin was sitting in the living room, sipping a cup of tea. "Have you heard the news?" she asked.

Taylor's heart sank. She doubted if the news was good. "No, I haven't."

"Teensy found her husband earlier today. He'd been killed. She's gone to take care of arrangements."

Taylor gasped. "Oh, no, not another one." Taylor sank into a chair. "She'd said she was almost done."

"What do you mean?" Mai asked.

"Nothing."

"You've got a lot a messages. Everybody from the shelter seems upset," Mai said.

"Apparently almost all of us connected with the shelter are suspects." Taylor sighed and went to listen to her messages.

When the thing was finished with him, he was so weak he could hardly move. Still he gasped, when the unseen force grasped him and forced him up against the cold, hard, metal wall of his cell. She approached him, rolling a tray. His eyes widened when he saw what was on it.

An assortment of shiny knives, sharp and lethal. Then he sagged against the invisible bonds holding him. It was time, and he was ready. He knew better than to hope for a quick, painless death.

She had a pleasant smile on her face. "I'm practically finished here. And you're all used up. You know that don't you? Time for me to move on. Get someone fresh and strong to take your place." She picked up a knife and looked at her reflection. "Do you remember the first time you hit me?" She turned to him and he regarded her with dull eyes. He wished she would shut up and get it over with.

"I see you don't. You beat me until I bled because I didn't have your dinner on the table on time. Remember?"

She eased the knife point near his eye and his natural fear took over. He nodded.

"I thought you would."

She took a step back and he let out his breath, not realizing he'd been holding it. He wanted to beg for mercy, a swift bullet to the head. But he knew she'd take pleasure in denying him.

She picked up two knives and rubbed the edges together, sharpening them. "A knife or a bullet to the gut is one of the most painful ways to die, you know that? Slow, too."

A deep, rich laugh came from within her. "I wish I could say I'm going to miss you, but sorry, I'm not. Nope, not going to miss you at all. The one I've chosen to take your place is tall and strong and handsome. He'll probably last much longer than you."

He whispered her name. "You have last words?" she asked.

"I'm sorry. I'm so sorry."

She regarded him steadily. "Truer words were never spoken."

A quick motion of her hand, and fire filled his guts. His eyes watered and little grunts came from his throat.

"Please, feel free to scream," she said with a smile. "We've only just begun."

***

Man after man died in a wash of blood and pain. The killer was an avenging angel, releasing women from the bonds of true evil.

"It's all relative after all, isn't it?" a voice whispered. "Depends on how you see things. On one hand, these men deserve to die. Each one is guilty of harm to a woman. Possibly a woman who loved him. Unforgivable." She was bringing righteous judgment, freeing these women to live in peace and harmony.

"It's a lie," Taylor screamed. "The end never justifies the means. Killing is always evil!"

"Oh, yeah? What does that say about your God who slew all those people in, say, it's hard to give one example, there's so many, Jericho? Pregnant women, babies in arms, even pets and livestock. What about those killings?"

"To slay the wicked and promote righteousness."

"My point entirely."

"It's not your place. Not my will but thine be done," Taylor whispered in despair.

"And whose will is that?"

The hand held a knife that had just gutted a man. Her hand. She turned to a mirror and looked into her own eyes. The eyes of a killer.

"Nooooo," she screamed.

She sat up in bed, the room dark. Beads of cold sweat plastered her T-shirt to her body. The dream had been terrible. She trembled in reaction, the metallic odor of blood still seeming to fill her nostrils.

She reached for the phone to call Stone. She needed him, wanted him so badly . . . Slowly she withdrew her hand. She'd played her best cards with him, and lost. She wouldn't beg him. She'd face this thing alone. Tears ran down her cheeks, and she brushed them away. She turned on the lamp. She couldn't tolerate the darkness. Then she sank back into her pillows, her eyes staring straight ahead, keeping a vigil. For what reason, she wasn't clear. She laid awake the rest of the night.

"I'm glad you decided to join our firm, Taylor," Brent took a Styrofoam cup of coffee from his secretary and handed it to Taylor. "You like it black, right?"

Taylor nodded. "Thank you for giving me a much needed job. I really appreciate you hooking me up like this, Brent."

"No problem. We go back a ways."

Taylor sipped her coffee and remembered all the angst and trauma Kara went through before she got together with Brent. It had been a picnic in the park for her and Stone by comparison. Then again, now there were no signs that she and Stone were ever going to actually get together. Stone couldn't have made it more clear that he didn't want her.

And in the face of that, what were a few bad dreams, sleepless nights, demons to fight?

"Taylor?"

She looked up at Brent. "Sorry, I missed what you were saying. I didn't sleep too well last night."

"I'm going to have to talk to Stone about that," Brent said with a grin. "Why don't you spend an hour or so with our human resources manager? Then I want you to spend the rest of the day reviewing some cases similar to the ones you'll be working on. Cathy has the files already. Just tell her when you're ready for them."

He stood. "Let me show you where personnel is, then we'll go see your office."

Taylor followed him out the door. He gestured to a closed door with a small plaque labeled Human Resources. "That's Jody's domain." He continued down the hall. "You'll be sharing the office with another woman. Eventually, you'll be working on the same caseload. You'll need to call her later today and confer on your working schedules. Essentially, you job share and you'll need to work opposite her."

He opened the door to a small, sunny office. Two desks were present, one overflowing with papers. "That's Jennifer's desk. The other one is yours."

Brent turned to the door. "I'll leave you to get settled in. Like I said, check with Jody first, then my secretary. Cathy has the files I want you to review." He smiled at her. "I hope you like it here, Taylor."

"I'm sure I will. Thank you again, Brent."

After he left, she walked to the window and looked out on the view of downtown Atlanta. Something nagged at her. A restless, uneasy feeling and she couldn't quite pinpoint the cause.

She returned to her desk and rifled through the drawers. Somebody had stocked her desk with new office supplies. A small business card lay by the phone. She picked it up. Jennifer Sidarin, the officemate whom she was supposed to call. They certainly were organized around here.

She drummed her fingers against the desk. The uneasy feeling persisted. Something was wrong. A small frown creased her brow as Taylor picked up her coffee and made her way to the human resources manager's office.

THIRTY-NINE

Stone got up bright and early, as was his habit, and was in his office before his secretary. He had a lot he wanted to do today. He had the feeling that today was the day everything would fall into place. He was so close to the answers he sought.

His speciality was analysis and deduction. Not necessarily combing the crime site for tiny bits of evidence, although he could do that, too. He had a gift for combining the evidence into a big picture and studying it for tiny blemishes and discrepancies. Human nature was generally very predictable.

He brewed himself a cup of coffee, then settled in front of the computer. Manila folders were heaped over his desk, each in messy disarray. Each folder was labeled with the name of someone connected with Helping Hands battered women's shelter, or the agency itself. Each folder was stuffed with documents and data.

He settled in to review everything again. As soon as it was nine, he'd make a few calls.

Hours later, a knock sounded at the door. His secretary entered, fresh coffee and a sandwich in hand. She placed the offering beside him wordlessly while he continued working.

He ate his sandwich slowly. Leaning back in his chair and staring at the ceiling. Then he nodded. Finally, he understood. The husbands, they were the key to the killer. And suddenly, as if someone had drawn him a map, he saw the pattern that pointed to the killer. Taylor was right, it was a woman.

He opened one of the folders, and scribbled an address on a note. He slid a gun out of his drawer into his holster. He was going to check out the address, and see if his hunch was correct. He turned to pick up the note, but he didn't see it amid all the disarray of papers. He flipped open the folder and scribbled the address down again. Then he stuck the folder back into the pile.

He wheeled as his hand touched the doorknob on his way out the door. He thought he heard a husky chuckle behind him. But when he turned, no one was there.

The words of the brief Taylor was trying to read blurred. Brent had treated her to lunch at a posh downtown restaurant, but her appetite was gone. She'd just had a salad.

She rubbed the back of her neck. Her head was pounding, focused on the tight muscles back there. She groped in her purse and gulped down two acetaminophen with stale coffee. She tried to refocus on the brief and suddenly gasped, making a jerky movement and spilling muddy brown coffee across pristine black and white pages. Pure fear and adrenaline had raced through her for no apparent reason.

Taylor stood with a swallowed oath and tried to brush the offending coffee away. Didn't work. She went into the bathroom to find some paper towels. Pulling handfuls of paper towels from the holder she caught sight of herself in the mirror and gasped again.

She leaned closer, not willing to believe her eyes. Instead of the reflection she expected to see, she saw white, gold, and blue colors swirling. Then the mirror cleared and she saw Stone, walking toward a house. Her heart almost froze when she saw the house almost inhale and exhale evil. The windows looked like malevolent eyes staring right at her. The walls dripped freshly shed blood. Stone stood in front of the door for a moment, then it opened like the red maw of a hungry beast to admit him.

She bit her lip and touched the mirror with a trembling hand. The surface was restored. Her own face reflected in the shiny silver. She hurried back to the office to call Stone. He must not leave his office until she got there.

"You just missed him," Stone's secretary said. "He rushed out the door in quite a hurry."

Taylor squeezed the telephone receiver so hard her hand hurt. "Do you have any idea where he went?" she asked trying to keep her voice calm.

"He'd been working on the computer, and thinking about that shelter murder case all day. Maybe he found something."

"It's urgent that I locate him. I'll be right over."

Ten minutes later she was going through the heap of manila folders on his desk. The sheer amount of data he'd amassed was incredible. He had entire dossiers on people she didn't know he knew of.

A half hour later she buried her face in her hands and tears stung her eyes. Nothing. Near despair, her eyes fell on a crumpled sticky note near the computer monitor. She picked it up, smoothed it out, and stared at the address scribbled there. That was it. She knew it beyond a doubt. She grabbed her purse and hurried out.

Stone checked his address and the house again. This was it, an older home in a stable, mixed Decatur neighborhood. He approached the house. It seemed dead and unlived in. Stone walked on the front porch and the boards creaked in protest. He rang the doorbell and waited a few minutes. Hearing nothing, he rang it again.

Then he knocked on the door and to his surprise it swung open. "Hello?" he called.

He heard nothing but a faint rustling and a hum, probably appliances. It wouldn't hurt to look around since he was here. The open door had seemed to welcome him.

The house was very neat, but a little old-fashioned, like his grandmother's house. Crocheted doilies lay over overstuffed upholstered chairs and a couch trimmed in wood with claw feet. An off odor permeated the house, but Stone couldn't place it.

Then he swung around. He thought he heard something from the basement. He entered the kitchen with its neat fifties appliances, and immediately saw the open door. Something made him hesitate, the hum was louder here, almost like an animal inhaling and exhaling. He clicked the light at the top of the stairs, it was dead.

Shining the beam of a small flashlight down the rickety stairs, he thought he heard a woman's chuckle again. "Who's there?" he called.

He walked down the stairs, wincing at the loud groan each step made. "Who's there?" he called again.

At the bottom of the stairs he paused to allow his eyes to adjust to the dim light. The sticky feel of cobwebs covered his face and he brushed them off. The smell was stronger down here, like something rotten. Then his eyes focused, and he saw with surprise what looked like a large metal box standing to his left. He shined his flashlight on it to examine it better. It was at least seven feet high and five or six feet wide. No way anybody got it down those basement steps, someone had to have put it together in the basement.

Then his eyes widened as he saw the wash of fresh blood oozing down the drain in the basement floor in front of it.

Stone stepped near the drain, shining his flashlight on the viscous maroon fluid. It came from the box. He circled the box, seeing a door with iron bars on the far side. A chill ran down his spine. It was a jail, a jail for a man. The door was open, seemingly beckoning him. He took a step closer, then another, certain he was going to find a body in there. He shined his flashlight in, but the tiny beam couldn't penetrate the thick impenetrable blackness within. Another step. Another.

Suddenly he felt something from behind him shove him into the cell. The clang of the iron barred door sounded behind him. He gave a cry and whirled, throwing himself against the bars. Locked. A woman's dry chuckle sounded. "Now, you're in a pickle aren't you?" she said. "Didn't anyone ever tell you what curiosity did to the cat?" His eyes widened with recognition as she stepped in front of his prison.

FORTY

Taylor got out of her car and stared at the house. It was the same one in her vision and she shuddered at the evil emanating from it. She spread her arms wide and spoke to the heavens and a sheath of white light immediately poured down and clothed her. She looked at her hand. Even it was glowing with an inner luminescence.

A human conduit was needed, an opening on this earthly plane for the continuing battle between good and evil to manifest in a physical sense. She had to bring the light, as the killer brought forth the darkness.

Despite the much welcome assistance she sensed near her, she wished she could wait in the car until it was over. She'd think those beings, and especially the Big Guy, would recognize that demon battle was not her forte and send someone more suited. But who was she to question the Big Guy?

"Indeed," she heard a light, silvery voice to her right.

She took a deep breath and walked toward the house. "You got my back, don't you?"

No answer, but she felt a little reassured.

Stone's eyes narrowed as he stared at the woman. "Guessed it was me? You're one smart boy." Then she chuckled. "Maybe not. You are in there, and I'm out here.

"The cage is iron," she said conversationally. "For your comfort and protection. Keeps my companion out until I let it in. It tends to be a little greedy. You'd last no time at all with unlimited access."

She reached out to unlock the door, and Stone's muscles tensed to jump out as soon as he heard the click.

"I don't mind if you don't thank me," she said, looking slightly miffed.

The door clicked and Stone leapt. A strangled scream came from his throat as he was slammed back against the metal wall of the cell by some unseen force. He blinked in disbelief as he was suspended in midair, his feet dangling, unable to move a muscle.

She stood in front of the open cell. "Sometimes it can be a little rough. Especially when it's very hungry."

She beamed at him. "The basement is fairly soundproof, so I don't mind if you scream. Releases tension, y'know."

Then the agony begun. His muscles strained against the pain, and he groaned. After a while, he couldn't help but shriek.

Taylor touched the door and it swung open. She gulped, and stepped over the threshold. Palpable gusts of psychic evil assailed her senses. They were strongest coming from that way. She walked to the kitchen and stared at the shut door.

Then she heard a strangled scream. It was Stone. She threw open the door and stumbled down the rickety wooden stairs. A large metal box sat in the middle of the basement, and Mai Lin stood in front of the far side.

Taylor drew up short, gasping with shock.

Mai Lin smiled at her. "Welcome to my modest home. Would you like some tea?"

Taylor stared at Mai and noticed she was standing within a chalk circle. A groan came from Stone and she ran to the box. Tears came to her eyes as she saw Stone pinned against the wall by a black mass. He writhed in agony, just like in her vision. Then the thing dropped Stone to the floor and poured out of the box. Toward her.

It slammed against her barrier of white light. She stretched her arms wide, and saw a gold light penetrate the ceiling and pour through the top of her head, issuing forth from her mouth in words in a language she didn't know.

She saw shapes of light struggling against the black mass. Mai was knocked out of the chalk circle and the blackness descended on her. Mai started screaming: high, shrill, panicked screams filled with pain. The light issued from her through her and penetrated the black mass. There was a sound like the whooshing of a vacuum being filled and the blackness was gone. Then the light drew in on itself and rushed through her, back to the heavens, leaving only the soft glowing white of her shield.

She stepped over the unconscious body of Mai Lin, and ran to Stone, gathering him in her arms. He lifted his head and stared at her. "Is the thing gone?"

"Vanquished."

"I don't suppose I'm dreaming, huh?"

"No, love, you're not dreaming." She softly kissed his lips before she pulled the cellular phone out of her pocket to call the police.

EPILOGUE

Taylor laid in Stone's arms, finally back at his apartment. Mai Lin had been led away by the police in handcuffs. It was over. Stone cleared his throat. "I've been meaning to ask you, what happened in that basement?"

She traced the line of his jaw with a lazy finger. "What did you see?"

"Nothing, really. I heard you coming down the stairs and you stood near Mai Lin. She said something to you, then you spread your arms and started babbling. In a few minutes Mai fell down and started screaming."

"It was a battle against good and evil. I wish you could have seen it. It was glorious."

"I hope you're not planning to go into the demon-battling business."

"No, I think not. Once in a lifetime is enough. Stone?"

"What, baby?"

"You know when I asked if we could live together. Why did you turn me down?"

He set her aside and took her hand. Unbidden tears rose in Taylor's eyes. This is where he told her that it was over between them.

"I don't want to live with you."

She turned her head, not bearing to hear more.

"Taylor. Listen to me. I don't believe in live-in situations.

I want to put a ring on your finger and walk down the aisle. I want us to buy a house, and fill it with children."

Tears ran down her cheeks, tears of joy. She threw her arms around him, speechless, the words caught in her throat.

"I love you, Taylor Cates, and if you don't marry me, I'll . . . I don't know what I'll do."

She touched his cheek. "There's nothing I'd rather do than spend the rest of my life with you."

Stone whooped, picked her up, and swung her around. Then he bent his head, and sealed the promise with a kiss.

Mai Lin tilted her head as if she was listening. Then a small smile touched her face. She was happy it had worked out for those kids. No hard feelings. Taylor had won the battle fair and square, but the war still raged. Those police were quite silly to believe that a jail cell could hold her. A new city, a new shelter. Her work continued.

"Do you have anything to add?" the social worker asked her.

She looked slowly around at the other women seated in the circle. "I'm happy for the women who lost their husbands, maybe now they'll be able to live." She unfolded her hands. "My daughter died. She was the love of my life, my only child . . ."

Dear Readers:

Thanks for joining me. While there's nothing better than a good romance with true love at the end, I do sometimes like the occasional something extra, such as the shivery thrill that I hope A MAGICAL MOMENT gave you. I always like hearing from you. Feel free to write me at P.O. Box 654, Topeka, KS 66601, include a stamped, self-addressed envelope for a reply. E-mail me at monica@comports.com, and my home page is located at http://comports.com/monica

Good reading!
Monica Jackson

COMING IN JULY

FIRE AND DESIRE   (1-58314-024-7, $4.99/$6.50)
by Brenda Jackson
Geologist Corithians Avery, and head foreman of Madaris Explorations, Trevor Grant, are assigned the same business trip to South America. Each has bittersweet memories of a night two years ago when she walked in on him—Trevor half-naked and she wearing nothing more than a black negligee. The hot climate is sure to rouse suppressed desires.

HEART OF STONE   (1-58314-025-5, $4.99/$6.50)
by Doris Johnson
Disillusioned with dating, wine shop manager Sydney Cox has settled for her a mundane life of work and lonely nights. Then unexpectedly, love knocks her down. Executive security manager Adam Stone enters the restaurant and literally runs into Sydney. The collision cracks the barriers surrounding their hearts . . . and allows love to creep in.

NIGHT HEAT   (1-58314-026-3, $4.99/$6.50)
by Simona Taylor
When Trinidad tour guide Rhea De Silva is assigned a group of American tourists at the last minute, things don't go too well. Journalist Marcus Lucien is on tour to depict a true to life picture of the island, even if the truth isn't always pretty. Rhea fears his candid article may deflect tourism. But the night heat makes the attraction between the two grow harder to resist.

UNDER YOUR SPELL   (1-58314-027-1, $4.99/$6.50)
by Marcia King-Gamble
Marley Greaves returns to San Simone for a job as research assistant to Dane Carmichael, anthropologist and author. Dane's reputation on the island has been clouded, but Marley is drawn to him entirely. So when strange things happen as they research Obeah practices, Marley sticks by him to help dispel the rumors . . . and the barrier around his heart.

Available wherever paperbacks are sold, or order direct from the Publisher. Send cover price plus 50¢ per copy for mailing and handling to BET Books, c/o Kensington Publishing Corp., Consumer Orders, or call (toll free) 888-345-BOOK, to place your order using Mastercard or Visa. Residents of New York, Washington, D.C. and Tennessee must include sales tax. DO NOT SEND CASH.

ROMANCES THAT SIZZLE
FROM ARABESQUE

AFTER DARK, by Bette Ford   (0-7860-0442-8, $4.99/$6.50)
Taylor Hendricks' brother is the top NBA draft choice. She wants to protect
him from the lure of fame and wealth, but meets basketball superstar Donald
Williams in an exclusive Detroit restaurant. Donald is determined to prove
that she is wrong about him. In this game all is at stake . . . including Taylor's
heart.

BEGUILED, by Eboni Snoe   (0-7860-0046-5, $4.99/$6.50)
When Raquel Mason agrees to impersonate a missing heiress for just one
night and plans go awry, a daring abduction makes her the captive of seductive
Nate Bowman. Together on a journey across exotic Caribbean seas to the
perilous wilds of Central America, desire looms in their hearts. But when the
masquerade is over, will their love end?

CONSPIRACY, by Margie Walker   (0-7860-0385-5, $4.99/$6.50)
Pauline Sinclair and Marcellus Cavanaugh had the love of a lifetime. Until
Pauline had to leave everything behind. Now she's back and their love is as
strong as ever. But when the President of Marcellus's company turns up dead
and Pauline is the prime suspect, they must risk all to their love.

FIRE AND ICE, by Carla Fredd   (0-7860-0190-9, $4.99/$6.50)
Years of being in the spotlight and a recent scandal regarding her ex-fianceé
and a supermodel, the daughter of a Georgia politician, Holly Aimes has turned
cold. But when work takes her to the home of late-night talk show host Mi-
chael Williams, his relentless determination melts her cool.

HIDDEN AGENDA, by Rochelle Alers   (0-7860-0384-7, $4.99/$6.50)
To regain her son from a vengeful father, Eve Blackwell places her trust in
dangerous and irresistible Matt Sterling to rescue her abducted son. He accepts
this last job before he turns a new leaf and becomes an honest rancher. As
they journey from Virginia to Mexico they must enter a charade of marriage.
But temptation is too strong for this to remain a sham.

INTIMATE BETRAYAL, by Donna Hill   (0-7860-0396-0, $4.99/$6.50)
Investigative reporter, Reese Delaware, and millionaire computer wizard, Maxwell Knight are both running from their pasts. When Reese is assigned to
profile Maxwell, they enter a steamy love affair. But when Reese begins to
piece her memory, she stumbles upon secrets that link her and Maxwell, and
threaten to destroy their newfound love.

*Available wherever paperbacks are sold, or order direct from the
Publisher. Send cover price plus 50¢ per copy for mailing and
handling to Kensington Publishing Corp., Consumer Orders,
or call (toll free) 888-345-BOOK, to place your order using
Mastercard or Visa. Residents of New York and Tennessee
must include sales tax. DO NOT SEND CASH.*

WARMHEARTED AFRICAN-AMERICAN ROMANCES BY *FRANCIS RAY*

FOREVER YOURS (0-7860-0483-5, $4.99/$6.50)
Victoria Chandler must find a husband or her grandparents will call in loans that support her chain of lingerie boutiques. She fixes a mock marriage to ranch owner Kane Taggert. The marriage will only last one year, and her business will be secure. The only problem is that Kane has other plans for Victoria. He'll cast a spell that will make her his forever.

HEART OF THE FALCON (0-7860-0483-5, $4.99/$6.50)
A passionate night with millionaire Daniel Falcon, leaves Madelyn Taggert enamored . . . and heartbroken. She never accepted that the long-time family friend would fulfill her dreams, only to see him walk away without regrets. After his parent's bitter marriage, the last thing Daniel expected was to be consumed by the need to have her for a lifetime.

INCOGNITO (0-7860-0364-2, $4.99/$6.50)
Owner of an advertising firm, Erin Cortland witnessed an awful crime and lived to tell about it. Frightened, she runs into the arms of Jake Hunter, the man sent to protect her. He doesn't want the job. He left the police force after a similar assignment ended in tragedy. But when he learns not only one man is after her and that he is falling in love, he will risk anything to protect her.

ONLY HERS (07860-0255-7, $4.99/$6.50)
St. Louis R.N. Shannon Johnson recently inherited a parcel of Texas land. She sought it as refuge until landowner Matt Taggart challenged her to prove she's got what it takes to work a sprawling ranch. She, on the other hand, soon challenges him to dare to love again.

SILKEN BETRAYAL (0-7860-0426-6, $4.99/$6.50)
The only man executive secretary Lauren Bennett needed was her five-year-old son Joshua. Her only intent was to keep Joshua away from powerful in-laws. Then Jordan Hamilton entered her life. He sought her because of a personal vendetta against her father-in-law. When Jordan develops strong feelings for Lauren and Joshua, he must choose revenge or love.

UNDENIABLE (07860-0125-9, $4.99/$6.50)
Wealthy Texas heiress Rachel Malone defied her powerful father and eloped with Logan Williams. But a trump-up assault charge set the whole town and Rachel against him and he fled Stanton with a heart full of pain. Eight years later, he's back and he wants revenge . . . and Rachel.

Available wherever paperbacks are sold, or order direct from the Publisher. Send cover price plus 50¢ per copy for mailing and handling to Kensington Publishing Corp., Consumer Orders, or call (toll free) 888-345-BOOK, to place your order using Mastercard or Visa. Residents of New York and Tennessee must include sales tax. DO NOT SEND CASH.

LOOK FOR THESE ARABESQUE ROMANCES